Comrades in Arms

War heroes, heartbreakers...husbands?

The close friendship between
Lieutenant Colonel Jack Trestain
and Major Finlay Urquhart was forged
in the heat of Waterloo's battlefield.

Famed for their daring and courage, these
are Wellington's most elite soldiers, but now
they're facing their biggest challenge yet—
falling in love!

If you enjoyed

The Soldier's Dark Secret

you'll love

The Soldier's Rebel Lover

the second instalment of this fabulously intense
and dramatic duet from Marguerite Kaye!

Praise for Marguerite Kaye

'A poignant, sensual historical romance that kept me reading late into the night.'
—*Romance Junkies* on
Rumours that Ruined a Lady

'Kaye offers up another sexy romp…with characters who stay with fans long after the last page.'
—*RT Book Reviews* on
Unwed and Unrepentant

'Each novella is a passionate love story in its own right; each a testament that love can survive everything—even war.'
—*RT Book Reviews* on *Never Forget Me*

'Daring. Dangerous. Delightful. Kaye's new Regency romance is a riveting and thrilling adventure.'
—*RT Book Reviews* on
Outrageous Confessions of Lady Deborah

THE SOLDIER'S REBEL LOVER

Marguerite Kaye

First published in Great Britain 2015
By Mills & Boon, an imprint of HarperCollins*Publishers*
1 London Bridge Street, London, SE1 9GF

Large Print edition 2016

© 2015 Marguerite Kaye

ISBN: 978-0-263-26278-0

Printed and bound in Great Britain
by CPI Antony Rowe, Chippenham, Wiltshire

Marguerite Kaye writes hot historical romances from her home in cold and usually rainy Scotland. Featuring Regency rakes, Highlanders and sheikhs, she has published almost thirty books and novellas. When she's not writing she enjoys walking, cycling (but only on the level), gardening (but only what she can eat) and cooking. She also likes to knit and occasionally drink martinis (though not at the same time). Find out more on her website: margueritekaye.com.

Visit the Author Profile page
at millsandboon.co.uk for more titles.

Chapter One

Basque Country, Spain—July 1813

Major Finlay Urquhart of the Ninety-Second Regiment of Foot scanned the rough terrain through the eyepiece of his field telescope, his senses on full alert. 'Got ye!' he whispered to himself with grim satisfaction.

The French arms dump was partially concealed, set in the lee of a nearby hillock. It was obviously a large cache and therefore a strategically important discovery, especially if it could be destroyed before Wellington began his siege of the nearby fortress at San Sebastian. There were no guards present that he could discern, but they could not be far away, and might return at any time. The French army was severely stretched in the aftermath of the Battle of Vitoria, where they had sustained heavy losses, but even against their presumably depleted defences, any planned assault on the arms cache would carry significant risk, since it was located some distance behind enemy lines.

As was he, Finlay reminded himself. The light was fading fast, and with it any chance of making it back to base tonight, for his journey would take him through some treacherous and hostile terrain. It would be much more prudent to hole up for the night under cover in the small, heavily wooded copse a couple of miles distant where he'd tethered his horse.

'Aye, and Prudence is my middle name, right enough,' Finlay muttered to himself. Despite the perilous nature of his situation, he couldn't help grinning at his own joke. With any luck, he could be back in camp and feasting on a hot breakfast not long after sunrise.

He could not have said what it was that put him on his guard. A change in the quality of the silence, perhaps. Maybe the fact that the hairs on the back of his neck were standing up. A sense, acute and undeniable, that he was not alone. Definitely. Finlay's hand moved automatically to the holster that held his pistol, but the failing light, and fear of the sound it would make when he primed it, made him hesitate and reach instead for his dirk, the lethal Scottish dagger he carried in his belt.

His ears pricked, Finlay listened intently. A faint scrabbling was coming from the ditch on the other side of the rough track. A rat? No, it sounded like something much larger. He waited on high alert, crouched in his own ditch, and was rewarded by the faint outline of a man's head peering cautiously out. No cap, but it could only be a French sentry, for who else would be concealed here, so close to the arms cache? He could wait it out and pray he was not discovered, but sixteen years in the army had taught Finlay the value of the pre-emptive strike. Taking the *sgian-dubh*, the other, shorter dagger he carried tucked into his hose, in his other hand, he launched himself at the enemy.

The Frenchman was in the act of aiming his pistol as Finlay threw himself at him, knocking his arm high and sending the gun spiralling harmlessly into the air. The man fought like a dervish despite his slight physique, but Finlay had experience and his own considerable brawn on his side. Within moments, he had the man subdued, wrists yanked painfully together behind his back, the glittering blade of the dirk only a hair's breadth from the French soldier's throat.

'Make one sound and, by all that is holy, I promise you it will be your last,' Finlay growled in guttural French.

His captive strained in Finlay's iron grasp. He tightened his grip on the man's wrists, noting with surprise how slender and delicate they were. Now that he was close up, Finlay could see he was not, in fact, wearing a French uniform. What was more, as he struggled frantically to free himself, it became clear that there was something much more profoundly incongruous about his captive.

'What the devil,' Finlay exclaimed, so surprised that he spoke the words in his native Gaelic. 'What the hell do you think you're playing at, woman,' he added, lowering his voice and switching to Castilian Spanish as he turned the female round to face him, 'creeping about in the dead of night in man's garb? Don't you realise I could have killed you?'

The woman threw back her head and glared at him. 'I might ask you the same question. What the hell do you think you are doing, creeping about in the night in woman's clothing? I could just as easily have killed you.'

The sheer audacity of her remark rendered him speechless for a moment, and then Finlay laughed. 'This, *señorita*, is a kilt, not a skirt, and you did not for a moment come close to killing me, though I don't doubt that you'd have tried if I'd given you half a chance. Why did you point a gun at me? Could you not see that I am wearing a British and not a French uniform? We are supposed to be on the same side.'

'If you could tell that my tunic was not a French uniform, why did you come leaping out of the darkness brandishing two blades like some savage?' she countered.

'Aye, well, fair enough,' Finlay said grudgingly, 'but that doesn't explain what you're doing out here dressed as a man. Are you alone?'

'I am here for the same purpose as you, I expect. To locate the position of this arms store.

And yes, I am alone. You can let me go now, I won't shoot you, I…'

'Wheesht!'

Finlay pulled them both back down into the ditch as the sound of horses' hooves grew louder. Three riders, and this time undoubtedly French. He turned to warn the woman at his side not to move a muscle, but there was no need; she was stock-still, as silent and tense as he. She was a plucky wee thing, that much was certain.

The horses drew closer and then stopped almost directly in front of them. One man dismounted, and Finlay slowly slid his pistol from its holster. Before he could stop her, the woman had wriggled a few feet away to pick up her own discarded weapon, careful to make no sound. Not just plucky, but cool-headed, then. Under cover of the ditch, he could barely see her, only sense the slim, coiled figure readying herself to attack. He shook his head imperceptibly, and to his relief she nodded her understanding. There were times when patience was a virtue. No point alerting the French to the fact that the arms cache had been discovered. It would only make any future assault on it more fraught with danger, as they would doubtless reinforce their defences.

After a few tense seconds, Finlay heard an unmistakable tinkling sound that was accompanied by tuneless whistling. This was followed by a long groan of satisfaction as a small cloud of steam rose into the night air. *'Zut alors!'* he heard a disembodied, and quite literally relieved voice say, and had to bite his lip not to laugh out loud. This whole bizarre episode was going to make a fine tale for the lads in the mess. Provided he made it safely back, that was. He himself was therefore equally relieved to see the soldier remount his horse before the trio set off in the direction of the arms cache, where presumably they would set up camp.

'We must move now, for they will almost certainly send out a patrol once they are settled.' The woman spoke in English. Her accent had a slight lisping quality that was undeniably charming.

One look at the sky, where a full moon was making its presence felt from behind the scudding clouds, made his mind up for him. Finlay nodded his agreement. 'My horse is hidden in a copse just over that ridge.'

'I know it. Let me lead the way, I know this terrain like the back of my hand.'

It went against the grain for him, but his instincts told him to trust her. They made their way along the ditch, inch by painfully silent inch, for half an hour as the moon rose higher and higher and the stars above them hung like lanterns suspended in the sky. Finlay was struck, as he was on every single clear night like this in Spain, by how much brighter and closer to earth they seemed compared to the tiny twinkling lights in the Argyll sky, back home in Scotland.

Ahead of him, the woman stopped and looked cautiously out of the ditch before standing up. 'We can follow this track here. It will take us over the ridge. Now that you have located the arms dump I presume the English army will destroy it?'

'It's a British army, with Scots and Irish and Welsh soldiers as well as English.'

'And you, I think, with that skirt, are Scottish?'

'Kilt. *Plaid* if you like, but not a skirt. Skirts are for women.'

He saw the glint of her teeth as she smiled at him. 'And you, soldier, are decidedly not a woman.'

Finlay surveyed her for the first time, in the fluorescent glow of the moon, and wondered how he could ever have thought *her* anything else. She was young, no more than twenty-three or four, he reckoned. Her rough woollen breeches were tucked into sturdy brown boots. Over her heavy tunic, the leather belts worn cross-wise held gunpowder, a pistol and a knife. The uniform of a partisan, a rebel fighter. But the long legs inside the breeches were shapely. The belt cinched a waist that even underneath the bulk of the tunic was slim. The hair pulled back from the face had been silky soft against his unshaven chin. And her face… The large, almond-shaped eyes under finely arched brows, the strong nose, the full lips—there could be no mistaking that for anything other than a woman, and a very attractive one, at that. 'We have established the reason for my presence. But what, may I ask, are you doing out here?' he asked.

Her smile faded. 'I told you, the same thing you are doing. Locating the French armaments.'

'But alone. And you are...'

'Female.' She stood straight, tossing her head and glaring at him. 'You think a woman is any less observant than a man?'

'Quite the contrary, but I do think sending a woman on her own on such a mission was a bloody stupid thing to do. These French soldiers would not necessarily have killed you straight away, lass,' Finlay said gently, 'if they had captured you.'

'I would not let them capture me. Under any circumstances,' she added darkly.

'You should not have been sent—assuming that whatever guerrilla group you belong to did actually authorise your foolhardy mission?'

She glowered at him again, opened her mouth to speak, then obviously thought better of it. 'We should not be standing here debating in the open. It is not safe.'

She had a point. She also clearly did not trust him, despite his uniform. And why should she, Finlay thought wryly as he allowed her to lead the way along the narrow track he'd followed earlier. The problem was, he needed her to trust him enough to tell him what her fellow partisans' plans were. If they meant to liberate the French weaponry and use it against them, it would save his men a job—and he could ill spare his men for such a mission, no matter how vital. Vitoria had knocked seven colours of shite out of them, and now Wellington was champing at the bit to attack the fortress towns of Pamplona and San Sebastian, despite the fact that desertion, sickness and sheer bloody exhaustion, to say nothing of the unseasonal and relentless rain, were having a serious impact on morale. If he could spare his men even one sortie…

Finlay frowned. He could not see how it was to be done. He knew no more about this woman than she knew about him. If he could at least find out who she took her orders from, for he was pretty certain he knew all the local guerrilla groups, and those he did not know his friend Jack, Wellington's master codebreaker, of a certainty would. If only he could get her to talk.

They were climbing steeply now, pebbles from the narrow rocky path skittering down behind them. The moon was high enough in the sky to cast ghostly shadows. The woman moved lithely, her long legs in their tight boots seemingly tireless as she set a pace that would have left some of Finlay's men gasping for breath. Raised in the Highlands, a childhood spent roaming the narrow sheep tracks on lower but equally rugged terrain, Finlay followed, his kilt swinging out behind him, his eyes alternating between his booted feet and the beguiling curve of his companion's shapely behind. There was a lot to be said for women in trousers.

There was a lot to be said for men wearing kilts, too. As an officer, he'd the right to trews, but Finlay had always preferred the freedom of his plaid. Other officers from other regiments, especially those up-their-own-arse cavalry, saw Finlay's loyalty to the kilt as one more piece of evidence of his barbarity. The Jock Upstart, Wellington had christened him when he had first, against all the odds and much against the duke's inclination, clambered out of the ranks. Finlay, smiling through very gritted teeth, had sworn to be true to this moniker forever. His plaid was just one of the many ways he maintained his rebellious streak. Sometimes subtly and subversively. Frequently, less so.

He wondered what this woman's family thought

of her wandering about the countryside armed to the teeth. Perhaps they didn't know. Perhaps she was married to a rebel warrior herself. It struck him, as it had often recently, how very different it was for the Spanish who fought alongside them, or who fought as this woman did, in their own underground guerrilla groups. Finlay was a soldier, doing the job he'd been trained to do, had been doing, man and boy. His cause was whatever his country and his commanding officer decreed it to be, his enemy whomever they nominated his enemy to be, and for the past few years it had been the French. He loathed the barbarities they had been responsible for, but he equally loathed the atrocities his own side, drunk on bloodlust and wine, had committed in the aftermath of Ciudad Rodrigo. But he did not hate the French indiscriminately. He admired their soldiers—they were worthy adversaries—and he would be a fool to do anything other than respect Napoleon's military genius.

Napoleon, however, had not invaded Finlay's homeland. The French army were not living off Finlay's family's croft, eating their oats and butchering their cattle. This woman, still striding out tirelessly as they crested the hill, was fighting for her country, her family, her village. And he, Finlay, might not be the enemy, but his men were still laying waste to the countryside in battle, laying siege to their ancient fortress towns and eating their hard-earned grain, even if they were paying a fair price for it. No wonder she had taken up arms. He'd bet his own sisters would do the same.

'What do you find amusing?'

They had come to a halt on the ridge. The copse where Finlay's horse was tethered was in the valley, about a hundred feet below. He hadn't realised he was smiling. 'I was trying to imagine my mother's reaction if she caught my sisters playing the soldier, as you are.'

The woman bristled. 'This is no game. Our sovereignty, our very existence is at stake.'

'I did not mean to trivialise the actions of you and your comrades, lass—*señorita*. In fact, I was thinking just then how much I admire what you are doing. And thinking my sisters would likely do the same, if our lands were invaded as yours have been.'

'You have many sisters?'

Finlay laughed. 'It feels like it at times, though there's only three of them.'

'And brothers?'

'Just the one. What about you?'

'Just the one,' she said, with a twisted smile. 'He is with our army, fighting alongside you English—British. I don't know where he is exactly.'

'You must worry about his safety.'

She shrugged. 'Of course, though if he was close at hand I would not have the opportunity to be so—' she indicated her tunic, her gun '—involved. And so it is perhaps for the best, since we can both fight for our country in our own way.'

'Your family don't object to your active participation?'

'My mother is dead. My father is—he is sympathetic. He turns the closed eye, I think that is what you say?'

'Blind eye. Your English is a lot better than my Spanish.'

Another shrug greeted this remark. 'I have been fortunate in my education. Papa—my father—is not one of those men who thinks that girls should learn only to cook and sew. Unlike my brother. Without Papa's support and encouragement I would not be here, and we would not have known about that cache of arms.'

'So your partisan group do intend to do something about it?'

The question was out before he could stop it. The result, he could have predicted if he'd given himself a chance to think. She folded her arms and turned away. 'As a soldier yourself, you cannot expect me to disclose sensitive military information like that to a complete stranger. I will accompany you to the copse down there, and then we must go our separate ways.'

Cursing under his breath in Gaelic, Finlay followed her, determined more than ever, now that he'd made it even harder for himself, to find a way of making her trust him. If he was to do so, he'd need to stop her leaving. Which meant abandoning his plans to be back at camp by dawn, bidding farewell to the prospect of anything more appetising than the hard biscuits he had in his knapsack. On the other hand, it was not as if a few hours in the company of such a bonny and intriguing lass would be any great hardship. Even if their situation was fraught with danger. Maybe precisely *because* their situation was fraught with danger.

Isabella watched the Scottish soldier stride over to his horse, which was tethered to a tree on a rope long enough to let the animal reach the stream burbling along the valley floor. She watched him as he quickly checked that the beast was content before hauling a large bundle that must be the saddle from where it had been concealed under a bush.

He was a big man, solid muscle and brawn, with a fine pair of powerful legs revealed by that shocking garment he wore, and a broad pair of shoulders evident under his red coat. She knew enough to tell that it was an officer's coat, though she had no idea what rank. He did not have the haughty manners of a typical Spanish officer. There was none of their pompousness and vainglorious pride in his demeanour. Perhaps it was different in the English army? British—she must remember to call them British.

His hair was the colour of autumn leaves. It glinted in the moonlight, and the stubble on his face seemed tinged with flecks of gold. His eyes… She could not tell the colour of his eyes, but she could see well enough that his face was a very attractive one. Not exactly handsome, but nonetheless, the kind of face that would always draw a second look. And a third. The smile he gave her now, as he walked back towards her, was the kind of smile that would ensure its recipient smiled back. She bit down firmly on her own lip, and equally firmly ignored the stir of response in her belly.

'Major Finlay Urquhart of the Ninety-Second Foot,' he said. 'I know it's a bit late in the day for introductions, but there you are. I am delighted to meet you, *señorita*…?'

'I—Isabella. You may call me Isabella.'

To her surprise he took her hand, bowing over it with a graceful flourish, brushing her fingertips with his lips. 'Isabella. A pleasure to make your acquaintance,' he said, as his smile darkened and took a decidedly wicked form.

'Major Urk…Urk…'

'Urquhart. It's pronounced Urk-hart. It might be easier if you called me Finlay.'

'Finlay,' Isabella repeated slowly, smiling.

'Yes, that is better. Well, Finlay, it has been very nice to meet you, but I must…'

'Don't go just yet.'

Truthfully, she did not want to, though truthfully, she did not want to admit that to herself. It was not the journey home that bothered her; she could do that blindfold. It was him. She ought—indeed, she had a duty—to discover what the British plans were with regard to the French arms dump. Reassured, she gave a little nod. 'I will stay for a moment,' Isabella conceded, 'and rest a little.'

'You don't sound in the least as if you need a rest.'

'I don't,' she said, instantly defensive, almost as instantly realising that she had contradicted herself. 'But I would welcome some water. I am parched.'

'Sit down. I'll bring you some.'

'I am perfectly able…'

'I'm sure you are, but I have a cup in my knapsack—it's a mite easier to use than your hands. Sit down there, I won't be a minute.'

Though she was loath to do as he bid her, loath to be waited on as if she was a mere woman,

Isabella sat. The water was cool and most welcome. She drank deeply, and consented to have more brought for the sake of placating the soldier, and for no other reason. *'Gracias.'*

'De nada.'

He sat down beside her, leaning back against the tree trunk. His eyes, she could see now, were a startlingly deep blue under heavy brows, which were drawn together in a faint frown. Despite the fiery glints in his hair, his skin was neither fair nor burned by the sun, but tanned deep brown.

'Well, now, Isabella, it seems to me that it would be daft for us both—my men and yours—to consider launching a sortie against this French arms dump, would it not? No point treading on each other's toes unnecessarily.'

His accent was strange, lilting, soft, and some of the words he spoke she could not translate, but she understand him only too well. He was going about it more subtly this time, but he was still interested in one thing only from her: what were the partisans' intentions with regard to the French arms cache? Fine and well, for that was also the only reason she was interested in him.

The thought made Isabella smile, and her smile made the soldier look at her quizzically, an eyebrow raised, his own sensual mouth quirking up on one side.

'I'd give a lot to know what is going on in that bonny head of yours, *señorita*. I mean,' he said, when she looked confused, 'I'd like to know what you are thinking.'

'I wager you would, soldier, but I'm not going to tell you.'

'Finlay. It's Finlay.'

'Finlay,' she repeated.

'Aye, that's it, you have it. There's not many use my name these days, apart from at home, that is. But it's been nigh on seven years since I've been there.'

'And where is home?' Isabella asked.

'A village in Argyll, not far from Oban. That's in the Highlands of Scotland. My family live in a wee cottage not unlike the ones you see in the villages hereabouts, and they farm, too, just like the villagers here, though they grow oats not wheat, and it's far too cold and wet for grapes, so there's no wine. Mind you, my father makes a fine whisky. He has a boat, too, for the fishing.'

Isabella stared at him in surprise. 'So your family are peasant stock? But you are an officer. I thought that all English officers were from grand English families. The Duke of Wellington, he is famous—'

'For saying that an officer must also be a gentleman,' Finlay interrupted her, making no attempt to hide his contempt. 'I'm the exception that proves the rule—an officer who is definitely not a gentleman,' he clarified. 'And I'll remind you, for the last time, that I'm not English. I'm Scottish.'

'I'm sorry. I think it is like calling a Basque person Spanish, no? I did not mean to insult you.'

'I've been called much worse, believe me. Are you from the area, then? I hope I've not insulted you by speaking Spanish. I'm afraid the only words I have in Basque I would not utter in front of a lady.'

The word was like a touchpaper to her. 'I am not a lady. I am a soldier. I may not wear a military uniform like my brother, but I, too, am fighting for the freedom of my country, Major Urka—Urko—Major Finlay.'

'By heavens, you've some temper on you. I've clearly touched a raw nerve there.'

'You have not, I am merely pointing out...'

He picked up one of her hands, which was curled into a very tight fist, and forced it open. She tried to resist but it was a pointless exercise; his big calloused hand had the strength of ten of hers. It was only when he let her go that she realised he could easily have hurt her, and had taken good care not to. Was he being chivalrous? Patronising? Was he showing her, tacitly, that a man was better, stronger than a woman? Why was it always so complicated? And why, despite his show of strength—or muted show of strength—did she feel no fear? She was alone in the dark of night with a complete stranger. A man who could overpower her and force himself on her if he wanted to. Her hand slid to her holster, though it was rather because she knew she ought to do so than because she thought she needed to.

'I won't harm you.' He was looking pointedly at her hand. 'You have my word. I have never in my life forced myself on a woman.'

He would have no need. And even though she

knew, as everyone knew after being so long at war, what many soldiers did to women in the aftermath of battle, she could not imagine that this man would. There had been a grimness in his voice when he'd warned her about the French soldiers; it spoke of experiences he would rather forget. But then everyone involved in this struggle, including her, shared those.

Isabella gave herself a shake. 'I believe you,' she said, realising that Finlay was still waiting on an answer.

'Good.'

His tone was curt, though he should be grateful for her trust. And she did trust him, which was extremely surprising and, little did he know it, very flattering. She glanced at him, as he sat, eyes closed, head thrown back, resting on his elbows. He did not look like the poor son of a farmer. He did not look like a peacock officer, either, and while he certainly didn't have the hands of a gentleman, he had the manners of one. No, that was not fair. He had not treated her as a fragile flower with no mind. He had treated her with respect, and she liked that. He would be a popular officer, she was willing to bet, and those were few and far between, if her brother was to be believed. She tried to imagine her brother wearing that skirt—kilt. He would look like a girl, while this man—no, there was nothing at all feminine about this man.

'Once again, lass, I'd give a lot to know what's going on in that head of yours.'

Caught staring, Isabella looked hurriedly away. 'I was thinking that you must be a very good soldier, to have become a major.'

Finlay laughed. 'That is a matter of opinion. Being a good soldier and a good officer don't necessarily go hand in hand. It's taken me a great deal more time and effort than most to get to where I am. As you said yourself, Wellington is not at all keen on the idea of commoners rising through the ranks.'

'In that, I think the Spanish and the English— British armies are the same,' Isabella said. 'Before the war, most of the officers were more concerned with the shine of their boots than the fact that some of their men had no boots at all. Things will be different when we have won our country back from the French.'

'You speak with conviction. It is not over yet.'

'No, but when it is…'

'Oh, when it is we can but hope that the world will turn in a different direction,' Finlay replied. 'Maybe they'll even allow women soldiers,' he added with a wry smile. 'Though if you asked me to tell the truth, I'd say that right now, the army is no fit life for anyone, man or woman. We've been fighting too hard for too long, and all we want is for it to be over.'

'That is all my people desire, too.'

'Aye, you're in the right of it. You must be desperate to see the back of all of us.'

'If you mean that we want you to go home…'

'To have your country back.'

'Yes.'

'And your life.'

'Yes,' Isabella said again, though with less certainty.

'Provided that it doesn't go back to exactly how it was before, eh?' Finlay said, as if he had read her mind. 'Now that you've had a wee—a small taste of freedom?'

'Yes.' Isabella smiled. 'A wee taste of freedom,' she repeated carefully. 'And you, too, you will be able to go back to your father's farm in

Scotland, and see all your loved ones. You will like that?'

'I will look forward to it,' he said, after a moment, sounding, to her surprise, as hesitant as she had.

'You do not wish to see your family?'

'Oh, aye, only I don't—ach, no point in talking about that. The war's not over yet. Once we've kicked the French out of Spain, we'll like as not have to chase them across France for a while. Which leads me back to that cache of arms.' He sat up, pushing his hair back from his forehead. 'Look, you don't know me and I don't know you, but these are unusual circumstances we find ourselves in. We can't allow the French to turn those guns on either of us, and I can make sure that they don't. Have I your assurance that the local rebel forces won't interfere and queer the pitch?'

'I don't know what that means, but regardless, I think it would be much better to leave it in our hands,' Isabella said firmly. 'We will put the arms to good use, and—and it would be excellent for morale and quite a coup if we were successful.'

Finlay pressed his fingertips together, frowning down at his hands. 'I'll be frank with you. I would quite happily agree to what you suggest if I could only be sure that the mission would be successfully accomplished. You understand, much as I'd like to, I can't just simply take your word for it.'

She bit back her instinctive retort, frowning now herself. 'If I told you that the information I have gathered tonight would go direct to El Fantasma, would that be enough to convince you?'

'You *know* El Fantasma?'

Isabella nodded.

Finlay looked unconvinced. 'He is like his name, a ghost. Everyone has heard of him, nobody knows him.'

'I do,' she said firmly. 'At least, I know how to get in touch with him.'

'Can you prove it?'

'I cannot. I can only give you my word.' She spoke proudly, held his gaze without blinking and was rewarded, finally, with a small nod of affirmation.

'You have three days to act. If I don't receive

word that you have been successful by then, I'll send my own men in to finish the job.'

'Thank you. You can be sure that word will be sent to you before the three days are up.'

He took the hand she held out, enveloping it in his own. 'You don't ask *where* to send word.'

With a smile of satisfaction, she told him exactly where his men were encamped. 'One of our men will find you.'

'I'm beginning to think they will.' He still had her hand in hers, but instead of shaking it as she had seen Englishmen do, he once again bent his head and brushed her fingertips with his lips. 'We have an agreement, then,' he said.

Once again, the touch of his lips on her skin gave her shivers. Isabella snatched her hand away. 'We have indeed,' she said quickly.

She had what she wanted; she was free to leave. Reluctantly, she made to get to her feet, but the Scotsman's hand on her arm stopped her. 'Stay until it's light, won't you? It's not safe for me to leave before then. Unlike you, I don't know the terrain. Also, it's been a while since I've had the company of a woman. It would be good to talk of something other than guns and field positions.'

'You think I cannot?'

'Why in the name of Hades are you so prickly? I'm not one of those men who think women have no mind of their own. If you met my mother, you'd know why.' He turned to look at her, his gaze disconcertingly direct. 'As to you women being the weaker sex—if ever I thought that, just seeing what the wives following the drum have to endure would change my mind. They have to be every bit as tough as their menfolk. Tougher, in some cases, when they have bairns with them. Though I'd be lying, mind, if I said I thought it was an appropriate life for them.'

He broke off, giving himself a little shake. 'Ach, I'm sorry, I didn't mean to rant at you. If you want to talk guns and tactics, then that's what we'll talk. Only indulge me with a few hours of your company, and grant me the pleasure of looking on your bonny face, for it will be a while, I reckon, until I get the chance to do either again.'

His smile was beguiling. The look he gave her

neither contrite nor beseeching, but—charming? He was not a man accustomed to being refused. On principle, she should refuse, but she was rather sick of principles, and what, after all, was the harm in allowing herself to be charmed for such a very short while?

Isabella permitted herself to smile back. 'I do not think a man like you has any trouble at all in finding female company.'

He laughed again, showing her a set of very white teeth, shifting on the ground, giving her a brief, shockingly tantalising glance of a muscled thigh as he did so. 'The trouble is, I'm a bit fussy about the female company I choose,' he said. 'I prefer to get to know a woman before I—before— What I mean is, I've a taste for conversation that I've not recently been able to indulge. Now, that makes me sound like I'm right up my own ar— I mean, like a right fop, and I'm not that.'

Isabella chuckled. 'I am not exactly sure what this fop is, but I am very sure it is not a label that fits you.'

'What I mean is, I like the company of women for their own sake.'

'And I think that women like the company of Major Urk—of Finlay.'

'Right now there's only one woman's company I'm interested in. Will you stay a few hours, Isabella?'

Why not? Her father would cover for her absence if necessary, but likely she'd be back in her bed before anyone noticed it had not been slept in. What harm could it do to indulge this man with a few hours' conversation? The fact that he had a beguiling smile and a handsome face and a very fine pair of legs had nothing to do with it. 'Why not?'

He smiled. 'Tell me a bit about yourself, then. Are you from these parts?'

'Hermoso Romero. It's not far from here. We have— My family has some land.'

'So they're farmers, peasant stock as you call it, just like mine?'

'They live off the land, yes.'

'And it's just you and your parents you say, for your brother's in the army?'

'Just me and my father. My mother is dead.'

'Oh, yes, you mentioned that. I'm sorry.'

'Thank you, but I never knew her. She died when I was very young.'

'Then, I'm very sorry for you indeed. A lassie needs her mother, especially if she's not got a sister.'

'I cannot miss what I have not had,' Isabella said stiffly.

Finlay opened his mouth to say something, thought the better of it, and shrugged, reaching over to pull his saddlebag towards him. 'Would you like something to eat? I'm hungry enough to eat a scabby-headed wean.'

'A— What did you say?'

'I said I'm very hungry. This is all I have, I'm afraid,' he said, passing her a handful of dry biscuits. 'It tastes better washed down with this, though,' he added, holding out a small silver flask. 'Whisky, from my father's own still. Try it.'

She sipped, then coughed as the fiery spirit caught the back of her throat. 'Thank you,' she said, returning the flask and wrinkling her nose, 'I think I will stick to water.'

'It is an acquired taste, right enough,' Finlay

said, putting the cap back on after taking, she noticed, only a very small sip himself. 'Tell me a bit more about yourself. For example, how does it happen that such a bonny lass is not married?'

'How does it happen that such a—bonny?—man is not married?'

Finlay laughed. 'No, no, you don't describe a man as bonny, unless you wish to impugn him. I'm not married because I'm a soldier, and being a soldier's wife is no life worth having. Since I am a career soldier, my single status is assured. Now I have explained myself. What about you?'

Isabella shrugged. 'While my country is at war and under occupation, I cannot think of anything else.'

'Aye, I can understand that. It's hard to imagine what peace will look like after all this time.' Finlay pulled a blanket from his saddle and offered it to her. 'Here, it's getting mighty cold.'

'I do not need…'

'For the love of— Come here, will you, and we'll share it, then.' Taking her by surprise, he pulled her towards him, throwing the blanket around them. He grabbed her arm as she tried to struggle free, and slid his own across her shoulders. 'I'd do the same for one of my own men if I had to,' he said.

'I don't believe you.'

'It's a sacrifice I'd be prepared to make—I hope. Luckily I've never had to put myself to the test.'

She felt the rumble of his laugher, and the warm puff of his breath on her hair. She had not noticed how cold it had become until he put the blanket around her. It would be churlish to push him away now, and a little silly, for then she would have to walk in the morning with stiff, cold limbs. She did not relax, but she no longer struggled, and allowed herself to lean back against the tree trunk. 'Tell me more about Scotland,' she said. 'Is it very different from Spain?'

'Very. For a start, there's the rain. The sky and the sea are more often grey than blue. Mind, all that rain makes for a green landscape. I think that's what I miss the most, the lush greenery that carpets the valleys and hills.'

'We have a lot of rain here in the north, in the winter.'

'Aye, but in Scotland, on the west coast, it rains most days in the summer, too. Are you sleepy? Should I stop babbling?'

Isabella smothered a yawn. 'No, if you mean should you stop talking. Tell me what other countries you have visited as a soldier.'

'Many campaigns. Egypt. Portugal. France. Ireland. America.'

'You are so lucky, I have never been out of Spain.'

'I'm not sure that you see the best of a country when you go there to fight.'

'No, but—tell me please. Describe what America is like. Is it the wild, untamed wilderness that I have heard tell of?'

'Once you leave the east coast, yes. And vast. A man could lose himself there.'

'Or find himself?'

Finlay was still musing on that thought when Isabella wriggled around under the blanket to look up at him. He tensed, willing his body not to respond to the supple curves of her. Her hair tickled his chin. He was inordinately grateful for the thick layers of clothing between them, and tried discreetly to shift his thigh away from hers. Concentrating his mind on answering her questions, he found she drew him out, that his desire, while it remained a constant background tingle, was subdued by his interest in her, by hers in him.

Eventually, as the moon sank and true darkness fell, they grew silent. He thought she slept, though he could not be sure. He thought he remained awake, though he could not be certain of that, either. They moved neither closer nor farther apart, and that, Finlay told himself, was as it should be.

In the morning he was glad of it. She stirred before sunrise, and he lay with his eyes closed, affording her some privacy. Only when she stood over him did he pretend to wake, getting to his feet, trying not to notice the way the water she had splashed on her face had dampened her hair, making a long tress of it cling to her cheek.

'You will find your way back to your own lines?' she asked.

He nodded. 'It'll be easier in daylight, provided I keep a weather eye out for French patrols.'

'I will send word when we have—when it is done, I promise.'

'I believe you.'

He took the hand she offered him. In the dawn light, her eyes seemed more golden than brown. He wanted to kiss that nervously smiling mouth of hers. He wanted, quite fervently, to have her body pressed against his, her arms around his neck. He took a step towards her. For a moment he felt it, the tug of desire between them, that unmistakable feeling, like the twisting of a very sharp knife in his guts. It was because he wanted to kiss her so much that he stopped himself, bent over her hand, clicking his heels together, then let her go. '*Adiós*, Isabella. Good luck. Please be careful. Stay safe.'

'Goodbye, Finlay. May God protect you and keep you from harm.'

She turned and slowly walked away, following the path of the stream as it meandered along the floor of the valley. Finlay watched her until she disappeared from sight behind a large outcrop of rock. Then he picked up his saddle, and within a few moments, just as the sun streaked the sky with pink-and-orange fingers, he, too, was on his way, heading in the opposite direction.

Chapter Two

England—autumn 1815

'So, Jack, are you going to spill the beans on why you had me hotfoot it down here? I'm intrigued. But then knowing you, you old fox, that was precisely your intention when you composed the enigmatic message I received.'

They were strolling in the grounds of Jack's brother's home, Trestain Manor, where he was currently residing, Finlay having arrived posthaste in answer to an urgent summons. Now he eyed his friend grimly. 'You're looking a bit rough around the edges, if you don't mind my saying so. Is this anything to do with the information I dug up for you regarding your wee painter lassie?'

'Her name is Celeste, and she is not, as I told

you in London, *my* wee painter lassie,' Jack snapped. 'Sorry. I'm just— What you told me helped me a lot, and I'm hoping to solve the rest of the puzzle now that I have permission from Wellington to delve into those secret files.'

'But things concerning the lassie herself don't look so hopeful?' Finlay asked carefully.

Jack shrugged. 'Let's just say I'm advancing on some fronts but have sustained some collateral damage on others.' The words were light-hearted but the tone of his friend's voice told Finlay the subject was not open for further discussion. 'The reason I asked you here is nothing to do with that, although indirectly it brought it about.'

Finlay rolled his eyes. 'Would you get to the point and stop talking in code, man!'

Jack smiled faintly. 'A habit that's difficult to break. It's a delicate matter, though, Finlay, and obviously everything I tell you is in the strictest confidence. I don't mean to insult your utter trustworthiness, but Wellington made me promise...'

'Wellington!'

'When I accosted him at that dinner I attended

on your behalf with my little problem of those secret files, he told me about a little problem of his own.' Jack's expression darkened. 'Save that it's not only the duke's problem, Finlay. I see it as very much mine. When we were in Spain, do you recall talk of a partisan commander called El Fantasma?'

'The Ghost! I'd have had to be deaf and dumb not to. He was a legend in the north during the Peninsular Campaign.'

'Yes, he was. The partisans in that area were incredibly effective in targeting the French supply lines thanks to him, and in intercepting mail. He was one of my most reliable and effective spies. The information he provided saved a great many lives.' Jack plucked a long piece of grass, and began to twine it around his finger. 'The thing is, Finlay, this El Fantasma knows some pretty compromising stuff, politically, that is. Some of the things that were done in the name of war—they wouldn't stand up to much scrutiny in the press.'

'Jack, none of the reality of war would sit well with the peacetime press.'

'You're right about that. To be honest, I think

it would be a good thing if some of it did come into the public domain. Since Waterloo, no one wants to know about the suffering of those who fought, the pittance they have to live on, the fact that the army has cast them aside, having no further need for them.' Jack broke off, fists clenched. 'Sorry, I know I'm preaching to the converted in you, and I've strayed from the point again. The problem, as far as the duke is concerned, is that, were El Fantasma to fall into the wrong hands, it could be extremely embarrassing, not to say damaging to his political career.'

'The wrong hands being...?'

'The Spanish government. Since Ferdinand was restored to the throne, the ruling elite has been cracking down on the former partisans and guerrillas who continue to speak out against them. Many of the more vocal liberals, the ones with influence, have been exiled, a significant number of them executed. El Fantasma, however, is still a thorn in their side. Rather more than a thorn, actually. You know that the freedom of the press in Spain is one of the many liberties that's been curtailed? Here, take a look at this.'

Jack handed Finlay what looked like a political pamphlet. It was written in a mixture of Spanish and Basque, from what he could determine, and the printed signature at the end was quite clearly that of El Fantasma, the small image of a spectre on the front page providing confirmation.

'This edition calls for the Constitution of 1812 to be restored, among many other things. Advocating that alone could get him hanged. I imagine the other editions espouse equally revolutionary views.' Jack was now frowning deeply. 'Wellington has been tipped off through one of his various diplomatic connections that the Spanish government are determined to flush El Fantasma out. He is a dangerous focal point and voice of anti-government rhetoric, and they intend to silence him once and for all. You can guess what that means.'

'It means I wouldn't like to be in his boots if they snare him.'

'And they will, Finlay. It's only a matter of time.'

'Which is what has put the wind up Wellington, I presume?'

Jack nodded. 'He says it is a matter of state security. It goes without saying that his concerns are partly driven by self-interest, but you know as well as I do how wide that man's sphere of influence is.'

'If the duke says it's a matter of state security, then undoubtedly it is. So he wants to get to El Fantasma before the Spanish do, I take it, and he's thinking that you are the man for the job, since a great deal of your information came from that very source?'

'El Fantasma did an enormous amount for us, and risked his life every day to do so. We owe it to him—*I* owe it to him personally, to make sure no harm comes to him. Which is where you come in.'

Finlay stared at his friend, his head reeling. 'Wellington wants me to go to Spain?'

'*I* want you to go to Spain. Wellington agreed to leave the matter in my hands. Since I'm the only person he could think of with the first clue of where to start, he had little option. I have his permission to act as I see fit and to use whatever resources I require. It's official business in that sense, though if anything goes wrong, of course, he'll deny all knowledge. In war and politics, there are always shades of grey, aren't there? Well, this is one instance. The Spanish want to silence our partisan. Our government, being afraid of what he might reveal in order to save his neck, also wants to silence him, Finlay. Do you see?'

'I do. And what, I'm wondering, is it you really want me to do for you?'

'Get El Fantasma out of Spain and the government's clutches by any means possible. Forcibly, if need be. It's for his own good. That will be difficult enough, but then there is the small matter of keeping him out of Wellington's clutches thereafter,' Jack said with a chilling smile. 'Here's how I think it can be achieved.'

Finlay listened in silence as Jack explained his plan and then let out a low whistle. 'You certainly haven't lost your touch, laddie. You do realise if the powers that be find out, it could be interpreted as a treasonable act,' he said, eyeing his friend with something akin to awe. 'It's a bold and possibly reckless strategy.'

'Precisely why I thought of you,' Jack quipped, though his face was serious. 'I know it's asking an enormous amount, but I can't think of anyone else I'd trust with the task. I would go myself, only I can't. I am not—not in the best of health, and there are things I am embroiled in here… If it could wait a few weeks, but I am not sure that it can, and so…'

'Jack, there's no need to explain yourself. Whatever is going on between you and your wee painter lassie is your business. I just hope the outcome is a good one,' Finlay said. 'Besides,' he continued hurriedly, for his friend was looking painfully embarrassed, 'can you not see that I'm bored out of my mind? Is this not the kind of scrape that you know fine and well I love beyond anything?'

He was rewarded with an awkward smile. 'I did think that you might be tempted, but…'

'Let me tell you something. When I got your note, I confess I was relieved. I'm not used to having all this free time. It doesn't suit me one whit. You know I've never been comfortable with mess life, and it's even worse now there's no battles to be fought, and the talk is all of dancing and parties and who is the fairest toast in the town and what particular shade of brown this Season's coats should be. I'm a man who needs to be doing something.'

Jack smiled, but his expression remained troubled. 'I thought the plan was for you to spend some time back in the Highlands.'

'I did go back, briefly,' Finlay replied, 'but—ach, I don't know. My brother has the croft well in hand, and I don't want to be standing on his toes, and...' He shook his head. 'It all seemed so tame and so very quiet.'

'I know what you mean,' Jack said wryly. 'Trestain Manor is hardly a cauldron of excitement, though it would be churlish of me to complain. My brother, Charlie, and his wife, Eleanor, have been good enough to take me in since I resigned my commission.' The two men sat down on the bank of a stream. 'What about you? Will you stay in the army, do you think, now that it looks like lasting peace has finally been achieved?'

Finlay shrugged. 'Soldiering is all I know. Anyway, no point thinking about the future when there's work to be done,' he said brusquely. 'It's agreed. I'll go to Spain and smuggle this El Fantasma out of the country, by hook or by crook. Just tell me what he looks like and where I might find him.'

Jack grimaced. 'That, I am afraid, is the first of many hurdles to be overcome. I have no idea what he looks like, never having met the man. The partisans operated in small, isolated groups to preserve anonymity. I dealt only with third parties—contacts of contacts, so to speak. Even assuming they have survived, which is by no means certain, many of them went into exile at the end of the war. It will be like looking for a needle in a haystack.' Jack ran his fingers through his hair. 'What you need is a starting point, and we don't have one.'

'Actually, I think we might have,' Finlay said slowly. 'Do you remember my tale of the occasion I attacked what I thought was a French guard, and it was…'

'A female Spanish partisan.'

Finlay smiled. 'Isabella, her name was. I've often wondered what became of her.'

Jack laughed. 'I'm sure her charms, as you described them to me, were grossly exaggerated. Moonlight and a dearth of females to compare her to will most certainly have coloured your view.'

'Not at all, she was a right bonny wee thing, and a brave one, too, but that's not what's important.'

'Now you're the one talking in riddles.'

'She claimed to know how to get in touch with El Fantasma. Now, I know virtually nothing about her. I don't even know for certain if she was telling the truth. It'd be clutching at straws. A very long shot, indeed. But in the absence of any other lead…'

'It is at least a potential starting point, although as a partisan, there's a good chance she may not have survived the war.'

Finlay grimaced. 'She didn't even tell me her full name. All I know is that she came from a place not far from where I found the arms cache. Roma? Roman? Romero? Aye, something Romero, I think that was it, but to be honest I can't be sure. If I could take a look at a map I reckon I could pinpoint it.'

'Don't go leaping into action just yet,' Jack cautioned. 'You'll need a cover story, papers, funds. I have contacts in London who will arrange everything you need, including passage on whatever naval ship is heading for Spanish waters. You may have to leave at very short notice.'

'If it means not having to take part in another mess discussion about the best way to tie a cravat, I'll go today.'

'I am very much in your debt. You will send me word, won't you, as soon as you are back safe in England?'

Finlay clasped his hand firmly. 'I will return, never fear. Where would Wellington be without his Jock Upstart?'

North of Spain—one month later

Finlay had endured a long journey, and since arriving in Spain, one increasingly redolent with memories of the campaign there, some of them very unpleasant indeed. Though more than two years had passed, the legacy of the war was evident in the ruined fortress port of San Sebastian where he had made landfall, and in the surrounding countryside as he travelled south through Pamplona, thankfully avoiding the site of that last bloody battle at Vitoria.

Here, in the wine-growing countryside of the La Rioja region, was his final destination. Hermoso Romero. He was still not absolutely certain he was heading for the right place, but it was the only one on the map that had anything approaching the name he thought the Spanish partisan had mentioned. It was not, as he had imagined, a small hamlet where her family had a farm, but as the Foreign Office research had revealed, a very large winery where presumably the partisan's family were employed to work on the estate, which was the largest in the region.

Finlay dismounted from his horse and shaded his eyes to gaze down into the valley. Hermoso Romero was a beautiful place, the pale yellow stone walls and the terracotta roofs mellowed by the late-autumn sunshine. The grapes had been harvested from the regimented lines of vines that fanned out on three sides from the house, while cypress trees formed a long windbreak on the fourth. The main house was a large building three storeys high, the middle section of which was graced with arched windows. What must be the working part of the estate was located to one side, built around a central courtyard, while at the back of the main block he could see what looked like a chapel, and some elegant private gardens contained by a low wall constructed of the same yellow stone.

Jack's mysterious contacts at the Foreign Office in London had done an impressively thorough job in providing Finlay with a cover story. The owner of the winery, Señor Xavier Romero, was by all accounts an extremely ambitious man, with a very high opinion of his Rioja wine. So when Señor Romero had been informed through a 'reliable' diplomatic source that an influential English wine merchant wished to pay him a visit to discuss a potential export deal, an invitation was immediately extended.

'He's likely to push the boat out a bit,' the man at the Foreign Office had warned Finlay. 'Be prepared to be courted. It would be advisable to crib up a little on the wine-production process if you can find the time.'

But time had been in very short supply. 'It is to be hoped that Señor Romero is more interested in allowing me to taste the wine than grilling me on my knowledge of grape varieties and vintages,' Finlay muttered, patting his pockets to reassure himself that his forged papers and letters of introduction were still in place. Though maintaining his alias was really the least of his problems. The scale of his task, the lack of information, the lack of any certainty at all, meant the odds of success were heavily stacked against him.

'So we are going down there,' he said, addressing his completely indifferent horse, 'filled with hope rather than expectation. Let's face it, laddie, there's a hundred reasons why this could be a wild goose chase. Would you like to hear some of them?'

The horse pawed at the ground, and Finlay chose to take this for assent. 'Let's see. First, there's the fact that though I think my partisan lass came from Hermoso Romero, I could be misremembering the name completely. Two years and a lot of water under the bridge since, it's likely is it not?'

He received no answer, and so continued, 'Then there's the lass herself. A woman who, if she did not actually fight with the guerrillas, most certainly was one of them. What are the chances of her having survived? And if she has, what are the chances of her remaining here, if indeed here is where she lived? And if she is alive, and she is here, how am I to know I can trust her? It's a dangerous thing, to espouse the liberal cause in Spain these days. My lass may well side with the royalists now—or at the very least, she'll simply keep her mouth shut and her nose clean and herself well clear of associating with the likes of El Fantasma, won't she?'

Receiving no answer once more, Finlay nodded to himself. 'And if by a miracle she is still alive *and* still a liberal, why in the name of Hades would she trust me enough to lead me to the great man? For all she knows, I could be out to snare him myself. And in a way, she'd be in the right of it, too. The Ghost. I have to find him, for I most certainly don't intend to let him haunt me for the rest of my life. So there you have it, what do you think of my chances now, lad?'

To this question, his horse did reply with a toss of his head. Finlay laughed. 'As low as that, eh? You're in the right of it, most likely, but devil take it if I don't try to prove you wrong all the same. I've never been a death-or-glory man, but I've always been a man who gives his all.'

Mounting his trusty steed and turning towards the wide, new-built road that wound down towards the winery, Finlay felt as he did surveying the field before a battle: excited, nervous, with every sense on high alert, dreading the start and at the same time wishing it could come more quickly. It was one of the worst feelings in the world, and one of the best. He felt, for the first time since Waterloo, truly alive with a sense of purpose. He had missed it greatly, he realised.

'Mr Urkerty. It is an immense pleasure to meet you. Welcome to Hermoso Romero.'

'Urquhart. Urk-hart.'

'Ah, yes, forgive me.' Xavier Romero, a good-looking man of about Finlay's own age, decided against a second attempt at the unfamiliar pronunciation, and instead shook his hand firmly. 'If you are not too tired after your long journey, I would very much like to take you on a short tour of my winery. I am anxious that you see the quality of what we produce here.'

'And I am just as anxious to sample it, *señor*.' Finlay had no sooner nodded his consent than he was escorted by his host back out of the front door, along the sweeping gravel walk and through another door that led into the courtyard he had spied from the top of the hill.

'Of course, the harvest is over for the year. It is a pity you could not have been here just a few weeks earlier. The soil here, as you will see when we go out into the vineyards tomorrow, is very heavy, mostly clay with some chalk. This gives the wine…'

Xavier Romero's English was extremely good. He seemed to require nothing from Finlay but nods and smiles, which was just as well, for he was clearly a man with a passion for the wine he made and all the technicalities of the process. From the briefing he had received, Finlay knew that Romero had served as a lieutenant in the Spanish army, fighting alongside several British regiments in the last two years of what the Spanish called the War of Independence, while their British allies referred to it as the Peninsular Campaign. Señor Romero's fellow British officers, two of whom Finlay had tracked down, had little to say of him other than that he seemed like a sound fellow, which Finlay took to mean that he was innocuous enough, and unlike the Jock Upstart, had the prerequisite amount of blue blood in his veins to fit in to the officers' cadre.

'We use oak barrels as they do in Bordeaux, but our grape varieties are very different. The main one is Tempranillo, as you will know, but...'

Señor Romero said nothing about his estate workers, a subject that interested Finlay much more than grape varieties, given the real nature of his business here. There was a small hamlet about a mile away, a cluster of cottages and farmland, planted with what looked like olive groves. Was it possible that the woman he had so fleetingly encountered lived in one of those cottages? He seemed to remember she said her family had some land.

Señor Romero was still pontificating. 'Of course, the estate is quiet at the moment while we wait for the first fermentation, but you should have seen it in September and October,' he said proudly, 'a veritable hive of activity. Grape picking is seasonal work. Once the harvest is in we have a big fiesta, which goes on for days. If only you had timed your visit better—but there, it cannot be helped.' His host pulled out a gold timepiece from his pocket and consulted it, a frown clouding his haughty visage. 'I apologise, Mr Urker, I got quite carried away. We must leave the rest of our tour until tomorrow, when I will do my best to answer the many questions I am sure you must have. I hope you do not mind, but tonight I have taken the liberty of arranging a small gathering in your honour. A few friends, only the best families in the area, you understand. Some of them produce Rioja, too. They will try to tell you it is superior to mine.' Señor Romero laughed gently. 'They are misguided.'

'I am sure that I will prefer your Rioja to anyone else's,' Finlay said.

He would make certain he did, even though he suspected he'd taste not a blind bit of difference between them.

As he wallowed in the luxury of a deep bath situated behind a screen in a luxurious bedchamber with a view out over the vineyards, Finlay was in fact starting to feel a wee bit guilty for raising his host's expectations, knowing that nothing would come of them. He hoped that two or three days at most would be sufficient for him to establish contact with the female partisan or to establish that she was not contactable, one way or another. The thought that she might be truly beyond any earthy communication was not one he wished to contemplate.

A glance at the elaborate clock on the mantel informed him that he had no time for contemplating anything other than getting himself dressed. He had refused the offer of a valet, but the evening clothes that he had, thankfully, packed at the last moment, had been pressed and laid out on the bed for him. Finlay dressed quickly. A brief assessment in the mirror assured him that he was neat as a pin and that his unruly hair was behaving itself for once. He would pass muster.

He gave his reflection a mocking bow and braced himself. Señor Romero had gone to a lot of trouble, but the idea of an evening spent making polite talk to the man's family and blue-blooded friends filled Finlay with guilty dread.

'Ah, Mr Urkery, here you are. Welcome, welcome.' Xavier Romero broke away from the small cluster of guests as Finlay entered the large vaulted room.

The collection of friends and family was significantly larger than Finlay had anticipated. This gathering reminded him of the glittering balls he had attended in Wellington's wake in Madrid. The scale of the room took his breath away. It was the full height of all three storeys of the building, with a vaulted ceiling, making it resemble the interior of a cathedral. The tall, arched windows were above head height and facing west, so that the fading evening sun cast golden rays over the assembled company of, Finlay reckoned, about a hundred if not more. The ladies' gowns in vivid colours of silk were high waisted and low-cut with puff sleeves as was the fashion in England, though their heads were dressed with the traditional mantilla of lace held in place with jewelled combs. The gentlemen, in contrast, seemed to be as Finlay was, dressed in black with pristine white shirts and starched cravats.

It was stifling in the room. Fans were fluttered, handkerchiefs used to mop brows. Jewels glinted; conversation buzzed. It was everything he hated. He had a very strong urge to turn tail and leave, but Xavier Romero was handing him a glass of sherry and telling him that he must before all else introduce his guest to his family.

As they made their way around the room, Finlay was the centre of attention. Women peeped at him over the tops of their fans. The men stared at him openly. He was probably the only outsider present. A small orchestra was tuning up. The acoustics of the place were impressive. That pretty woman over there in the red dress was making it very clear she would not be averse to an invitation to dance. She had a mischievous look that appealed to him. He would ask his host to introduce them later.

'Ah, at last. Allow me the honour of introducing you to my wife. Consuela, my dear, this is Mr Urkery, the wine merchant from England who is our guest of honour. I am afraid my wife speaks very little English.'

'No matter, I speak some, admittedly very bad, Spanish,' Finlay said, switching to that language as he made his bow. 'Finlay Urquhart—that is Urk-hart—at your service, Señora Romero. It is an honour.' The woman who gave him her hand was young and very beautiful, with night-black hair, soft, pretty features and a plump, voluptuous figure. 'And a pleasure,' Finlay said, smiling. 'Your husband is a very lucky man, if I may be so bold as to say so.'

Beside him, Xavier Romero managed to look both flattered and discomfited. 'Mr Urkerty is going to introduce our Rioja to the English, my love,' he said, edging closer to his wife. 'I am pleased to say that he believes, as I do, that they should drink wine from the vineyards of their allies, not Bordeaux from the vineyards of their former enemies. It is long past time that they did so, do you not agree, Mr Urkyhart? They have been happy to import as much port as your Portuguese friends in Oporto can supply. Now you and I, we will make sure that Rioja, too, takes its rightful place in the cellars of England, no?'

'The cellars of Scotland being too full of whisky, I suppose you're thinking,' Finlay said with an ironic little smile.

Fortunately, Romero simply looked confused by this barb. 'I must introduce you to—' He broke off, frowning, and scanning the room. 'You will excuse me for just a second while I fetch my sister. She has obviously forgotten that I specifically told her...'

He spoke sharply, clearly irked by his sister's non-compliance. Finlay had already taken a dislike to his host. Despite his attempt at ob-sequiousness, he had an air of entitlement that grated. Señor Xavier Romero considered him-self as superior as his wine, his wife and sister mere chattels in his service. Finlay felt a twinge of sympathy for the tall woman about ten feet away whose shoulder Romero was gently prod-ding.

She wore a white lace mantilla. From the back, it obscured her hair and shoulders com-pletely. Her gown was white silk embroidered with green leaves and trimmed with gold thread. Her figure was slim rather than curvaceous. She turned around, the lace of her mantilla floating out from the jewelled comb that kept it in place, and Finlay, not a man often at a loss for words, felt his jaw drop as their eyes met.

Dark chestnut hair. Almond-shaped, golden eyes. A full sensuous mouth. A beautiful face. A shockingly familiar face. Merciful heavens, but the person he had come on a wild goose chase to attempt to track down had, astonishingly, landed in his lap. The gods were indeed smiling on him.

Finlay's fleeting elation quickly faded as two thoughts struck him forcibly. First, she might very publicly blow his cover wide open. And second, she was clearly not who she had said she was. Extreme caution was required. Resisting the urge to storm across the room and cover her mouth with his hand before she could betray him, he forced himself to wait and watch.

That she recognised him was beyond a doubt in those first seconds. The shock he felt was mirrored in her own expression. Her mouth opened; her eyes widened. For an appalling moment he thought she was going to cry out in horror, then she flicked open her fan and hid behind it. Relief flooded him. She no more wanted him to acknowledge her than he wanted her to acknowledge him. He was safe. For the time being.

'May I present my sister? Isabella, this is Mr Urkyhart.'

'Urk-hart,' Finlay corrected wearily. 'Señorita Romero. It is a pleasure.'

'Mr Urquhart.' Isabella made her shaky curtsy. Her heart was pounding, her mouth quite dry. It was undoubtedly him. The English wine merchant bowing over her hand was the Scottish major she had encountered in a ditch more than two years ago. The man she had spent the night with. *Dios mio*, what was he doing here?

She gazed beseechingly at him. She had forgotten how very blue his eyes were. He was clean-shaven, his auburn hair brushed neatly back from his forehead. He was not wearing his kilt. If only she had mastered the Spanish art of communicating with her fan, she could beg him not to betray her secret partisan past. He had said nothing yet. She had to find a way of ensuring he kept silent about their previous encounter.

She slanted a glance at her brother. Xavier had made such a song and dance about this visit, seeing it as his chance to finally have his Rioja recognised as the great wine he believed it to be. Grudgingly—very grudgingly—Isabella admitted that her brother knew what he was talking about, but still, she had very much resented his command that they do all they could to make the man's visit memorable. If Xavier only asked rather than ordered it might be different. When she was feeling generous, Isabella put his tendency to command rather than request down to his years in the army. But she, too, had given orders during the war, and she had not returned to play the dictator.

Her brother drew her one of his looks. 'The first dance is about to start. I believe Gabriel wishes...'

Isabella threw the wine merchant another beseeching glance. Fortunately, he seemed to be able to read this look easily. 'If you would do me the honour, Señorita Romero, I would very much like to dance with you.'

'Gracias.' In a daze, she took his arm, propelling him towards the dance floor before Xavier could protest or stake Gabriel's prior claim.

'This,' the Scotsman said to her *sotto voce* as they joined the set, 'is rather a turn up for the books. A very unexpected surprise, to put it mildly.'

The vague, ludicrous hope that he had not recognised her, or that he would ignore their previous meeting completely, fled. Isabella felt quite sick. The first chords of the dance were struck, forcing them to separate. She cast an anxious glance around her. They had spoken in whispers, but even if Xavier was not watching, that cold little mouse of his wife would be.

As the dance began, fortunately one that required only simple steps as they progressed up the line, she tried desperately to regain her equilibrium. The shock of seeing the Scottish soldier again, and in such incongruous circumstances, had fractured her usually immaculate composure. There was too much at stake. She had to pull herself together.

He was alive. In the shock of the meeting, this salient fact had escaped her. She had occasionally wondered what had become of him as the conflict in Spain had drawn to a close and the British and French had taken their battles into the Pyrenees. He had clearly survived that false end to the war. He must have left the army then and established himself in business. He had obviously done very well indeed for himself, though that was not really surprising. He had struck her as a very, very determined and resourceful man.

He had also struck her as a very attractive man. That had been no trick of the moonlight, and judging by the way every other woman in the room was slanting him glances, she was not the only one to think so. She was drawn to him just as she had been before, despite the fact that he could turn her world upside down. When he had brushed a kiss to her fingertips, the memory of his lips on her skin all that time ago had come rushing back with unexpected force. Isabella had no idea whether it was this, or the reality of his touch now, or the underlying terror of exposure that made her shiver. Whichever, it had taken her by surprise, for she had not thought of him in a long time.

He cut as fine a figure in his evening clothes as he had in his Scottish plaid. The tight breeches clung to his muscled legs; the coat made the most of his broad shoulders. She couldn't help comparing him to Gabriel, the man whom Xavier was eager for her to marry. There was no doubt her brother's friend was more handsome, but Gabriel's was the kind of beauty that reminded Isabella of a work of art. She could admire it, she could see he was aesthetically pleasing, but there was none of the almost feral pull that she felt towards this mysterious Scotsman.

Finally, the dance brought them together. 'May I compliment you on your *toilette*,' he said with a devilish smile. 'So very different from the outfit you wore the last time we met, though I must confess, your gown does not do justice as your trousers did to your delightful derrière.'

Colour flamed in her face. She ought to be outraged, but Isabella was briefly, shockingly inclined to laugh. 'A gentleman does not remark on a lady's derrière.'

'I seem to recall telling you when last we met that I am not a gentleman, *señorita*. And now I come to think of it, I recall also that you took umbrage at being called a lady.'

She had forgotten what that particular smile of his did to her, and how very difficult it was to resist smiling back as the dance parted them once more. He was dangerous, dangerous, dangerous.

'I never got the chance to thank you,' he said when they next crossed the set. 'I'm told your guerrillas did a very thorough job.'

They circled, hands brushing lightly. 'Of course

we did,' Isabella replied in a whisper. 'Did you think I would not keep my word?'

He could not answer, for they were once again on opposite sides of the floor, but he shook his head and silently mouthed the word *no*.

The set moved up. They were separated by ten or twelve feet of dance floor, but she was aware of him watching her. She tried to keep her eyes demurely lowered, but could not resist glancing over at him every now and then. She was merely doing what every other woman in the room was doing. He was the only stranger at the ball, but it was not that that made the female guests flutter their lashes and their fans. Hadn't she recognised that night they had met, that he was a man who would attract a second and a third glance? Here was the proof of it, and there, in that sensual smile and those sea-blue eyes, was the warning she ought to heed. *Dangerous, dangerous, dangerous*, Isabella repeated to herself.

She had to make sure he did not talk. She had to! This thought plummeted her back to earth. When next the dance brought them together she rushed into speech. 'I must ask you to keep our previous acquaintance a secret.' There was no mistaking the urgency in her voice, but this was not a time for subtlety. 'Please,' she said. 'It is very important.'

'Why is that?'

The music was coming to an end. Isabella's heart was pounding. 'I will explain, I promise you, but not here.'

She made her curtsy, and the Scotsman made his bow. 'Where?'

'Promise me you will say nothing,' Isabella hissed, 'until we talk.'

He frowned, seemingly quite unaware of the urgency. She wanted to scream. She wanted to grab at his coat sleeve and shake him. Instead, she forced herself to wait what seemed like an eternity for him to consider, though it must have been mere seconds before he finally asked her where, and when.

Consuela was beckoning. Gabriel was by her side. Isabella began to panic. 'Tomorrow morning. Meet me in the courtyard behind the chapel at eight. Promise me...'

He nodded, his expression still quite unreadable. 'Until tomorrow.'

He had not promised, and now it was too late.

'Isabella.' Consuela arrived with Gabriel in tow. 'I have assured Señor Torres that you will give him your hand for this next dance.'

Gabriel's smile would have most other ladies swooning. Isabella, who had become adept at mimicking other ladies' responses, was tonight incapable of producing more than a forced smile.

'Indeed, I hope that you will,' Gabriel said, 'else I will think you prefer the company of an Englishman to a true Spaniard, and that will break my heart.'

Isabella stared at him blankly. 'Mr Urquhart is Scottish, not English.'

'A minor distinction.'

'Indeed, it is not.'

The Scotsman spoke the same words as she did at the same time. A small, embarrassed silence ensued. 'Mr Urquhart was just explaining the difference to me while we danced. To call a Scottish man English is like calling a Basque man Spanish.'

Another silence met this well-intentioned remark. Isabella resorted to her fan. Gabriel stared off into the distance. The visitor made a flourishing bow. 'Señora Romero, would it offend your husband if I asked for the hand of his beautiful wife for the next dance?'

Consuela coloured and gave the faintest of nods. 'If you will excuse us.' Gabriel made a very small bow as the orchestra struck up the introductory chords.

The Scotsman made no effort to return Gabriel's bow, Isabella noticed, and felt, in the way his hand tightened on her arm, that Gabriel had noticed, too. He swept her onto the dance floor. Looking over her shoulder, Isabella saw Consuela smile and blush coquettishly in response to some remark made by Mr Urquhart.

'You are looking very lovely tonight. There is no other woman in the room who can hold a candle to you.'

Gabriel's compliments, like his smile, were practised and meaningless. He was rich, he was well born and he was handsome. He had no cause to doubt that he was an excellent catch, and enjoyed enthusiastic encouragement of his suit from Xavier. Isabella was nearly twenty-six. Too old, in the eyes of most of her acquaintance, to hope for such an excellent match. To be wooed by Gabriel Torres was flattering indeed.

Looking at him now, as he executed one of the more complex dance steps with precision, Isabella could nonetheless summon nothing stronger than indifference.

Chapter Three

Finlay threw open the doors that led out from his bedchamber onto the balcony and sucked in the cold night air. It had been a very long evening. He was fair knackered, to use one of his Glaswegian sergeant's phrases, but his mind was alert, his thoughts racing, just like in the old days. He stared up at the stars that hung like huge silver disks, struck anew by how much brighter they seemed to shine in the sky than at home.

Home. It had not felt at all like home when he'd gone back. Ach, his ma and da had been the same. And his sisters, and his brother, too. None of them had changed. Their lives, the landscape had not altered, but he had, and there was no point pretending otherwise. He hated himself for it, but he couldn't help but see the croft and the village and his family and their friends as his fellow officers would view them. No, he didn't share their contempt for them, and yes, he still loved his family, but if he had to spend the rest of his life there he'd go stark staring mad. He would rail against the provincial predictability and cosy safety of it, the very things that he had thought he'd crave after the bedlam of war.

'I'm just a big ungrateful tumshie,' he muttered, 'with ideas well above my station.' But no matter how guilty he felt, he knew that if he left the army and returned to Oban, he'd make his family every bit as miserable as he.

He had never been anything other than a soldier. He had surrendered his real family long ago, and had no idea what he would do without the one he had adopted in the army. If he did choose to leave, that was. And what would he do with himself, if he did?

Sighing, Finlay leaned on the stone balustrade and gazed out over the formal gardens of Hermoso Romero. The future would have to take care of itself. Fortunately, he had plenty other things to occupy his mind. Such as rethinking his strategy in the light of this evening's extraordinary turn of events.

Calm and clarity of mind returned. A light breeze had picked up, making the tall cypress trees bend and sway gracefully in the moonlight like flamenco dancers. Finlay shivered in his shirtsleeves and, returning to his chamber, stretched out on top of the bed. It had been a major shock to see Señorita Romero at the dance tonight, but it had been a much, much bigger shock for her. The lass had been scared out of her wits that he'd betray her, and that was all for the good, making it highly unlikely she'd betray him first. Even if she did, he had a plausible cover story to explain his presence here. He just had to stick to it.

He pondered this course of action, staring up at the shadow from his candle dancing on the corniced ceiling, and decided that there was a great deal of merit in it. Gradually, the miracle of having found his partisan right here, in plain view, began to supersede his concerns for his own safety. He only had to bide his time and see how the land lay with her. Not all ex-guerrillas and partisans were liberals. If she espoused her brother's politics, then she represented everything El Fantasma railed against in his illegal pamphlets.

Finlay frowned at this. She'd seemed a feisty thing during those few hours they'd shared together under the stars. He'd admired her, the way she stood up for herself. Tonight, he'd seen a glimpse of that fire when they were dancing, but for the rest of the evening she'd behaved like a shy, retiring wee mouse with little to say for herself.

'In other words, Finlay, just exactly like an unmarried high-born Spanish lady. Which is exactly what she is, now that the war is over.'

Though two years ago she had implied she was a farmer's daughter. Why? Like as not, it had simply been a ruse to hide her identity. One thing, her being a female partisan with a gun he'd encountered in a ditch. Quite another, if that partisan was a lady, the sister of the biggest local landowner. He smiled to himself. That would cause quite a stir were it discovered. Though now he came to think of it, there had been mention of a father. She had seemed right fond of him, too, but he obviously wasn't around, presumably dead. Poor lass. Whatever her politics, if she had any, it must be tough trying to fit back into this privileged and class-conscious world. He could sympathise with that, and then some.

Watch and wait, that was what he needed to do. Spend a bit of time in her company, find out if he could trust her, and encourage her to trust him. It would be no hardship. She was every bit as bonny as he remembered. Jack had been wrong about that one. Finlay rolled off the bed and undressed quickly before snuffing the candle and clambering between the sheets. He was looking forward to his early-morning encounter with Señorita Romero.

Isabella was at the assignation point early. She wore one of her favourite gowns—dark blue merino with long sleeves that covered her knuckles, the bodice, cuffs and hem trimmed simply with cream embroidery. She had eschewed a shawl or pelisse, the woollen dress offering sufficient protection from the early-morning chill. The colour and the simple style suited her, she knew. Dressing for a man was not something that sat well with her, but this man held the sword of Damocles over her head, and if it helped to look well, then she would make every effort to do so.

She was nervous, though a long night's reflection had helped her regain most of her habitual composure. It had also revealed to her some fundamental issues to be addressed. Her reaction had been too extreme. Her fear must have been obvious. She reassured herself once more that the Scotsman's having said nothing so far made it less likely that he would say anything at all. As she watched his tall figure striding across the grass towards her, Isabella tried very hard to convince herself of this.

'*Buenos días.* You're looking bonny this fine morning, Señorita Romero.'

'Thank you. I trust you slept well?'

'Like a baby. Shall we get away from the main house? There's that many windows looking out on us, I'm sure you'd rather we were not observed.'

'I'm sure the feeling is mutual, Mr Urquhart.'

He smiled enigmatically, either oblivious to her implied threat, or indifferent. 'I'm glad you've finally mastered my name, but I seem to recall you calling me Finlay before.'

'As I recall, you were a major in the British army at the time.' Isabella headed for the walkway flanked by two rows of cypress trees where they would not be observed. 'Your life has taken a very different turn since then. It seems rather remarkable for a soldier to transform himself into a prosperous wine merchant.'

'No more remarkable than for a partisan to transform herself into a lady.'

'I am not *transformed*,' Isabella said sharply. 'I am merely *returned*.'

'Returned.' He eyed her speculatively. 'I wonder, *señorita*, if anyone knows that you were ever away. I suspect not. It would certainly explain why my appearance last night terrified you out of your wits.'

He spoke softly, but his tone was all the more menacing for that. 'I was taken aback, that is all,' Isabella replied.

'No. *I* was taken aback. You looked like an ensign confronted with a bayonet for the first time.'

'If you are implying that I would run away from facing the enemy...'

He laughed. 'Are you implying that I am the enemy?'

'Are you? If so, I fail to see how my coming here quite alone could be construed as running away.'

The conversation was not progressing as she had planned, mostly because she had signally failed to play her part. It was his fault. This Scotsman, he made her speak without thinking. She had to regroup her thoughts, stick to what she had rehearsed. She had to remember there was no shame in it, that the means justified the end. 'You are right,' Isabella said with what she knew to be a forlorn little smile. 'I was afraid.'

'Because that brother of yours has no idea that you fought with the guerrillas?'

'My brother is a very influential man, Mr Urquhart, and his estate is the largest in La Rioja. It would be most embarrassing to him if it was discovered that his sister was…that she acted in an—an unladylike manner.' *To say the least!*

'Unladylike. That is one way of putting it.'

'You have another way?' she asked sharply.

He smiled at her. 'You were fighting for your country, just as he was. I'd say what you did was brave and honourable. If you were my sister, I'd be proud of you.'

His praise, so unexpected and so very rare, made her flush with pleasure. 'Thank you.'

'I meant it.' He caught her hand, bringing them both to a halt. '*Señorita*, I have been remiss. Your father, I take it he passed away? Please accept my condolences. You gave me the impression that you were very fond of him.'

'Yes. We were very close.' A lump rose in her throat. Papa had always preferred his daughter to his son, yet it was to Xavier that all of the condolences had been given when Papa died, just as it had been Xavier who had received all the gratitude and admiration for fighting for his country. 'It happened just after the end of the war. At least Papa lived to see peace return to his beloved Spain.'

'And now you have had peace for two years. Is it what you imagined or hoped? Does the world turn in a different direction?'

'I think it was you who expressed that hope, actually.' Isabella shrugged, pulling her hands free before turning away. 'As far as my brother is concerned, the world turns in exactly the same manner as it did before the war. He has a very modern approach to wine, but in every other respect Xavier, like our king, prefers the old ways.'

Despite herself, she had been unable to keep the edge of bitterness out of her voice and the Scotsman noticed. 'I take it that you do not share your brother's views?'

'Mr Urquhart, I am a woman, and in the eyes of the law I am my brother's property now that I am no longer my father's, and will remain so until I am my husband's.'

'You have changed a great deal in two years, if what you're telling me is that you don't have any views at all.'

The temptation to contradict him almost overwhelmed her, but the dangers of doing so restrained her. Isabella forced a brittle smile. 'We have both changed a great deal, I think. Neither of us are soldiers now. You are a businessman. I am a lady. I would therefore very much appreciate it if you kept what you know of my past to yourself. To expose me would cause my brother a great deal of embarrassment.'

'I'd say embarrassment was putting it mildly.'

'What do you mean?'

'If it was discovered that your brother was nourishing a liberal viper in his midst...'

'I am not a viper!'

His sea-blue eyes sparkled with amusement. 'I note you do not deny being a liberal.'

Too late yet again, she realised she had betrayed herself. 'Mr Urquhart, you are here to do business with my brother. Lucrative business for you, I believe, for there is substance to his boasts. You will not find a better Rioja than ours. Surely you cannot be thinking of putting such a deal in jeopardy? Please,' she urged when he made no reply, swallowing the last remnants of her pride, 'whatever you think of me, whatever you know of my past, you understand that it can only hurt Xavier.'

He frowned, pushing his hair back from his brow, though it was cut considerably shorter than before, and there was no need. 'Very well, Señorita Romero, you have my word that I will keep quiet about your patriotic past. After all, we Scots have a well-earned reputation for being canny and shrewd businessmen with an eye for a profit,' he concluded wryly.

'Thank you. I— Thank you.' Her relief was

apparent in her voice, but so it should be. 'It is better, I think, for the past to remain in the past now the war is over.' They were Xavier's words, and often uttered. Isabella rolled her eyes metaphorically as she spoke them.

The Scotsman, however, looked—sad? 'You think so?' he asked. 'You really want to forget it happened?' He leaned back against the trunk of a tree, head back, looking up at the pale expanse of sky visible through the foliage. 'All that sacrifice, all those lives lost. Now that Boney is stuck on an island in the middle of the Atlantic, at least we are done with wars for a while.'

'And there is no more requirement for soldiers to fight them,' Isabella said softly, as understanding dawned. And empathy.

'No, there's not.' He stood up, rolling his shoulders. 'So now I buy and sell wine, and you sit at home embroidering or knitting or whatever it is fine Spanish ladies do.'

She couldn't help but laugh. 'Oh, if you want an example of the perfect Spanish lady, you must look to my sister-in-law. Consuela can set a perfect stitch, sing a perfect song, bear a perfect child, and all the while smiling a perfect smile. She is a bloodless creature.'

'I think she is simply very young and very shy and very overwhelmed by all this,' Finlay said, nodding back at the house. 'She misses her sisters.'

'She told you all that while you were dancing? It is more than she has ever seen fit to tell me.' Isabella shook her head incredulously. 'You must have misunderstood. Her family would be welcome to visit any time. She only has to issue an invitation.' She waited for him to answer her implied question, but he said nothing. 'What is it, what did she say to you?'

'I never break a confidence. You'll have to ask her yourself.'

'A confidence! You only met her last night, and she is confiding in you.'

'I'm sorry, I didn't mean to offend you.'

The Scotsman touched her cheek. Isabella jerked away. 'Why should I be offended? Consuela is very beautiful, and you are very charming, and if she chose to speak to you of matters that—well, that is none of my business.'

'She is indeed beautiful, but in the manner of

a painting, you know. You can admire her, and you are happy to look at her, but as to anything else…'

'But that is exactly what I was thinking about Gabriel only last night.'

'The Adonis who looked down his nose at me? What is he to you?'

It was none of his business, but it was so refreshing to talk to a man who actually spoke what was on his mind and expected her to return the favour. 'He is my brother's best friend. They were in the army together. My brother hopes to make a match between us. It would be a very good match for me.'

'But it would also be—what was your phrase—bloodless.'

'What do you mean?'

'I mean you don't find the idea of kissing him appealing. You see, that's the difference between you and your brother's wife. While I'm more than happy to look at her, I don't feel the slightest inclination to kiss her.'

Isabella's mouth went dry, and her pulses fluttered. The Scotsman's fingers circled her wrist loosely. She could easily free herself. His other hand rested on her shoulder. She seemed to be standing very close to him. 'I am very glad,' she said, 'because I think Xavier's hospitality has limits.'

He laughed softly. 'You know that I would very much like to kiss you, don't you?'

'I think you wanted to, two years ago.'

'It's something I've often regretted, that I did not.'

Her heart was pounding wildly. She was playing with fire, but she was enjoying it far too much to stop. She was so rarely afforded the freedom to be herself. It was exhilarating. 'It is something I, too, have regretted, that you did not,' Isabella said daringly.

She had surprised him. She could see from the way his eyes darkened that she had also aroused him, and that knowledge heightened her own awareness of him. 'There is nothing worse than regret,' he said.

'Nothing,' she agreed.

He made no move for a long moment, and despite the longing twisting inside her, she had reached the limits of her boldness. If he did not kiss her now, he never would. If he did not kiss her now, she would always wonder. If he did not kiss her…

He kissed her. His lips touched hers with the softness of a whisper. She closed her eyes and stepped forward into his embrace. A hand slid around her waist, another cupped her cheek. His kiss was so gentle, she hardly dared move lest he break it. His mouth was warm on hers. It felt odd, different, in the nicest way possible. She angled her head. She slid her arm around him. He gave a tiny sigh and pulled her closer and kissed her again. Not so gently, but still carefully.

She had never been kissed like this before. She let him coax her mouth open. It didn't cross her mind that her ignorance would betray her or make her seem foolish; she thought only that she wanted to kiss him back, and so she did. His fingers curled into her hair. Her fingers curled into his coat. She could feel the hardness of his body against hers. He was so much bigger than her, but it didn't make her feel weak. He felt so warm; she felt so secure against the solid bulk of him. He was making her feel very hot. His tongue touched hers, and she leaped back in astonishment.

He cursed. At least it sounded like a curse, though the language was foreign to her. 'I'm sorry,' he said, raking his hand through his hair again. 'I didn't realise...'

Isabella flushed with mortification. He would think her a child. 'Please,' she said, turning away, 'let us forget about it.'

Any other man would be happy to do exactly what she asked, to spare himself the embarrassment of an apology if nothing else. This man, she ought to have remembered, was not like any other man. He caught her arm, pulling her back to face him. 'I am truly sorry. I went too far, and mistook your experience.'

Isabella was too proud to look at the ground, and she could not bear pity. 'No, you mistook my enjoyment,' she said, giving him a haughty look. 'I think it is not always true that good things come to those who wait.'

For a split second, he looked as if she had slapped him and then, to her astonishment, he burst out laughing. 'That's me told, then. I must be more out of practice than I realised.'

'I do not think a man like you lacks women to—to practise on.'

'Now that, *señorita*, was quite uncalled for. I remember quite clearly that one of the things I told you that night was that I'm not the kind of man who has a taste for kissing any and every available woman. Not that it's any of your business, but in the two years since last we met, there has been only one woman in my life, and that fleeting *affaire* ended in Brussels nearly four months ago.'

There was not a trace of humour in his voice now. He released her, taking several paces back. The look he gave her would be quite intimidating if she was the kind of woman to allow herself to be intimidated. The kind of woman she pretended to be. But Isabella was beyond playing such a part for now. 'Your women—or your lack of women—are none of my business,' she said, anxious more than anything to close the subject.

But the Scotsman seemed determined to prolong it. 'No, they are not, save that I wouldn't have kissed you if there had been any woman in my life, and I would sure as hell have *stopped* kissing you if you'd given me the least bit of an idea that you didn't want me to. I told you—*an-*

other thing I remember telling you very clearly—that I never, ever force myself on a woman.'

He was angry, though he was trying very hard not to show it. She had to acknowledge that he had a right. 'I'm sorry.' Isabella closed her eyes. 'You were right. I have not...I lack—I lack the experience you attributed to me. I'm sorry. It was my fault, not yours.'

She was blushing. It had cost her dear, that admission, and she shouldn't have been forced to make it. His anger dissipated like melting snow. Finlay touched her cheek gently. Her eyes fluttered open. 'No, you are too generous. It was my fault. I got carried away, and forgot that you are not the woman I spent the night with two years ago, but a lady whose innocence I quite forgot to take account of. Will you forgive me?'

'There is nothing to forgive.'

'I took advantage. Your brother...'

Her big almond-shaped eyes flashed at him. 'Do not bring Xavier into this. Who I choose to kiss or not to kiss has nothing to do with my brother.'

Finlay was pretty sure that Xavier held a very

different opinion on the subject. And he was, on reflection, pretty certain that an innocent like Isabella should not be choosing to kiss any man until she was betrothed. That she was an innocent, after that kiss there could be no doubt, but he was struggling to reconcile the lady who claimed to be feart of offending her brother with the one who crept about behind enemy lines brandishing a gun.

They came to the end of the cypress walk. 'I will leave you here,' Isabella said. 'I hope that we have an understanding between us now?'

'I believe we do,' Finlay said with a smile he hoped was reassuring. He believed quite the contrary, but what to do about it, he needed to consider. He watched her go, standing in the shadow of one of the tall trees. She walked with the long, graceful stride he remembered until she came within sight of the house, when she stopped abruptly, looking up at one of the windows. When she resumed, her walk had that slow, floating grace that made her look as if she was gliding. He could tell from the line of her neck that her gaze was demurely lowered.

Was she playing the part of a lady for whoever

was watching, or had she played the part of the feisty partisan to keep Finlay sweet—and quiet? Had she kissed him for the same reason? Had he initiated the kiss or she? He could remember only that he had wanted to kiss her more than he'd wanted to kiss any woman for quite some time. Had she pretended to enjoy it as much as he had?

He cursed in Gaelic under his breath. 'Kisses are not the point here,' he told himself. 'Forget the kisses and concentrate on what you came here for. You need to get her to give you the information you need, or decide she's not going to, in which case you will need to rethink your strategy.'

Consulting his pocket watch, he cursed again. Señor Romero would be waiting to take him on the promised tour of the vineyards, a prospect Finlay was far from relishing, not least for fear of betraying his own ignorance. It was such a waste of time, too, and he had no idea how much time he had if he was to beat the Spanish to El Fantasma. It would be much more constructive to spend the time with Isabella. Much more constructive, and considerably more appealing, Finlay thought, shuddering as he anticipated long hours of Xavier's obsequious condescension. He had to find a way of swapping the brother for the sister after today. It would be a challenge, but Finlay relished a challenge.

Isabella sat in the shade of a tree while her horse drank from a small stream. Taking advantage of the fact that Xavier was too engrossed in showing the Scotsman around the estate to wonder what his sister was doing, she had ridden out without an escort. She was hot and tired, but the tension she had hoped to work off was, if anything, aggravated.

She had to clear her head. She had to try to think straight. Take a step back. Gain perspective. Something. Isabella got to her feet and pulled off the long boots and stockings she wore under her riding habit. Picking up her skirts, she scrabbled down the banks into the stream, gasping as the icy water that tumbled down from the mountains caressed her skin.

It was painful and exhilarating at the same time. It struck her as pathetic that she was reduced to obtaining pleasure from paddling in a mountain stream. When Finlay Urquhart had kissed her this morning, it had been just like this, only more. Who would have thought that a man's lips could have such an effect? She had felt wild, locked in his embrace. She had felt strangely free.

But what a stupid mess she had made of it afterwards. Isabella waded over to a large boulder in the middle of the burbling water and sat down, tilting her face up to the sun. Gabriel had never attempted to kiss her. Was it because it would be improper until they were betrothed, or because he did not want to? She tried to imagine kissing Gabriel, but instead of his dark good looks, she could picture only the Scotsman's fascinating blue eyes, his wicked smile, the glint of his auburn hair. There was a recklessness about him that had appealed to her that night they had spent together two years ago. It still appealed.

Xavier would be utterly furious if he knew that his sister had been kissing a mere wine merchant. Isabella laughed, but her smile faded almost immediately. She had behaved shockingly. She had spoken much too freely. But, oh, it had been so good to do so. For long moments, she had been herself with the Scotsman. It had been a relief not to pretend that the Isabella he'd met before had never existed. It had felt so good. She longed to be that woman again, just for a little while. She would like to spend more time in his company, to cross conversational swords with him. He spoke to her as if she had a mind of her own. It made her realise, sadly, that almost no other man of her acquaintance did, save those she knew from the war, and they were now in a minority of one.

Had she been rash? He had given her his word not to betray her. He had given her his word once before, and kept it. Major Finlay Urquhart had been an honourable man. Was there such a thing as an honourable wine merchant? The incongruity of his choice of profession struck her anew. He was a man of action. A man who had taken on the task of surveillance himself when he could surely have sent one of his men. Just as she had. A man who liked to make his own decisions. Just as she did. Not a man who would relish haggling over the price of a hogshead of wine, caught in the middle between supplier and buyer, she would have thought. The man she had met that fateful night and the man he appeared to be now seemed almost incompatible. There was something about Mr Finlay Urquhart, wine merchant to the gentry, that did not quite ring true.

Sliding down from the boulder, Isabella picked her way over the slippery stones back to the shore, pulling her stockings and boots on over her numbed feet. She ought not to be wasting time thinking about a man who would be walking out of her life for good in a few days. She ought to be considering her own future.

Could she really contemplate becoming Señora Gabriel Torres? She tried to imagine spending her days engaged in domestic pursuits. It was not the housekeeping or the children that she rebelled against; it was not even surrendering herself to the care of a man, for in the eyes of the law, she was Xavier's property until he gave her up. What appalled her the most was the surrender of her mind. She would not be expected to think beyond what to put on the table for dinner. Her opinions would not be consulted. She would not be permitted to discuss politics or business. What was it the Scotsman had said this morning? Embroidery and knitting. Isabella had always taken perverse pride in being very bad at both. She was not about to learn now.

Yet she must marry, for Xavier was set on it, and he could make her continued presence in his house unpleasant. Gabriel was rich, he was handsome, he was popular, she reminded herself. He was an excellent match.

'And at my great age, I cannot expect to do better, according to my brother,' she said to herself as she prepared to mount her horse. 'Loath as I am to admit it, Xavier is right. If I do not accept Gabriel soon, he will find someone else, and then where will I be? Better the devil you know, perhaps?'

She settled her skirts around her, thinking as she always did, how much she missed the freedom of riding astride in breeches. As the wife of Gabriel Torres, there would be no question of her ever doing that again. Exasperated, she dismissed the question of her future. Right now, she had a contradictory, disconcertingly attractive Scotsman to deal with. Really, for Xavier's sake she needed to ensure that he was what he claimed to be, and if that meant spending more time in his company, so be it. Having happily reconciled her inclination with her duty, Isabella tapped her heels lightly against her horse's flank and headed in the direction of home.

It had been, as Finlay had predicted it would be, a long and tedious day. He had not thought anyone could discourse at such length on the subject of viticulture, but Xavier Romero seemed to be tireless. His passion for all things Rioja led him to expound at length on soil types, grape varieties, vine diseases, pest control, pruning methods, harvesting methods and the weather, from frost, to hail, to sun and humidity. Fortunately, his enthusiasm was second only to his love of his own voice. Finlay had contributed very little to the conversation, if such it could be called. His head, however, was throbbing as if they had drunk six bottles of Rioja when in fact the only thing they hadn't done was sample the blasted stuff.

They were quitting the stables when Señorita Romero arrived. Alone, and on horseback, when she saw her brother, she could not disguise her dismay. 'Xavier, I thought you would still be out with Mr Urquhart.'

'Where is your groom?'

'He was busy elsewhere. I am quite capable of saddling a horse and going for a ride.'

Her tone was mild, though Finlay thought he saw a flash of anger in her eyes. She dismounted with a rustle of her skirts, and a tantalising glimpse of leather riding boots. How long were they? he wondered, momentarily distracted. Did they stretch to her knee, or higher still?

Xavier clicked his fingers to summon a stable hand. Isabella handed over her reins to the boy with a friendly smile. Her brother however, was not happy. 'I have told you several times that it is most improper for a sister of mine to ride about the countryside without an escort.'

'I have been riding about this countryside all my life. Everyone knows me, I know everyone. Papa never insisted I take a groom.'

'Our father was far too lenient with you. Besides, it is I who is now custodian of Hermoso Romero,' her brother replied stiffly. 'Your reputation is a reflection on me. It will be said that I cannot take care of my own sister, if you are seen out alone. It will be said that I do not treat her with respect.'

'Then, you can reply that you trust me to be on my own. That is treating me with respect. That is what Papa would say.'

Romero seemed with difficulty to control his temper. For some reason, Finlay noticed with interest, the subject was a sore point with him. 'Our father is dead,' he said, speaking sharply to his sister. 'It is clear to me that you have been completely overindulged. I do not envy Gabriel the schooling of you.'

There was no mistaking the flash in the *señorita*'s golden eyes at this remark, though she clasped her hands tightly round her riding crop and did not rise to the bait. Finlay however, who had been standing quietly to one side, could not resist. 'She is not a child, Romero.'

'She is a woman. It is almost the same thing,' the other man snapped. 'Excuse me, but this is none of your concern, Mr Urkarty.'

'I beg your pardon, *señor*.' Finlay spoke through clenched teeth, although his smile was conciliatory—he hoped. 'Señorita Romero strikes me as a most competent horsewoman.'

'Naturally. It is in her blood.'

The arrogance of the man! 'And she has, I understand, been accustomed to riding out alone while your father was alive, without damaging her reputation?'

'That is not the point, Mr Urkarty.'

'No, Señor Romero, you are quite right, it is not. The point is to choose your battles more carefully. I have three sisters of my own, and so speak from experience. A little leeway in small matters will buy you a great deal of credit when it comes to the larger ones.'

Romero's temper hung in the balance for a few moments. The man was not accustomed to being contradicted, that was for certain. Finlay shot a warning glance at the object of their conversation, but her eyes were fixed firmly on her boots. Unlike her brother, she knew when to keep her mouth shut.

Finally, Romero spoke. 'Three sisters,' he said with a smile every bit as forced as Finlay's. 'I confess, I don't envy you that. Perhaps it is because I have only the one that I am overprotective. Very well, I will take your advice, Mr Urkety. Provided she confines herself to our estate, I do not see why—you see Isabella, how magnanimous I can be.'

'I— Thank you, Xavier.'

Her brother, however, was distracted by the return of his stable hand carrying a note. Señorita Romero turned to Finlay. 'I must thank you, too, Mr Urquhart,' she said softly. 'Every time I am permitted to slip my leash a little, I will think of you.'

Her smile was demure, but her eyes were stormy. 'If it was in my power I would cut your leash completely,' Finlay replied. 'You know, I...'

An exclamation from Romero made them both turn around. 'It is Estebe, who is in charge of the winery. The man has fallen from a tree, would you believe.'

'Oh, no, Xavier, is he badly injured?'

Romero frowned. 'A broken leg. It is very inconvenient, for I had intended he take Mr Urkety on a tour of the cellars tomorrow. I have urgent business elsewhere, which I am loath to cancel, but...'

'Cannot Señorita Romero escort me instead?' Finlay asked.

'Oh, yes, please allow me to take Estebe's place,' Isabella urged. 'While you were at war, while Papa's health was failing, I helped Estebe a great deal. Of course I know that compared to you and Estebe, I am a mere novice, but I do know the history of our home and of the wine, and I am sure that is something Mr Urquhart will wish to be able to impart to his customers.'

Romero pursed his lips. 'It would be most irregular.'

'Aye, but your sister speaks the truth,' Finlay corroborated, masking his surprise. 'My customers like to know a bit about the background and provenance of the wines they are being asked to pay a pretty penny for. And I would hate to deflect you from important business.'

'Very well. Yes, when you put it that way.' Romero smiled thinly at his sister. 'Another favour granted, Isabella. I hope you are keeping count. You may supervise some tastings, brief Mr Urkety on the history, perhaps even compile some notes for him. She writes a fair enough hand, Mr Urkety, I will grant her that. And now, if you will excuse me, I must return to the house. I will see you both at dinner.'

Señorita Romero watched him go before turning to Finlay. 'If I was not cursed with the brain of a mere woman, I would suspect you of very manipulative behaviour, Mr Urquhart.'

'Ach, now, I wouldn't put it quite as strongly as that.'

She narrowed her eyes at him. 'How would you put it?'

'Now, there, you see, you've put me on the spot, for if I was to confess that your brother's company is not nearly as appealing to me as yours, you would likely accuse me of being condescending rather than manipulative. But don't, I beg you, try to pull the wool over my eyes.'

'What do you mean, Mr Urquhart?'

'It's Finlay.' Glancing over his shoulder, he caught her hand and pulled her into the shelter of the stable door, out of sight of prying eyes. 'I can understand why you don't want your brother to know anything about your past. I have promised to keep that between us, and I keep my promises. But what I don't understand, my fair former partisan, is why you're so determined to hide your true self behind a demure facade. What are you trying to conceal?'

If he had not been watching her so closely he would have missed the flicker of fear in her eyes. It was quickly masked. 'I don't know what you're talking about, Mr Urquhart.'

'Finlay.'

She closed the distance between them to whisper in his ear, 'I am not concealing anything, Finlay. I assure you.'

'No?' Her hair tickled his cheek. Her smile was beguiling. Her eyes gleamed. Not a trace of the demure lady now; this woman made his blood heat. She made him lose his train of thought, distracting him with the proximity of that mouth, the memory of that kiss this morning.

But this was business, life-and-death business, not pleasure. He stepped away from temptation. 'As my friend Jack is wont to say, "I'll believe you, thousands wouldn't."'

Chapter Four

Isabella peeled an orange and carefully separated it into segments. Xavier had breakfasted hours ago, setting off on his business trip to Pamplona before the sun had risen. Across the large, ornately laid table in the breakfast room, Finlay had finished his substantial selection of ham, cheese and bread, and was taking a second cup of coffee. He was chatting to Consuela about the latest French fashions. Isabella knew nothing about such things, and so could not tell if he was extremely knowledgeable or merely extremely plausible. Her sister-in-law was more animated than Isabella had ever seen her. Several times she had broken into a ripple of girlish laughter. Now, she was reading him a mock lecture, wagging her pretty beringed finger at him and fluttering her long lashes. Consuela never teased Xavier like this, but then Xavier, though handsome, had not a fraction of Finlay's charm and even less interest than Isabella in women's fripperies.

She ate a piece of her orange. The fruit was at its best at this time of year, succulently sweet, rather like Consuela. And that, Isabella reprimanded herself, was a shrewish remark quite unworthy of her.

She slanted a look at Finlay. He caught her eye and flashed her a smile. She looked down at her plate. It had seemed complicit, that smile. As if they had a secret. As if they knew something Consuela did not. A flutter of nerves sent her back to her coffee cup. She took a reviving sip, reminding herself that Finlay had no grounds for whatever suspicions he was nurturing. If he challenged her again about playing the demure lady, she would invoke the need to behave as her brother expected her to while under his roof. And in the meantime, she would pursue her own suspicions regarding him.

'Xavier tells me that you are taking Mr Urquhart on a tour of the wine cellars,' Consuela said, getting to her feet. 'That was generous of you.

They are horrible, Mr Urquhart, cold and I am sure swarming with rats. It is no wonder my husband is reluctant to go down there. I only wonder that Isabella is so fond of them. Now you will excuse me, if you please. I must go and tend to my son.'

'So your brother is uncomfortable in his own wine cellars,' Finlay said, closing the door behind Consuela. 'That explains why he was so easily persuaded to allow his sister to spend time in the company of a mere wine merchant.'

'It is not the dark or the rats Xavier fears, it is the fact that the cellars are so far underground. He has never liked them.'

'And yet you, according to the lovely Señora Romero, are very fond of them.'

'I don't share my brother's temperament. I have been wondering, Mr Urquhart—Finlay—what it was that made you turn to the trading of wine, when you left the army?'

'It is a lucrative business. As a canny Scot, that was reason enough.'

'With the right contacts I am sure that it is indeed lucrative. I wonder, you see, since you told me that you had not been home to England—I beg your pardon, Scotland—for so many years, I wonder how you have managed to establish sufficient customers so quickly.'

Isabella took a sip of coffee, but kept her eyes on Finlay. Did his eyes flicker? Did his fingers tighten on his cup? She could not be sure.

'I'm wondering,' he replied, 'if it is any of your business. Are you worried that I'll sell your brother's wine to someone who has not the palate to tell the difference between your fine Rioja and the stuff they drink from the barrel in the village bodegas? Are you thinking I should test the colour of a man's blood before I sell to him? Blue—yes, you can have as much as you like. Red—no, sorry, laddie, not good enough.'

He was still sitting, seemingly relaxed, at the table, but there was an edge to his voice that should have warned her to drop the subject. Isabella popped another segment of orange into her mouth. 'It is not a question of blood, Mr— Finlay. It is a question of money.'

'They all too often go hand in hand, I find, *señorita*. One begets the other. Lack of one tends to mean lack of the other.'

'But you are the son of a farmer, and yet you

became a major in Wellington's army, and now you are a wealthy merchant. You are, as I seem to remember you telling me before, the— I forget the English phrase.'

'The exception that proves the rule.'

Isabella nodded. 'That was it.'

'The Jock Upstart, is what Wellington calls— called me. A man who does not know his allotted place in the scheme of things.'

'The Jock Upstart,' Isabella repeated slowly. 'Ah, I see, because it rhymes with Urquhart. That is clever. Though also condescending.'

'Add in licentious, ruthless and charming, and you have encapsulated the essence of the Duke of Wellington, taking the fact that he is on the whole a brilliant strategist as given.'

Isabella raised her brows. 'You don't like him very much.'

'No, but then he does not like me very much, either. It doesn't stop him thinking me useful.'

'You use the present tense, I think?' Isabella asked sharply. 'But you have left the army…'

This time she was sure she saw a flicker of unease in his eyes, though he smiled blandly.

'Useful in terms of supplying him with the best wine in Spain. If your brother will sell it to me.'

Isabella could not argue with the sense of this, though still, she was sure he was not telling the whole truth. 'You know, for a man who is so successful, you are very—I don't know, contradictory? You look down your nose at the Duke of Wellington and at my brother, and at me, too, I think, and you say to yourself, you are our equal, if not our superior. But you don't really believe it.'

'What precisely do you mean by that?'

She had no idea what she had meant, save to rile him into betraying himself. He was sitting perfectly still, but his expression was forbidding. She ought to back down, but she was exceeding tired of biting her tongue and eating her words and quelling her so unladylike thoughts. 'You don't realise how lucky you are,' Isabella said. 'You are a man.'

'I'm lucky because I'm a man? You'll have to explain yourself a bit more, if you please.'

On the contrary, what she ought to do was keep her mouth closed. Isabella pushed her plate away with some force. 'It is obvious. When you walk into a room, people do not think, there is that—what was it?—Jock Upstart? They don't think about your family tree or your bloodlines or any of those things. They think, there is a man who knows who he is. A confident man. A man who commands respect as well as admiration. Do you think my brother would be taking such pains to cultivate you if he thought anything else?'

'I'm still not getting your point, lass.'

Exasperated, she jumped to her feet and threw back the curtains that kept the sunlight Consuela dreaded from the room. 'You are a man! Do you not understand, that is the most salient point! You can do what you want with your life, make of it what you want. I am a mere woman. All I have is my bloodline and my family tree. When I walk into a room, people think, there is Señorita Romero, sister of Xavier Romero, whose dowry would make an excellent addition to our family coffers.'

'That's not what I think when you walk into a room, I can tell you, and I'd be very surprised indeed if it was the first thing any man thought.'

'If you are going to mention my derrière again...'

His low chuckle made her turn away from the window. The wicked look was back in his eyes. 'There, that's the problem, you see. When you walk into a room, you do not make a man want to treat you like a lady. Well, not this man, at any event. And that was a compliment, incidentally, just in case you weren't sure.'

Isabella folded her arms. 'You make it very difficult to argue with you.'

'I wasn't aware that we've been arguing.'

'I think that behind the bravado, you have a very low opinion of yourself, Major Finlay Urquhart.'

'No, Señorita Romero, I leave that to other people.'

'You don't. That is what we were arguing about.' Smiling triumphantly, Isabella got to her feet. 'You see, contrary to popular opinion, I am not just a pretty face,' she said, patting Finlay lightly on the cheek. 'I will meet you at the winery in half an hour, Mr Urquhart, and you shall have your tour of the cellars. Although I am sure an acknowledged expert such as your-self should be giving me the tour.'

She left that remark hanging in the air as she swept from the room.

The entrance to the wine cellars was through a huge trapdoor set in the floor of the main press-ing room. The heavy oak and iron hinges were lifted by means of a pulley that Isabella attached to the ringed handle. Finlay found it turned very easily, revealing a steep set of stone steps disap-pearing into the gloom below.

'This is the original entrance. There is another, much wider one, cut when oak casks were intro-duced to the process, but I thought you would like to see this,' Isabella said.

She was wearing a long cloak over her cotton gown. The thick walls of the winery's working buildings kept the rooms cool. The air coming up from the cellar entrance was chilly. Finlay was glad of his coat. Isabella lit two lamps and handed him one. 'Be careful—the steps are very worn in places.'

His instinct was to insist on going first, but he managed to restrain himself and follow in her wake, just as he had done on the hillside track two years previously. The staircase was narrow enough for him to touch the rock on either side. In places as they descended, the arched roof was no more than a few inches from the top of his head. Isabella moved sure-footedly, swiftly enough for her cloak to flutter out behind her. Señora Romero was in the right of it; Isabella was obviously no stranger to this place.

As they stopped at the bottom of the steps and Finlay lifted his lamp high, he whistled. 'What a place for a wean to play.'

'Wane?'

'Wean, bairn, child,' he clarified.

'Ah, yes. When I was a little girl I loved to come here.'

'I'll bet you did. It's absolutely cavernous.'

'Oh, this is just the beginning. Wait till you see.'

The passageway led off in both directions. They turned to the right through an arched entranceway into a wider corridor, one side of which was stacked high with oak barrels. The individual cellars themselves led off the passage, each with vaulted ceilings cut directly out of the limestone. Dusty bottles, some shrouded with cobwebs, lay in wooden racks, stacked along every wall and set in islands on the stone floors.

'Each cellar is devoted to a different vintage,' Isabella told him, pointing to the marked boards. 'Farther along there are some very old vintages, indeed. This year's wine is still maturing in the casks, which are stored on the other side of the cellars.'

The lamps made shadows on the pale limestone. As they made their way farther into the cellars the rooms became smaller, the ceilings lower. 'So you and your brother played here as children, then,' Finlay said, looking round one of the smallest rooms, where the bottles were encrusted by a thick film of dust.

'I told you, Xavier has a fear of very small spaces, he rarely comes down here if he can help it.'

'And you—you are not afraid of the rats, *señorita*? I'd imagine there are plenty down here.'

'They are more afraid of me than I of them.'

There seemed to be another archway at the end of the room, smaller than the rest, and the gap covered by one of the tall wine racks. 'What's through here?' Finlay asked.

'Nothing. It is blocked off.' Isabella put her lamp down on a small table in the centre of the room, and after a few moments' pondering in front of one of the racks, selected a bottle. Blowing the dust off the neck, she produced a corkscrew from a cupboard built into the table and expertly opened the bottle, sniffing the cork delicately. 'It is far too cold, of course, and it should be allowed to breathe, but this is one of our better wines, I think you'll find.'

Two glasses were produced from the same cupboard. They sat down on the stools by the table, and Isabella poured the wine. *'Salud!'*

'Salud!' The wine was soft and fruity, to Finlay's untutored palate. 'It's very nice,' he said, taking a second appreciative sip.

Isabella laughed. 'I hope you manage to be a little more enthusiastic with Xavier.'

'It's extremely nice?' he suggested, grinning.

Isabella picked up her glass. 'You must first talk to him about the nose,' she said, swirling the wine around before sniffing. 'So this one, it is sweet, like cherry, do you smell it?'

Finlay nodded, mimicking her actions, though his eyes were on Isabella. She was explaining the layers of taste now, swirling the wine around in her mouth. There was a cobweb clinging to her hair. Her eyes really were golden, like a tiger's. And her mouth— He had an absurd wish to be the wine swirling around in her mouth. Her lips would taste of it. What had she said, cherries? Yes, her lips would taste of cherries, and…

'You are not tasting, Mr—Finlay.'

He took a sip of wine. 'Cherries,' he said.

'And?'

'Strawberries,' he answered, looking at her mouth.

'Really? I do not…'

Finlay leaned over to touch his lips to hers. 'Strawberries,' he said. 'Definitely.' He tucked back a silky strand of hair from her face and pressed his mouth to the pulse behind her ear. 'Lavender?'

'My soap.'

Her voice was low, breathy. Her fingers touched his hair. He pressed fluttering kisses down the column of her neck, then placed his lips on the pulse at her throat. 'Lavender.'

'Yes,' she agreed.

He lifted his head. She was looking at him, her lips slightly parted, tense, waiting for what he would do next. Nothing, was what he ought to do. He bent his head and kissed her again. Her lips clung to his. Her fingers curled into the sleeve of his coat. He was trying to muster the courage to stop when her tongue touched his.

Finlay slid his arms around her, under her cloak. Isabella swayed towards him on her stool, her mouth pressed to his. She tasted so sweet. Wine and strawberries and a sizzling heat that sent the blood surging to his groin. Their kisses became wilder, deeper. Her fingers tangled in his hair, fluttered over his cheek, curled into his shoulders. He flattened his hands over the narrow span of her back. He could feel her shoulder blades through the cotton of her gown, the complicated strings and boning of her corsets. He licked along her plump lower lip, kissing each corner of her mouth.

'You taste delightful,' he said. 'Delicious. Like vintage wine.'

She kissed him deeply, her tongue tangling with his. Fast learner. Very fast. He could not keep up with her. 'Vintage kisses,' Finlay said. 'If only they could be bottled, you would have an elixir beyond price.'

He kissed her eyelids. He kissed her nose. He kissed her mouth again. And again. And again. Their knees bumped as they tried to get closer. He was hard. It would not do at all to get any closer. It was all he wanted. He kissed her again. She gave a tiny whimper that sent his pulses racing.

Slowly, he lifted his head and let her go. Her mouth was dark pink. Her eyes were wide, dark. He could feel the flush of passion on his cheeks, and lower down—Finlay shifted uncomfortably on the stool. 'I don't expect you'll believe me if I tell you I'd resolved not to do that,' he said.

'We could blame it on the wine.'

'We've not even finished one glass yet.'

Isabella picked hers up and swallowed the contents in a single gulp. 'That was sacrilege,' she said, wiping her lips.

'Then, we must not waste a drop.' Finlay licked the wine from the back of her hand. She shuddered. He didn't mean to, but somehow his lips found hers again, and somehow they were kissing again, and this time they were very different kisses. Dark and hot, tongues stroking, touching, thrusting. The kind of kisses that demanded more. The stools clattered to the stone floor as they stood, pressing their bodies hard against each other, still kissing, and kissing and kissing, until Finlay knocked against the table, and the wine bottle fell over and the precious wine began to spill out over the wood and drip onto the stone floor.

He grabbed it and set it upright. There was less than a third left.

'Now, that really is sacrilege,' Isabella said.

'Or a warning. I should not have— I did not mean— Have you any idea how ravishing you look?' Finlay groaned. 'What am I thinking!'

'I sincerely hope that it is not leading to an apology.'

He laughed drily. 'I'm not sorry, though I should be.'

'Good, because neither am I.' Isabella was tidying her hair, concentrating on adjusting the fastenings of her cloak, pouring the last of the wine. Finally, she met his eyes. 'I wanted you to kiss me. I wanted—after the last time, I wanted to get it right.'

'You got it a trifle too right.'

'Did I?'

'I'd have thought, from the way I couldn't keep my hands off you, that it was obvious.' Finlay brushed the cobweb from her hair. 'But I should not have taken advantage.'

She flinched away from him, the light dying from her eyes. 'You think I kissed you because you wanted me to, and not because I wanted to?'

'No, I don't. You really are a prickly—but you probably have cause. Look at me. Please.' He touched her cheek gently. 'The fact is that I've a deal of experience in these things and you have none. To put it bluntly, I am not a seducer of virgins.'

She coloured, but held his gaze. 'It was just a few kisses, Finlay.'

He laughed softly. 'There, you see, your innocence is showing if that's what you think. Those were the kind of kisses to keep a man awake at night, wanting more. Now, shall we drink this excellent wine and get on with the rest of the tour?'

* * *

She took him back through the wine vaults to the barrel vaults, and began to explain the process of ageing. The cellars were so familiar to her that Isabella could lead the way without a lamp if necessary. The questions Finlay was asking were intelligent enough. Some wine merchants knew more, true, but not all. Their field of expertise was in the tasting. Had Finlay been teasing her when he had pretended to know nothing of the nose? Or flirting? Back up the stairs to the main winery, she took him through to the coopering shed. Here he surprised her, clearly knowing a great deal more than she of the process.

'From my father,' he told her when she asked. 'He learned from his father, who most likely learned from his. There has always been a still in our family for the whisky.'

Isabella perched on the top of a finished barrel to watch as he ran his hands over the staves waiting to be formed into another barrel. 'Will you take it over from your father, then—the farm, making the whisky?'

Finlay turned his attention to one of the finished barrels. 'I used to joke about it in the mess, my wee Highland hame.' He picked up a coopering hammer. 'Some of them—the other officers, I mean—to hear them talk, you'd think I was born in a sheep pen. They think everyone north of Glasgow lives off porridge and neeps— that's turnip, which I know you have here.' He grinned. 'I used to come up with some fine tall tales for them.'

'Tell me what it is really like,' Isabella said. 'Your family farm, and the place where they live—it is by the sea, yes? You said before that your father has a fishing boat.'

'He does. Nothing fancy, just a single sail. They are built wide and shallow where I come from, not like the Spanish fishing boats, and they catch very different fish.'

'And the farm?'

'We call it a croft. Our farmers are crofters, which means they do a bit of everything. The croft sits up on the hill above the village. The house is long and low, with a thatched roof. Half of it forms the barn for the beasts. We have harsh winters, and it rains a lot. Warm rain in the summer, freezing in the winter. I don't miss that at all.'

'And your sisters, do they live in the farm—croft? I think you said you had four?'

'Three. It can feel like five or six mind, when they are all in the same room. Mhairi, Sheena and Jean. They are all married now, with their own crofts, and have a gaggle of bairns between them.'

He talked of them all with obvious affection. As she listened, Isabella couldn't help comparing his childhood with her own. It had been harsh, there was no doubt about it, though he did not dwell on it, but they were obviously a loving family.

'You have been back then, since the war?' she asked. 'I think you told me it had been many years since you had been home.'

Finlay's smile faded. 'Aye, I've been back.'

'After such a long time away, you must have found it very changed.'

He looked troubled. 'No, it was almost exactly the same.'

'And your family, they were all well?'

'Aye.' He put the hammer down with a sigh.

'They were all very well, and very pleased to see me, and I—ach, it doesn't matter.'

'It obviously does.'

'What I meant was, I don't want to talk about it.'

'I can see that from the way you are scowling at me.'

'I don't scowl.'

She wrinkled her face into a fair imitation of his expression. 'What is that, then?'

Finlay was forced to laugh. 'What it means is, when I say I don't want to talk about something, I don't want to talk about it.'

'After the war,' Isabella said, picking her words carefully, 'I found it very difficult to go back to being Señorita Romero again. I felt as if I was acting a part.'

'You look to me as if you're still acting. Not now, but with other people, your brother—'

'Who thinks it's high time I was married,' Isabella interrupted hurriedly. He *was* suspicious. It was imprudent of her to have embarked upon this comparison between them, but she had never been able to discuss how she felt before, and most likely would never be able to discuss it again. 'Xavier is right,' she continued. 'I am much older than most Spanish brides, but I—I don't know.' She shrugged. 'I am afraid Gabriel will be disappointed in his side of the bargain. He is a nice man. He is a perfect husband for me. Everyone thinks so. Perfect. Only I am not sure that I could be such a perfect wife. Or—or want to be. Do you understand what I mean?'

Finlay shrugged, picking up the hammer again, turning it over in his hand.

Deflated, Isabella slid down from the barrel. 'Never mind.'

He caught her arm as she passed him. 'I do understand.' His smile was crooked. 'I do. It's what I thought I wanted, what I used to think about on the nights before a battle, when it seemed morning would never come. Going back to the croft. Taking over from my father. Settling down. It's what I always thought I'd do, when peace came. Thing is, I never really thought peace would come, and now it's here…'

'You are not so sure anymore?'

He flinched. 'That's the problem,' he said sadly. 'It's one thing I'm very sure of. I'm not cut out to be a crofter.'

'So that is why you became a wine merchant?' She waited, but he merely shrugged. 'Do you miss the war, Finlay?'

'Not exactly. Certainly not the bloodshed and the suffering.'

'But the excitement of it. Knowing you made a difference, that your contribution was vital. Knowing that so many men relied on you. The responsibility.' Isabella smiled. 'And the danger.'

'Aye. All of that. People don't understand it, but the army has been my life.'

'It was my life, too, for a time, during the occupation. I miss it, too, just as you do.'

'Do you? Aye, I can see that you might, though it's not the same.'

The empathy she was feeling trickled away. 'Why not? Why is it not the same? Because I am a…'

'For the love of— It has nothing to do with your being a woman, if that's what you were about to say. What a chip on your shoulder you have,' Finlay exclaimed. 'It is not the same because I have spent my entire adult life in the army. I know nothing else, whereas you had a life before, and a life to come back to. The war here has been over two years. You must be accustomed to peacetime life by now.'

She clenched her fists and was about to retort angrily, when the incongruity of his remark struck her. 'Your entire adult life has been in the military? You told me you left the army when Napoleon was sent to Elba, which was nearly two years ago, and since then you have been assiduously building up your wine business.'

Finlay waved his hand dismissively. 'What I meant is that the army has dominated my life so much that it feels as if I have always been a soldier. And speaking of my new career,' he said, looking at his watch, 'it is high time we were getting back to change for dinner. It wouldn't enhance my negotiating position with your brother if I were to insult him by having the bad manners to keep his wife waiting.'

In his room, taking a quick bath before dinner, Finlay cursed himself for a fool. What an eejit he'd been, to get caught out so easily. Luckily it had not been too costly a faux pas but he would have to be much more careful in future.

'Aye, for example, please refrain from mentioning over dinner that you fought at Waterloo a matter of months ago, Finlay, there's a good chap!'

The fair Isabella was as sharp as a tack, and he had once again allowed himself to be sidetracked by those big eyes of hers, and those luscious lips. He poured another jug of hot water over his head. He wasn't doing her justice. Her kisses were delightful, sure enough, but it was her, Isabella herself, who intrigued him. She was an enigmatic mixture, and a fascinating creature. 'And a gie clever one, you'd do well to remember, Finlay Urquhart.'

He'd recovered the situation, but only temporarily. Her suspicions had been aroused, which meant he had to be a step ahead of her by the morning.

He'd think of something. He always did. In the meantime, there were other, more delightful things to think of. Such as the fact that Isabella's chamber was only a few doors down the corridor. Most likely she was taking a bath, too. Her hair would be all damp curls, clinging to her back. Her face would be flushed from the heat of the water. She'd be lying back as he was, her eyes closed, as his were. The water would be lapping at her breasts. There would be tantalising glimpses of her nipples through the suds. Her soapy body would be slippery to the touch, and when the bubbles burst as the water cooled, so much more would be revealed...

Chapter Five

Consuela placed the letter she had received on the breakfast table and poured herself a cup of chocolate. 'It is a brief note from Xavier. Unfortunately he will be detained in Pamplona for a further few days. Isabella, he asks that you ensure Mr Urquhart is given a comprehensive tour of all aspects of the work of the estate. To that end, you are to take him to visit Estebe, the head winemaker, and—but here, you may as well read it for yourself.' Consuela pushed the letter across the table.

Isabella took the letter, raising her brows at the list of tasks her brother had compiled for her. Necessity and greed had forced Xavier into trusting her with an important task. Though not enough to actually write to her himself.

'Mr Urquhart is tardy this morning,' Consuela said, eyeing the clock.

Isabella, who had been anxiously thinking the same thing, began to rearrange the bread on her plate. 'You like our foreign guest, don't you?'

Consuela bristled slightly. 'I hope you are not implying that my behaviour has been improper in any way?'

'Not at all. Only that he is very handsome and extremely charming. All women like him, I think. Even I do.' *Though I am fairly certain he is a fraud and not who he purports to be.* The butterflies in her tummy started beating their wings again. She wished that there was another conclusion, but once again decided there was not.

'Isabella, you know that it would not be appropriate, or wise, to grow to like this man too much? He *is* charming, but he is a wine merchant. You think I am empty-headed. I know you do, because you never discuss anything of any import with me save my son, and...'

'Consuela, I...'

'No, let me speak for once. You think that because I say nothing I don't see what's happening under my nose, but I do. The way you look at Mr Urquhart… You have never looked at Gabriel like that.'

'Gabriel has never looked at me the way Mr Urquhart does.'

Consuela, to her surprise, giggled. 'Mr Urquhart looks at you as if he would like to have you for his dinner. I think that it would be very nice, to be Mr Urquhart's dinner, to be devoured by him.'

'What on earth can you mean by that?'

Her sister-in-law gave her a coy look. 'You must trust me on that, and you must wait to find out for yourself when you are married. You *are* going to marry Gabriel, aren't you?'

'Everyone seems to expect it, but my feelings for him are tepid at best, since we are being frank.'

Consuela rolled her eyes. 'I forget you have no mother to guide you. I will tell you, then, what my mother told me. Love blossoms after marriage, not before. It is perfectly natural, when you think about it. Until a woman truly knows her husband, as his wife, she can have no reason to love him any more than she loves any other suitor.'

'Do you love Xavier?'

Consuela looked surprised. 'But of course. He is my husband. It happened just as my mother predicted. She is never wrong. It will happen to you, too, when you marry Gabriel.'

Love was not a subject to which Isabella had given much consideration, and it was not one that much interested her, either. Consuela's persistence, though, made one thing clear that had not occurred to Isabella before. 'It would suit you for me to be married off and gone from Hermoso Romero, wouldn't it? I am sorry. I have endeavoured not to interfere in the running of your household since you arrived as Xavier's bride two years ago. I have been at pains to give you your place, but you must appreciate that I have been de facto mistress of Hermoso Romero for many years.'

'I do understand that, and I assure you, it is not a big problem for me. I don't dislike you. I don't see you as a threat, Isabella, though I know you think I do. Xavier thinks that because you are his sister and I am his wife, that you should also be my sister. But you're not,' Consuela said simply. 'The truth is I would love my real sister to come here to live, but while you are here Xavier will not countenance it. So for that reason, you understand, your presence is—inconvenient.'

'Oh.' Isabella felt like a fool. She also felt—rejected. 'I had no idea.'

'You have never asked. I am very relieved that you have broached the subject now.'

Mortified, she remembered that Finlay had hinted she do so. What a fool she had been. 'Yes. I see.' Isabella smiled weakly. 'I am sorry.'

'It is easily remedied. Gabriel Torres is waiting only for a sign from you and he will propose. I am glad we have cleared the air. And now here is Mr Urquhart at last.' Consuela rose from the table. 'I have had a letter from my husband. Isabella will explain. You must excuse me. I promised to take my son for a drive in the carriage today.'

The door closed on a swish of silken skirts. 'My sister-in-law has just informed me that I am to marry Gabriel in order to allow *her* sister to come and live here in my place,' Isabella said dully. 'But you knew that, didn't you?'

'I did, yes. I'm sorry.'

'There is no need. At least now I understand my position.'

'It's a damned unfair one. This has been your home much longer that it's been hers.'

Her own thoughts exactly. Hearing them expressed aloud made Isabella feel marginally better. Finlay had poured himself a cup of coffee, though he had not sat down. He had a tiny nick on his chin, a cut from shaving. There was a rebellious kink of hair standing up like a question mark at his hairline. It was oddly endearing. He was wearing buckskin breeches and top boots. She wondered if his legs had lost their tan. Looking up, she caught his eye. 'Do you miss wearing your kilt?' she asked.

'In London, it caused more bother than it was worth. Ladies either found it indecent or intriguing. A fair few found it to be both. I was never quite sure whether it was indecently intriguing or intriguingly indecent! Do you miss wearing your breeches?'

'Yes, I do.' Isabella smiled faintly. 'In Spain, we pretend that ladies do not have legs, you know.'

Finlay laughed. 'It is no different for ladies in England.'

'You seem to know a lot about English ladies and fashion, unless you were inventing it for Consuela's benefit.'

'I've been to my fair share of balls and formal dinners.'

'Do you know the steps to this new dance, the waltz? Xavier thinks it is too shocking to be danced in polite society.'

'I reckon I could teach you. Do you want to be shocked, Isabella?'

She began to rearrange the untouched bread on her plate again. 'Your turning up here is quite shocking enough. Since you left the army, though, you will have had little time for balls and parties, I would imagine, while building your business. All work and no play, as the saying goes.'

Silence fell. Finlay poured another cup of coffee, but still did not sit down. He was waiting for her to speak. A knot formed in her stomach. 'I have something...' Isabella cleared her throat. 'We need to talk,' she said.

'I agree, we do.'

'Finlay, I do not profess to know why you are here, but it is of a certainty not to purchase wine.'

'No, I'm not.' He finished his coffee in one gulp. 'Take a walk with me, and I'll tell you the real reason I am here.'

Isabella had pulled a fringed shawl around her shoulders. Her gown was simple but elegant, the plain white material relieved by a bold pattern of what looked to be strawberries running around the hem and diagonally across the skirt. The high waist suited her tall, slim figure. Her feet were clad not in the delicate slippers favoured by her sister-in-law, but in much more sturdy and practical boots. She kept pace easily at his side as they walked, despite her narrow skirts. There were gold highlights in her hair, sparked to life by the weak winter sunshine. The cold morning air caught in his lungs, their breath visible as they continued on their way.

On balance, Finlay had come to the conclusion overnight that Isabella would not betray him. He had pondered the possibility of inventing another story to fob her off for a few more days, but quickly abandoned that idea. Though he disliked Xavier Romero, Finlay disliked the lies he was obliged to tell the man even more, the false expectations he was raising.

But lying to Isabella… That was a whole different kettle of fish. There had existed, from the very first time they had met, an unmistakable spark between them that he, for one, had never experienced before. It went against the grain with him not to be straight with her, though he was fairly certain she was doing a fair bit of dissembling herself. If she was, as he hoped, merely protecting his quarry, he could not blame her for that. In fact, it was a rather admirable display of loyalty.

He led the way past the chapel, along the cypress tree walk and out onto a path that climbed between the serried ranks of vines to an ancient wooden bench with a panoramic view out over the estate. Isabella did not speak as they snaked their way up the hillside. He sensed her tension as they sat down, saw it in the rigid way she held herself, her hands clasped together under her shawl.

'Right, then,' Finlay said. 'I'll speak first and save you the trouble of asking. I'm not a wine merchant. In fact, I'm still a soldier, same as I've always been.'

Isabella jumped to her feet. 'So everything you have told me has been a lie?'

'No! Not all. My family, the croft, all that is true.'

'But you did not leave the army when Napoleon was sent to Elba? You presumably fought at Waterloo, then?'

'Aye.' He grabbed her wrist and pulled her back onto the bench. 'Who I fought and when are beside the point. Listen to me now, because it's vitally important. Lives are at stake here, including my own if things go badly. I had no option but to lie to you until I knew whether or not I could trust you. It's been two years since we met after all, and a lot can change in two years. When I arrived here, I wasn't even certain that I'd be able to find you.'

'Find me? You mean you came here looking for me?'

Finlay grinned. 'I came looking for a wee peasant lassie, and there you were in that fine white lace mantilla and that silk gown, not only a lady, but the sister of the estate owner. I couldn't believe it. I damn near panicked, I can tell you.'

'You hid it very well,' Isabella responded tartly. 'Unlike me.'

'Aye, that was one of the things that set me off wondering about you from the first, but then when you explained about your brother, and I could see for myself he was no friend of the liberal cause, I thought that was the cause of your panic. But the real Isabella kept popping through the lady's demure facade that you have clearly donned since the end of the war. I am hoping I'm not the only one who is not what he appears. In fact, I am staking quite a lot on it.'

'Why?' she asked baldly.

'You told me once that you knew how to get in touch with a partisan known as El Fantasma, in order to convince me that the partisans be allowed to attack a French arms cache. The fact that they succeeded proves to me that your claim was genuine. El Fantasma is clearly known to you.' He felt her flinch at the name, and though she said nothing, it was enough. 'Isabella, the man is in deep trouble. I think you know where he might be found. I think you might still be involved in some way with his cause. I need you to take me to him.'

'Take you to him?' she repeated blankly.

'To El Fantasma. His life is at risk.'

'For El Fantasma there are always risks.' Isabella waved her hand dismissively. 'You think he cares about that?'

'Frankly, he'd be a fool not to care. There's bravery and then there's sheer recklessness.'

She narrowed her eyes. 'Perhaps he thinks that the cause he fights for is more important than anything else.'

'More important even than his life?' Finlay snapped. 'Isabella, the British government believe that your Spanish government are determined to track him down, and the net is closing around him. I'm here to prevent that happening.'

'What!' she exclaimed incredulously. 'You cannot mean—are you saying that you have been sent here to *rescue* El Fantasma?'

'That's the gist of it.'

'You don't think that's incredibly presumptuous? I am very sure he neither wants nor needs to be rescued.'

He shook his head, taken aback by her vehemence. 'How can you be so certain?'

Isabella bit her lip, eyeing him speculatively, then gave a little shrug, followed by an enigmatic smile. 'Because,' she said, 'I am El Fantasma.'

It took Finlay a full minute to unscramble his reeling senses before he could muster a response. '*You* are The Ghost? *You* are El Fantasma? By all that is— I can't believe it.'

'No,' she said, drawing him an arch look, 'you did not for a moment consider it could be me, did you?'

'Not for a single second,' he admitted frankly. She was beaming at him now, her golden eyes shining with a mixture of pride and glee. Finlay burst into laughter. It was ridiculous, outrageous, fantastical, though in a way it made an awful lot of sense. 'Good Lord, does that brother of yours know?' he asked.

Isabella tossed her head. 'Of course not. No one knows, save for my deputy, Estebe.'

'Estebe! By all that is…' Finlay cursed under his breath.

'Estebe himself has four deputies, though they do not know each other, of course, and below that—but you know how partisan groups are structured to protect anonymity and preserve security, I think. Estebe helps me with the printing press we use to publish our propaganda pamphlets. It is…'

'Hidden in the winery cellars.' Finlay finished for her as the pieces began to tumble into place.

Isabella's smile faded. 'How did you know?'

'I didn't, but it's obvious now that I—' He broke off, shaking his head. 'Have you any idea how dangerous a game you're playing?'

'It is not a game, and I am not stupid. Of course I know it is dangerous, but what does that matter, when we have so much at stake?'

'Aye, such as the lives of your family. Your brother. For God's sake, Isabella, that printing press in his cellar— If it was discovered…'

'It will not be.' Her voice hardened. 'You do not understand, Finlay. We are fighting for our future.'

'I think it's you who doesn't understand. What I'm trying to tell you is that if you carry on, you'll have no future.'

Her eyes blazed. 'If we stop, if we give up, the future will not be worth having! We sacrificed so much during the war—has it to be for nothing? We must fight on, if not with guns, then with words. Those in power do not want to hear what we have to say, but we will continue to say it until they listen.'

She spoke with such conviction, such passion, that he was momentarily disarmed. He could not doubt her claim to be the infamous partisan, but however inspiring she was, it was her very idealism that worried him, for it made her quite reckless and completely, misguidedly without fear. He'd seen far too many brave men slaughtered. A dose of healthy fear was essential to survival, in his book—not that he'd admit to it himself, mind.

'I'm not doubting your sincerity, or indeed your cause,' Finlay said, choosing his words carefully, eager not to estrange her further.

'I am glad to hear that.'

'Aye, but this government of yours, the men in Madrid who wield the power here in Spain, to put it bluntly, the louder you shout, the more determined they will be to shut you up.'

Isabella tossed her head again. 'Do you not see, the very fact that they wish to do so is evidence of El Fantasma's success? As the voice of protest grows, so, too, does our power to change things. We will force them to listen, Finlay. We will force them to act.' She caught at his jacket sleeve, giving his arm a shake to emphasise her point. 'Yes, it is dangerous because we say what they do not want to hear, but how much more dangerous would it be to remain silent?'

Silent was what she would be, as the grave, if she was not careful, but she looked so magnificent standing there, a fervent light in her eyes, a flush on her cheeks, a proud smile on her delightful lips, that Finlay found himself quite torn. She was so sure she was right, and he was equally certain she was wrong, but he could not bring himself to destroy her illusions. Not yet.

'You're a very brave lass. I still can't quite believe that you are The Ghost,' he said. Here he'd been, thinking the hard part of his mission was going to be tracking El Fantasma down, but the really tricky thing was going to be persuading her to come away with him. The irony of it, the sheer unlikelihood of it, made him shake his hand, marvelling at this twist of fate. Isabella was still clutching at his jacket. Finlay took her hand between his, fascinated by the slenderness of it, how delicate it looked in his own rough paw. 'I'm still struggling to take it in,' he said ruefully.

She chuckled. 'We are neither of us what we appear to be, it seems.'

'That's for certain.'

'And now we can stop pretending.'

'That is very true,' he said, much struck by this. He smiled, revelling in the simple pleasure of looking at her for the first time without any barricades or withheld secrets between them. 'You do know,' he said, 'that I haven't been pretending all the time. I did not pretend to enjoy your company. I did not pretend to enjoy your conversation.'

'Since we are in the business of confessions,' she said, 'I will admit that I, too, have very much enjoyed our conversations. Being alone with you, I have not had to pretend to be the dutiful, and frankly boring, Lady Isabella.'

Did she know how bewitching her smile was? Did she realise what it did to him, that smile?

And the way she looked at him with those big eyes of hers... Did she know she was playing with fire? Almost without meaning to—almost—he pulled her closer. 'Above all, you do know that I did not pretend to enjoy kissing you, don't you?'

'No? Why, then, did you kiss me, Major Urquhart?'

He tried to remind himself that she was an innocent, but the demure Spanish lady she purported to be was nowhere to be seen in this feisty, bold, brave, beautiful woman smiling seductively up at him. 'I kissed you,' Finlay said roughly, 'for the very simple reason that you are irresistible.'

'I think that is what is known as serendipity,' Isabella replied, 'for it's the very same reason I kissed you back.'

'Serendipity,' Finlay said, sliding his arm around her waist. 'I've always wondered what it tasted like.'

'Strawberries, and lavender, and vintage wine, I believe is how you described it.'

'No,' he said decidedly. 'It tastes of nothing

other than essence of you. The most intoxicating and delicious taste imaginable.'

There was a different quality to Finlay's smile that excited Isabella. There was something different in the way he looked at her, too, a gleam in his sea-blue eyes, as if he could not quite believe what he was seeing. There was a very different quality to their kiss, too. This time it was he who was tentative, she who was daring. He kissed her as if he was not sure who he was kissing. She kissed him back with the boldness, the wild elation she felt at finally being able to reveal her true self.

Her response ensured he was not tentative for long. The pressure of his lips increased as she opened her mouth. The touch of his tongue on hers set her aflame. His hands slid down to cup her bottom, pulling her hard up against him. She slid her hands under his coat, flattening her palms against the smooth silk of his waistcoat, feeling the rippling of his muscles as she touched him, up the length of his spine, back down, to the waistband of his breeches.

His mouth was hot on hers. She closed her

eyes, the sunlight dappling crimson inside her lids, and slid her hands over the smooth leather of his breeches to the taut muscles of his buttocks. He moaned, plunging his tongue into her mouth. She could feel the unmistakable ridge of his arousal pressing between her thighs. Heat trickled through her. She felt potent, wild, that intense, fierce focus from the old days. The pinpoint of danger, though this time the threat was not of capture but surrender.

Still they kissed. His jacket fell to the ground. They were on the bench now, and she was splayed on top of him, her skirts rucked high, his erection pressing against her. She flattened her palms over his shoulders. His breath was ragged. His kisses grew wilder and more passionate. Her own lips pressed against his, as if they would meld. His hand on her breast made her gasp. Her nipple hardened sweetly, painfully beneath her corset. She wanted to moan with frustration for the layers that lay between them, his skin, her nipple. She dug her fingers into his hair, clutching the soft silkiness, tilting her hips to rub herself against him, panting as his mouth devoured hers, as his hand tightened on her breast, as something inside her tightened like a knot, too.

She tensed her thighs against his. More kisses. Behind her closed lids, crimson, blood red. Her blood hot. Danger. She remembered then, seeing him that first night at the ball. Dangerous. He was dangerous. He was so delightfully dangerous. And she was so unafraid.

Finlay muttered something soft in what she assumed must be Gaelic, and dragged his mouth from hers. Gently, he began to disentangle himself from her. 'I'm sorry. I don't know what I— I didn't mean to— And here, of all places. What the devil was I thinking!'

His eyes were dark, his pupils dilated. His hair was in wild disarray. The pins had come out of hers. Isabella knew she ought to be shocked at her own behaviour, but all she could think about was the tension inside her, the urgent need for release, the feeling of hanging on a precipice, desperate to let go, the slow realisation that she would instead have to clamber back down to reality. 'I don't believe either of us was thinking,' she said, trying to herd her errant thoughts into some sort of coherency.

'No, I don't suppose we were.' Finlay stooped to gather some of her hairpins from the ground, handing them to her with a rueful smile. 'You are the most distracting lass I've ever come across. I look at you, and my head says one thing and my body something else entirely.'

'My body is not in the least bit interested in what my head is saying at this moment.'

Finlay's eyes darkened. 'Dear heavens, nor is mine.' He reached for her, then pulled his hand away as if he had been burned. 'We need to talk. We need to decide—you are El Fantasma. I still can't get my head around that one.' He gave himself a little shake. 'Aye. Right. El Fantasma. We need to think about what we do next. I had already taken the precaution of making some prior arrangements on the assumption I would track him—you—down, but…'

His words brought Isabella tumbling firmly back to earth. 'I am not interested in your arrangements. There's nothing to think about, nothing to discuss,' she said sharply. 'Now you know the truth, you can return to England forthwith and tell the Duke of Wellington that El

Fantasma thanks him for his concern but has no desire for, or need of rescue.'

He stared at her for a long moment. She could not read his thoughts. In truth, she did not really wish to contemplate his leaving here, not just yet. It would be a huge relief to be able to be herself for a little while longer, in this beguiling man's company.

'Isabella, can you not see…'

'Finlay, can you not see!' She grabbed his arm. 'I know what I am doing. You have no right to interfere.'

'I'm trying to save your life.'

'And I am trying to save many, many other lives,' she declared hotly. 'I wish I had not told you.'

He paused in the act of putting his coat on. 'Why did you?'

'I don't know. I've never told anyone else. I suppose I hoped you would understand.' She began to stick pins randomly into her hair. 'I thought that you would see we were similar. You were wrong when you told me I don't know what it is to be a soldier, don't you see? I *am* a soldier, just like you. You cannot expect me to do anything other than stay and fight this battle, when it is exactly what you would do if the roles were reversed.'

He was silent for a long time, his brow furrowed. When he spoke again, it was with a deliberate detachment. 'There's little to be gained by us arguing from implacably opposed viewpoints. We both have a lot to digest and reflect on. I'm going for a wee walk. I'll see you at dinner.'

He turned and began to make his way up the track, leaving Isabella to stare at his retreating back, fighting the urge to call him back to convince him of the validity of her case and the equally strong urge to call him back and demand that he finish what he had started.

Finlay strode off up the hill towards the tree line. *Is fheàrr teicheadh math na droch fhuireach.* Better a good retreat than a bad stand. He was not running away, but though it went against the grain with him to leave Isabella alone after all that had happened, he knew if he stayed it would be a strategic miscalculation.

'You need to start thinking with your head, and stop letting yourself be driven by your other body parts, my lad,' he muttered under his breath. He could feel Isabella's eyes on him as he climbed the steep path. He quickened his pace, forcing himself to ignore the urge to look back. Upward, onward, away he marched, just short of a run, enjoying the way the exercise made his heart beat faster, the way the fresh air stabbed at his lungs. And finally, as he cleared the tree line and emerged on the next ridge and his calf muscles began to protest, finally, his head began to clear itself of the fog of confusion triggered by this latest bewildering turn of events.

He stopped, taking deep, recuperative breaths, and looked at the landscape spread out below him. Ochre soil, the warm yellow stone of Hermoso Romero, the regimented row of pruned vines, the soft green foliage of cypress trees, the pale winter blue of the sky and the silvery lemon of the winter sun. It was a beautiful place, no doubt about it. If he lived here, he'd be loath to leave. But it wasn't all this beauty that made Isabella determined to remain here—it was all the things you couldn't see. The poverty. The injustice. The constraints of the old ways. The same feudal culture that made her brother the region's biggest landowner and one of its most influential men. It was ironic that Xavier Romero represented all the things Isabella wanted to change.

'And I can't blame her for fighting for change, since by and large I share her views,' Finlay said, smiling to himself as he recalled the fire in Isabella's eyes as she had spoken of El Fantasma's cause. He squatted down on his heels, wiping the sweat from his forehead. The death of the old ways, a new beginning, a new world. Hadn't he been fighting for the same things himself?

His face hardened. Waterloo, the battle that had finally defeated Napoleon, the battle that had brought peace to Europe, had taken place five months ago. He sat back heavily, causing a limestone rock to clatter down the path. Peace was a fine thing and to be welcomed. No more death. No more bloodshed. He had not lied when he'd told Isabella he didn't miss that. Peace would bring prosperity, the press said.

'To the likes of Wellington, to those who had always been prosperous, aye, that it would, but what about the rest of us?' Finlay muttered. London was already full of ex-soldiers, cast out of the military once their usefulness had expired, reduced to begging on the streets. Back home, in the Highlands, things were just the same as ever, the crofters just as poor as ever. And it was as Jack had said—no one wanted to know. Nothing had really changed, despite all the sacrifice. Was this what he'd fought for?

Here in Spain, it was worse. Here in Spain, they'd taken a few more steps backwards. But Isabella had not given up. Isabella was still fighting, though it was, in Finlay's opinion, a very lost cause, indeed. Did that make her wrong? Was her deluded optimism better or worse than his pragmatism?

An unanswerable question. But one thing he did know, Isabella's deluded optimism was clouding her judgement. She thought herself a hardened soldier, she thought her cause more important than her life, but she had no idea. It was all very well to wave away a theoretical threat, but the reality was something else entirely. Finlay, all too easily able to imagine what would happen if she was caught, shuddered at the horrors Isabella would be forced to endure. Indeed, not only Isabella, but her brother and his wife, too, like as not. Yet she seemed quite unable to grasp this fact. Or mayhap she simply didn't want to acknowledge it? Aye, that was more likely.

He picked up a rock and threw it so forcefully down the mountainside that the limestone split into a cloud of powder. Reluctant as he was to spell it out to her, that was what he had to do. Better to fill her head with horrors than to have to face the reality of them, surely? He picked up another small rock, rolling it over in his palm. The idea was extremely unpalatable. Isabella's idealism was her Achilles' heel but it was also her shield. What right had he to tell her to stop fighting her battles? What right had he to destroy her illusions? None, and what was more, he did not want to.

Yet what he wanted was quite beside the point. The case was simple. Isabella's life was in mortal danger. Finlay had been sent here to get El Fantasma out of Spain. He was here under Wellington's, albeit indirect, orders. More important, he was here to keep a solemn promise made to Jack. More important still, if he could not get Isabella to see sense, she might very easily be taken, tortured or executed before he spirited her away.

Still, the thought of acting against her very decided wishes and taking matters into his own hands gave him pause. Finlay got to his feet and hurled the rock down the mountainside. One more chance. He'd give her one more chance to see sense. There was time yet for that.

Chapter Six

Isabella pushed her papers aside with a sigh of frustration. El Fantasma's next pamphlet was due to be printed this week, but Estebe was still confined to bed, and though she could set the type and do all the preparation, she could not work the printing press alone. She scanned the piece she was working on, making a few changes before casting it aside once more. There was nothing wrong with it, but nor did it contain anything fresh. The demand for the pamphlets was increasing, but when would talk turn to action?

Would it ever take that definitive step? Pulling back the long voile curtains, Isabella threw a soft cashmere shawl over her nightdress, opened the window and stepped out onto her balcony. The night air was invigorating. It had a sharpness to it that told her winter was not too far away. There would be snow on the mountains soon, perhaps within a few weeks. And before that, perhaps within as little as a few days, Finlay would be gone.

It was for the best, she told herself, gazing up at the stars with the usual pang of regret that she could no longer look at them through the telescope with Papa. Another thing Xavier had appropriated. Star gazing, it seemed, was not a pastime fit for females, though neither was it a pastime her brother had shown any inclination to take up. She wished that she could love Xavier as she ought. She wished that she could trust him with her secret. She wished that he could see her for who she truly was. She sighed, irked with herself. There were more important things to wish for.

Her brother was no fool, and Finlay knew as much about wine as she did about Paris fashions. The moment Xavier stopped boasting and pontificating about his precious Rioja and started asking searching questions, Finlay's cover would be blown. How did he plan to extricate himself? He would not go to the lengths of placing an order, she was fairly certain. 'No, of that I am absolutely certain,' Isabella said aloud. 'Lies, they do not sit well with Finlay Urquhart.'

Leaning on the balustrade, she looked out along the side of the house. She could see the adjacent balcony that served as Finlay's bedchamber. The room was dark, the window to his balcony closed. Was he sleeping? She pictured him sprawled on his back, one arm above his head. His nightshirt would be open at the neck. Though perhaps he did not wear one? Would his chest be smooth? No, a smattering of hair. Dark auburn, it would be. She closed her eyes, recalling his contours under her hand. He was solid, not slim like Gabriel. Yes, that was it. Solid.

Today, on the hillside, he had given her a taste of what Consuela had hinted at. Remembering the way he had touched her, kissed her, the feel of his lips on hers, his tongue, his hands—she wanted more. The urgent tension he had left her with, that tightly furled feeling inside her had given her just a flavour of what could exist between a man and a woman. How much more was there to experience?

She shivered. What had Consuela meant when she said that she would like to be devoured?

Isabella didn't like to think of Finlay devouring any other woman, though he had doubtless savoured many. She tried to imagine kissing Gabriel as she had kissed Finlay, but it was no use. Gabriel would be shocked to the core. A good Spanish woman went to her wedding bed innocent of such things. Isabella turned away from the stars and headed back inside. How she very much did not want to be a good Spanish woman!

It was late. The warming pan was cold on her feet. She pulled it out from under the blankets and set it on the hearth before getting back into bed. The very few who had known her in the past as El Fantasma treated her as an honorary man. They had respected her. Some had feared her. All had obeyed her orders unquestioningly. Finlay had been excited by her revelation. He had not seen her as a threat, but a challenge. To him, she was no honorary man. Not an equal precisely, but— Was there such a thing as equal and different? He made her feel less masculine and wholly feminine. It was very strange. And really, not the point at all.

She plumped her pillow and turned onto her

other side. There was a point, but she couldn't remember— Ah, yes, now she did. Lies. Finlay did not like to tell lies. His deceit made him extremely uncomfortable, which meant there must be a very, very important reason for him to resort to it.

Isabella sat up in bed and began to unravel her long plait. What if the net truly was closing in on El Fantasma? Certainly, the more vociferous liberals were now being persecuted. El Fantasma stood for all that the government wished to repress. He was subversive, but was he really dangerous enough for the state to pursue him?

The idea was much more thrilling than frightening. If it was true, it meant they really were starting to make a difference. Isabella ran her fingers through her hair and began to divide it up and plait it again. There were times when it felt as if the country she had fought for had gone backwards since the end of the war. It was not just the withdrawal of the constitution or the persecution of its supporters, it was the return of the Inquisition, the loss of freedom of the press. All that bloodshed, all that sacrifice, to go back to how things were before. She had put her life on the line for her country, for change. No politician in Madrid was going to stop her speaking out! None! She would not allow it. Absolutely, she would not!

And as to danger? For a moment, recalling just how vociferous Finlay had been, Isabella felt a little bit sick. She hadn't ever considered the risk to Xavier of the printing press being found in his cellars. 'But who would find it!' She tied her plait tightly. The sickness faded. 'This to danger,' she said, snapping her fingers. 'We cannot stop now. The fight must go on.'

The problem, she mused, was that Finlay did not understand. If she could make him see how important their cause was then he would leave, explain to the great Duke of Wellington that El Fantasma was in no need of rescue. Tomorrow, she would show him, quite literally. Smiling, Isabella snuggled back down under her sheets. Tomorrow, Finlay would start to see things her way.

'I should have guessed.' The small wine cellar looked just as it had when Isabella had brought him here a few days ago, though the bottle and the glasses had gone from the table. 'It's behind here, then?' Finlay studied the wall that she had claimed to be blocked. 'How does one gain access?'

Isabella pulled a wine bottle out and slipped her hand in behind the rack covering the lower part of the wall, and he heard a small click. 'Will you help me? You need to push that way.'

He did as she indicated, and the rack slid with ease along the wall to reveal a small wooden door. Isabella stood back to allow him through as soon as she had turned her key in the lock. He had to stoop. Holding the lamp high, he was surprised to find that this secret cellar was nearly twice the size of the one they had come through.

The bulky wooden printing press stood on three sets of trestles. It took up most of the floor space and would, when the frame holding the paper was extended, make the place very cramped indeed. A long table covered most of one wall, stacked with paper, trays of type, bottles of ink and all the other accoutrements necessary to the production of El Fantasma's pamphlets. The press was about seven feet long and the same height in the middle, Finlay reckoned. 'I take it you brought it in here in pieces and then assembled it,' he said, eyeing the small doorway.

'Estebe assisted me. It took us three nights to bring all the parts down through the cellars.'

'It's as well that brother of yours has his phobia,' Finlay said. 'Does anyone else know of this place?'

'Not now that Papa...' Isabella turned away, busying herself with lighting another lamp. 'Only Estebe and I know, now that Papa is no longer with us. During the war, we stored arms here.'

'We? You mean your father knew?'

'Not about the printing press, that was after he— After.' Isabella turned around, smiling sadly. 'But the arms—yes, it was his idea to use this place. It was he who had the new door fitted.'

'Aye, but what I meant was, did he know what you were up to?'

'Oh, yes,' she said, with a whimsical smile. 'My father was a very influential man, Finlay, and a very enlightened one. He had access to a great deal of privileged information, you know. How do you think El Fantasma came to be so well informed?'

'Your father knew you were El Fantasma, the partisan! Hell's bells, how many more of these revelations are you going to hit me with!'

Isabella laughed at his astonishment. 'Only one more. My father was actually the original El Fantasma. All I did was act as his liaison between certain trusted guerrillas at first, and then gradually, as he became sick and as I became more…adept?—then I took over. You see, you could describe it as the family business.'

'I doubt your brother would see it that way,' Finlay responded drily.

Isabella's expression hardened. 'I told you, my father was a very enlightened man. As his son, Xavier was destined to take on the legacy of Hermoso Romero, and Papa made sure that he was fit for that purpose. Expensive schooling. The army. The management of the estate. The production of the wine. Xavier will do the same for his son. To me, Papa bequeathed El Fantasma. I do not interfere with my brother's management of his legacy. My own legacy is none of Xavier's concern.'

It was not so much the words as the tone in which she spoke that made Finlay's heart sink. She sounded as he did, when giving orders. Cool, calm and utterly implacable. He wasn't simply dealing with a woman on a mission to bring about change. Isabella's dreams were also her father's. How the devil was he to convince her that she had to give them up forever?

'You will not,' she said. 'Persuade me to give El Fantasma up,' she clarified, 'if that is what you were thinking?'

'So you're a mind reader now, are you?'

She shrugged. 'I know that you are not a man who countenances failure. I made it very clear yesterday that I would reject any offer of rescue, but your orders are nonetheless to rescue me, and Major Finlay Urquhart is a soldier who, I suspect, never fails to obey an order.'

'You're quite wrong there, lass,' he said harshly. 'If I hadn't been quite so capable of insubordination, I'd be Colonel Urquhart by now, at the very least.'

Isabella spread a sheaf of pages out on the

table in front of her. 'Instead, you are the Jock Upstart—have I that right?'

'You do.'

'Then, they will not be so very surprised, your superiors, when you disobey this particular order,' she said, glancing over her shoulder. 'Once you have seen for yourself how important El Fantasma's work is, I am hoping you will agree that they were quite misguided when they sent you here.'

So she was laying down the gauntlet. He was not surprised. Though it would have made his life a damned sight easier if she'd turned around and agreed with him, he'd have been disappointed. And maybe a wee bit sceptical, too. Isabella was not the type to simply roll over. 'I'm afraid it is you who are misguided, lass,' Finlay said, shaking his head.

'No,' Isabella said firmly. 'No, you will not ever persuade me to that way of thinking, so instead I must persuade you to think differently. Come, see for yourself.'

Why not? he thought, joining her at the table. She deserved a fair hearing, even if the outcome was already, in his mind, decided.

Joining her at the table, he saw she had a large rectangular frame set in front of her. 'This will be the front page of our next pamphlet.' Isabella began to select tiny blocks of characters to place into it. 'You see, all the letters have to be inserted in reverse. I used to practise with a mirror. Even after two years, I am still very slow.'

She didn't look slow. Finlay watched her reaching for the individual characters with only a cursory glance, the columns of the page forming at an impressive speed. 'This is called a forme,' she said, indicating the frame. 'When it is finished, it sits on the coffin, that flat bed on the press there, and you can apply the ink if you wish. We may as well take advantage of your presence and do some printing. It requires two people to operate the press, and with Estebe out of commission I have been unable to print anything. Unless assisting El Fantasma counts as insubordination?'

Treason, more like. Finlay sighed to himself. This pamphlet was never going to see the light of day if he had anything to do with it. Not that his so-called superiors gave a damn about El Fantasma's pamphlets or, frankly, his cause.

'This is El Fantasma's symbol.' Isabella held up the small woodcut on which was embossed the inverted shape of the phantom.

'Aye, I saw that on one of your pamphlets back in England.'

'Really?' Isabella exclaimed. 'I had not realised our message had spread so far and wide.'

She looked so pleased, he could not bring himself to burst her bubble. 'What symbol would you use for me, then?' Finlay asked instead.

Continuing to set characters into the frame at speed, she pursed her lips. 'A man in a kilt? Though I think that would be too difficult to cut.'

'And it might be mistaken for a woman in a skirt.'

She turned to him, her eyes dancing. 'No one would mistake you in a plaid for a woman in a skirt.'

'Any more than anyone would mistake you in a pair of breeches for a man.'

'Yet I fooled you, did I not?'

'For a few moments, in the dark. The minute I held you in my arms, I knew unmistakably what you were.'

* * *

Isabella's heart did that funny skipping lurch it seemed to have developed since Finlay's arrival in Spain. 'You make it sound as if we were dancing,' she said, trying to ignore it. 'In fact, we were rolling around in a ditch.'

'I've rolled around in a few ditches in my time,' he replied, with one of his devilish smiles, 'but I reckon that was the most memorable. And the most enjoyable.'

'You are easily amused,' she told him, trying and failing to suppress her own smile.

'On the contrary. You undersell yourself, lass.'

Lass. It meant *girl.* Young woman. The way he said it, in that lilting accent of his, it felt more like a caress than a word. That smile of his was fascinating. How could a man smile in one way and seem merely amused, another and seem so—so tempting? Isabella dragged her eyes away. Now was not the time to be tempted to do anything other than finish the pamphlet.

'And you, I think, overrate yourself, Finlay Urquhart,' she said firmly. 'I am not going to be charmed into kissing you.'

'Not now, or not ever?'

'Oh,' Isabella said, smiling in what she hoped was a saucy way as she turned back to her work, 'I never say never. Now, are you going to help me or not?'

Without waiting for a reply, she picked up the completed forme and slotted it carefully into position on the stone coffin bed of the press. Next, she measured ink onto the wool-stuffed pads and handed one to Finlay. 'It must be applied very evenly. Watch, I will show you.' She did so, then handed him the second pad. 'Good. Careful now. Excellent.'

He had a deft touch, she noted. Trying to keep her mind firmly on the work in hand, Isabella turned her attention to dampening the paper. She had brought Finlay here this morning to persuade him that his mission was pointless. El Fantasma did not need to be rescued. El Fantasma was needed here. Yet here they were, printing El Fantasma's latest pamphlet together, and all Isabella could think of was kissing!

And Finlay wasn't helping, with that smile of his, and that tempting mouth of his, and those sea-blue eyes. Why did he have to be so—so distracting? Why could not the Duke of Wellington have sent a much older man with liver spots on his bald pate, or a man who did not like to wash or clean his teeth, or a man with those spindly legs and knobbly knees she hated, or—or any man, other than Finlay Urquhart!

Finlay Urquhart, who looked at her as if he would like her for dinner. Yes, she would like to be Finlay's dinner, whatever that meant, though she should not be thinking of dinner or kisses or any of these things at the moment, Isabella scolded herself. The paper. The ink. The setting of type. Those were the things she ought to be thinking about.

She put the first piece of paper into position, frowning hard. 'The first press will soak up any excess of ink,' she said, refusing to look at Finlay. 'Now it is a case of turning this handle, and we will see.'

He turned the handle and the press rolled into motion. Isabella checked the results. 'Almost perfect,' she said, keeping her eyes on the page. 'Now, if you will turn, I will set. We require at least two hundred copies.'

'As well I'm a big brawny Highlander, then,' Finlay said.

Without thinking, she lifted her eyes. He had flexed his arms. His smile was mocking, teasing. Why did he have to smile at all? She wished he would not. 'Browny?'

'Brawny. It means…'

'Strong.' Before she could stop herself, she touched his flexed muscle. 'I thought so yesterday when—' Isabella broke off, blushing foolishly and busied herself with the paper.

Finlay turned the press. Another sheet was spread out to dry. Another sheet inserted. He turned the press. They worked well together, their actions dovetailing seamlessly. He said nothing, though she was aware of him slanting her covert glances. He understood the power of silence. He had given her more than enough to think about. Too much. She couldn't think. She didn't want to think. She inserted another piece of paper. He checked the ink without her having to ask. The press turned and turned and turned.

It was hot work. Finlay took off his coat and waistcoat. They each drank a glass of the cool water that came from the well under the cellars. The press turned with metronomic regularity. Finlay removed his cravat. Isabella undid the top button at her throat. His shirt clung to his chest. She could see a smattering of hair, just as she had imagined. She could see the dark circles of his nipples. Her own tightened in response. A bead of sweat trickled down her back. Only twenty more sheets. Only ten.

'Done.'

Finlay drew a fresh bucket from the well. They drank thirstily. He dipped his handkerchief into the icy water and ran it over his brow, his neck, his throat. Watching him, Isabella's own throat constricted. He caught her looking, and heat of a different kind flared between them.

He dipped the handkerchief into the bucket again. He touched the cool linen to her brow. To her temples. To her cheeks. 'Hot,' she said.

'Hot,' he repeated.

Another dip. A trickle of water on the back of her neck. Then round over her collarbone to the damp skin at the base of her throat. Her heart was pounding. He must be able to feel it. Was his the same? She raised her hand to touch him, felt the damp of his shirt, heard the sharp intake of his breath, then he caught her wrist.

'Wait,' he said.

'Wait?' Isabella blinked at him stupidly. *What was she doing?*

'This,' Finlay said, 'between us, I don't want it misconstrued. I will not have you thinking I seduced you in order to persuade you to come away with me.'

'I told you I had no intention of kissing you. You will never persuade me to come away with you.'

'Never say never, is what you said.'

'Do you think I would kiss you in order to persuade you to leave me alone?'

'I'd like to think not. I'd be sore offended if I thought you were playing me like a fish on a line.'

Was he teasing her? She didn't think so. 'I wonder how a man who turns every head in a room can think such a thing possible,' Isabella said. 'Every lass would want to kiss you, I think. Even my very proper sister-in-law says that she would like to be your dinner. I asked her what she meant, but she wouldn't tell me.'

Finlay still held her hand, but when she flattened it over his chest, he made no protest. 'I wouldn't describe you as a mere dinner,' he said.

'You are a feast. A banquet. Dinner doesn't do you justice.'

His words conjured up such images, of his mouth on her breasts, of his tongue on her skin, tasting her, savouring her, relishing her. She imagined herself spread naked for him on a damask cloth, and a wrenching twist of desire made her shudder. 'Consuela cannot have meant—*that*,' Isabella said, shocked at her lurid imagination.

Finlay's laugh was low, his voice husky. 'Well, I'm not sure exactly what you mean by *that*, but I reckon she did.'

This assertion, Isabella found more shocking than anything. 'She would not!'

He eyed her with some amusement. 'You're surely not thinking that your sister-in-law is one of these women who sees lovemaking as a marital duty without pleasure?'

'Her husband is my brother. I have not thought of it at all.'

'Have you not seen the way the pair of them look at each other?'

Isabella didn't like the way Finlay was looking at her. It made her feel foolish. 'You've heard the way Xavier talks. My brother is interested in Consuela as the mother of his children and nothing more.'

His response was to shake his head, smiling in a way that made her both embarrassed and uncertain. 'Aye, that's what he'd like the world to believe, for it is not the done thing, is it, for a man to admit he's in thrall to his wife? You are not the only one in this household to lead a double life.'

Was he right? Certainly, Consuela had said that she loved Xavier, but Isabella had assumed she meant in a—a wifely way. A dutiful way. She had assumed that Consuela was as bloodless as—well, as bloodless as Isabella assumed a dutiful Spanish wife would be. She had assumed that there was nothing more to Consuela than the blank, cold, demure facade she presented, until Finlay suggested she look again.

'You must think me very arrogant,' she said, turning away from him, feeling very small. 'It is no wonder that Consuela wishes to replace me with one of her own sisters. I have made no attempt to get to know her. Worse, I have assumed there was nothing worth knowing.'

'Now you're being daft.' Finlay caught her shoulder, turning her back around to face him. 'Look at all this,' he said, waving at the stack of drying pamphlets. 'You've been carrying the burden of El Fantasma for two years all alone, fighting for more years than that for your country. You'd be more than entitled to boast about what you've achieved, instead of which, what you're concerned about is not having done enough.'

'That is no excuse. Consuela is family.'

'That's true. She's your brother's wife, which makes her, in the way of things, above you in the hierarchy. Has she made any attempt to understand you? Has she confided in you?'

'No, but...'

'You were here first. That's not Consuela's fault, but your brother must have known you had the running of the place while he was off at the war. Has he tried to understand your feelings?'

'He has tried to marry me off to his best friend. In Xavier's eyes, that is taking care of me, I suppose, though I doubt very much if Gabriel would be so eager to offer for me if he knew his new bride was El Fantasma.'

She meant it as a poor attempt at a joke, but Finlay did not smile. 'Is that what you're thinking? To give it up and marry Torres?'

'No.' Her denial took her aback, for her tone was quite decisive. Was it only a few days ago, she had been contemplating quite the opposite?

'Why not?' Finlay spoke sharply.

Isabella shook her head in confusion. 'I can't,' she said, again with absolute certainly. 'If I told him the truth he would not wish to marry me, and if I married him I could not tell him the truth.'

It was a perfectly logical, perfectly reasonable, perfectly honourable response. Finlay looked unconvinced. 'If you loved him…'

'That has nothing to do with it. Consuela assures me that I would, after we were married but—you know this is none of your business, Finlay.'

'Far be it for me to contradict your sister-in-law,' he continued, ignoring her. 'It may be true that love follows the wedding vows, but I reckon there has to be something there first of all.'

'What something?'

'A wee spark. Do you think of kissing him? Do you imagine making love to him?'

'No!' A lie. More accurately, she had tried and failed. She prayed that her flush of embarrassment could be attributed to the heat from the press. 'It is not possible to imagine what one has not experienced. As you have pointed out on several occasions, I am a virgin,' she said baldly.

'It didn't stop your imagination a wee minute ago.'

'What...?'

'When I said you were not a dinner, but a banquet.' Finlay's eyes were alight with devilment once more. 'What was it that you imagined?'

'Nothing. I have no idea what you meant by it.'

'One of the problems I have with you is that I look at you and I have far too many ideas.'

Her skin was tingling. The tingling was spreading. 'What kind of ideas?'

'Indecent ones. Ideas I couldn't possibly put into words.'

Finlay's upper lip was beaded with sweat. It took Isabella's every ounce of self-restraint not to lick it. His cheeks were high with colour. She could see his chest moving under his sweat-damped shirt. Was his heart beating as fast as hers? Did he ache, as she did, for the touch of his skin on hers? She would not make the first move. She could not bear it if he did not. 'If not words, what about actions?' Isabella asked. 'An appetiser, perhaps?'

'This sort of thing, do you mean?' He kissed her. A fleeting, soft and utterly delicious kiss, his tongue licking into the corner of her mouth, his hand resting lightly on her breast, and then she was free.

'I believe it is customary to serve more than one appetiser at a banquet.' Surrendering to temptation, Isabella licked the sweat from his upper lip, allowing her breasts to brush fleetingly against his chest.

Finlay moaned and kissed her ardently. 'That's the problem with an appetiser,' he said, gently easing her away.

Isabella looked at him blankly.

'It leaves one wanting more. A great deal more.' He checked his pocket watch and picked up his waistcoat. 'Talking of appetites, I think it would be prudent if we both cleaned off all

this rather incriminating ink before joining Consuela for dinner.'

'Yes, of course. Dinner,' Isabella said. But her
thoughts were not of food.

Chapter Seven

'I thought I might show you a little more of our beautiful countryside today,' Isabella said, 'since I think it would be unwise for me to take you to visit Estebe as Xavier requested. Your knowledge of wine is so sparse, he would be suspicious of you within a few minutes. If Xavier asks, we will need to concoct a story to explain why we—'

'Is your brother due back today?' Finlay interrupted.

'No, but when he does return, we need to have a plausible explanation for not visiting Estebe. Xavier will be most displeased that I have disobeyed his direct instructions.'

'I am not planning to be here when your brother returns.' Finlay was not planning to be here beyond tomorrow, and he was not planning to leave alone, either, though it was clear that his plans and Isabella's did not currently coincide.

Her face had fallen momentarily at his terse tone, but she recovered with a determined smile. 'I did not think you would go so far as to place an order for Xavier's precious Rioja that would not be fulfilled, but as he is not likely to be home for a few days yet, you do not have to rush off on his account.'

'Isabella, it's not your brother I'm worried about.'

'No, but—you did not expect to find El Fantasma so quickly, did you? I mean, if you had not found me, or if I could not lead you to him, or if it turned out that I could, but it took some time to arrange—' She broke off, looking flustered. 'What I mean is, you must have anticipated having to spend a considerable amount of time in Spain searching for El Fantasma. Having achieved your objective with relative ease, why not reward yourself with a tiny hiatus from your duties as a soldier while the opportunity presents itself? You must admit, the Hermoso Romero estate is a beguiling place.'

She was blushing. She looked so enchanting,

it was all Finlay could do to stop himself from leaning across the breakfast table to kiss her. Of course, he knew she was not indifferent to him, and he was certainly not indifferent to her, but he suspected that their mutual attraction was more to do with the heightened tension of the situation they found themselves in than anything else.

Still, he wished she hadn't dangled further temptation in front of him. He took a sip of coffee and took another, unwanted, slice of cured ham. Señora Romero had not joined them this morning, leaving them to breakfast alone. There was something very appealing in looking at Isabella across the breakfast cups. She would be even more appealing if they were taking breakfast together in their bedchamber, her hair down, wearing a lacy gown and nothing else. He had always been a man who preferred to contemplate the forthcoming day in solitude, but…

What the devil was he thinking of? 'It is indeed a beguiling place, but not as beguiling as one of its inhabitants. However,' Finlay added quickly, 'I'm here on a mission, not on holiday, and my objective is far from achieved.' Ach!

Now Isabella looked as if he'd slapped her. 'I'll tell you what,' he added, softening his tone, 'why don't we ride out, like you suggest? We need to talk, but there's no necessity for us to do it here. A good gallop and some fresh air would be most welcome.'

'I would like that. I know some lovely spots hereabouts. But as for needing to talk, I'm afraid there is nothing to discuss, Finlay. We must agree to differ.' She crossed her arms, looking mulish. 'I am not in need of rescue. I told you...'

'And I listened. Now it's your turn to listen to me. No,' he said, when she opened her mouth to protest again, 'you're not being fair. You've had your say, now it's only right that you let me have mine.'

'The world is not a fair place.'

'Doesn't El Fantasma advocate free speech for all and a fair hearing?'

She laughed, holding up her hands in surrender. 'You use my own rhetoric against me! I call that very unfair, indeed. But all is fair in love and war, that is what you will say, no? I shall go and change. Meet me at the stables in half an hour.'

He caught her arm as she made for the door. 'We're not at war, Isabella.'

'No.'

Their eyes met and held. Her mouth softened into a sensual curve. The urge to touch her, to kiss her, simply to hold her tightly against him was so strong, it almost overpowered him. 'No,' Finlay said, letting her go, 'we are not at war.'

As to the other, he thought, as the door closed behind her, he would be a fool to contemplate it. And Major Finlay Urquhart had never been guilty of being a fool.

A couple of hours later, they were sitting side by side on a blanket, leaning against an overturned tree in a pretty glade at the edge of a forest located some distance from the estate. The sun had obligingly come out, and there were only the slightest, puffiest of clouds in the pale blue winter sky. Isabella opened the top button of her jacket and lifted her face to the warmth. Finlay had taken off his coat, and sat in his waistcoat and shirtsleeves. His leather-clad leg was not touching her skirts, his arm was not brushing hers, but she was so aware of him, it was almost as if they were. She didn't want him to leave. Not yet.

No, not yet. She hadn't realised until he'd turned up out of the blue how lonely she had been. She had her cause but precious little else. She hadn't realised how rarely she was her true self. Not even with Estebe could she talk as she did with Finlay, and she had never, ever thought of kissing Estebe. Now she seemed to do nothing else but think of kissing Finlay.

He shifted against the tree and she opened her eyes to find him studying her intently. 'What is it? Have I dust on my nose?' She brushed her face roughly, not for fear of dust but to conceal the effect his gaze had on her. She felt flustered and flattered in equal measure. She wrinkled her nose. 'Has it gone?'

Finlay grimaced. 'Stop being so endearing. For pity's sake, it's difficult enough having to say what I have to say, without...'

'Then, don't say it, Finlay.'

'I have no choice.'

'Not yet.' She knew, absolutely, that what he had to say would signal the end, and she so desperately didn't want it to end. 'Not yet,' she said again, smoothing her hand over his hair, his cheek.

He turned his face, his lips brushing a kiss on her palm, then, taking her by the wrist, he kissed each of her fingers. 'Why did it have to be you?' he murmured. 'Why do you have to be so irresistible?'

'Then, do not resist.' She caught his hand and did as he had done, brushing her lips over his palm, her tongue over each of his fingertips. His eyes flickered shut as he inhaled sharply. She pushed the cuff of his sleeve back, kissing the pulse on his wrist. And then his mouth found hers and she forgot everything save for the taste of him and his touch and his drugging, sweet, heady kisses.

He whispered her name as he kissed her. He said her name like no other did, his soft, lilting accent making a caress of it as his hands stroked her cheeks, her neck, unfastening the buttons of her riding coat to slide inside and cup her breasts. She kissed him back hungrily, her own hands roaming over his back, his shoulders. She held him tightly to her, pressed herself against him, for fear he would stop. She could not bear it if he stopped, not this time.

He kissed the tops of her breasts above the gown of her habit. She laced her fingers into his hair. Her corsets felt too tight. She was hot. Her nipples were hard under his caress, aching for more. *'Más,'* she whispered urgently.

Finlay muttered some gentle endearment in his native tongue. His eyes were dark, his cheeks flushed. His neckcloth was undone, his waistcoat open. She could sense him wrestling with his conscience. She did not want his conscience to win. 'Please do not stop,' she said, made shameless with desire.

He groaned. 'Don't look at me like that. How am I to resist you when you look at me like that?'

'Then, don't.' She pulled him back towards her. 'Don't resist,' she said, and kissed him fiercely.

This time he obeyed her command. His kisses were harder, his breath became more ragged, his hands touched her more surely, cupping her breasts, making her arch up with pleasure. He slid his hand under the skirts of her habit, stroking his way up her leg, over her stocking, her garter, to the soft flesh of her thigh. Her body pulsed and throbbed. Her skin tingled. Inside her, the tension, the heat, pooled between her legs. Finlay's skin was hot, too, under the linen of his shirt, his nipple hard against her flattened palm. His eyes, intent on hers, reflected the fire building inside her.

'Are you sure?' he asked.

'*Si*. Yes. Sure,' she answered. Though she was not at all sure what he meant, she was sure she wanted it, and when his hand cupped her sex, when he slid his finger inside her, she was certain, whimpering with delight. 'Yes, yes, yes,' she said as he touched her. 'Yes.'

She surrendered to it, to him, to the exquisite pleasure of the tension his touch was building, lying back on the blanket, his body half-covering hers. She closed her eyes as he kissed her again, lost in the pleasure of his mouth, his tongue, his touch. Stroking. Thrusting. Stroking inside her, moving instinctively with him, clinging on to the knot until she could bear it no longer, and it exploded, forcing a strange, guttural cry from her as she shuddered and pulsed, clinging to his shoulders to anchor her, convinced that if she let go of him she might fly straight up into the pale blue winter sky and burst into flames like a firework.

Isabella lay sprawled on the blanket, half-covered by his body, the embodiment of temptation, the image of sated delight. Her eyes fluttered open, and Finlay could not resist kissing her one last time. His erection throbbed. It took him every ounce of willpower to move away from her. He could not believe he'd allowed himself to go this far.

He sat up abruptly. 'Enough,' he said, aloud this time. Her smile faded. There was hurt in her eyes, and confusion. Steeling himself, Finlay grabbed his jacket and shrugged it on, deliberately putting some distance between them.

Isabella, too, sat up, buttoning her jacket, the glow fading from her cheeks, her expression hardening. 'For the avoidance of doubt, do not even think of apologising. What happened was entirely at my instigation. I did not realise that you were so reluctant. Or indeed that my own— enthusiasm—was so one-sided.'

Finlay cursed. 'It's not that. How can you

think that?' he said, reaching for her instinctively. 'If you mattered less to me, this would all be a damned sight easier. I've never wanted a woman so much. Did I not tell you only a few moments ago, I've never met a woman like you?'

'Then, why—I don't understand. Why are you sorry for—for what happened, if I am not?'

She was blushing adorably. He wanted to kiss her. He wanted to hold her. He didn't want to let her go. It was this thought that stopped him in his tracks and forced him to do exactly that. 'Enough,' Finlay said once more. 'The time has come to stop faffing about. I want you to sit down, and I want you to listen to me.'

His tone brooked no argument. He spoke as he would to his men, and he told himself that from now on that was how he had to think of her. She was one of his lieutenants, not to be reasoned with or cajoled, but to be informed of his orders, and instructed to discharge them forthwith. Isabella cast him a resentful look, but she sat down on top of the overturned tree and looked at him expectantly. Good. Fine. Finlay put his hands behind his back and stood a few steps away. 'Right, then. Here's the bald truth of the matter.'

He told her in plain, unvarnished facts what Jack had told him when he had briefed him. 'Two years ago,' he concluded, 'you were a partisan fighting in a legitimate war for your country. That war is over now. Yes, for El Fantasma and his supporters, the fight goes on, but it's no longer legal. El Fantasma, his supporters… They're not soldiers in the eyes of the law, they are traitors. You are the enemy within, Isabella, and if you carry on as you are doing, I doubt very much you'll live to see your next birthday.'

She was pale, but still defiant. 'They will never catch me. No one will ever suspect that El Fantasma is a woman.'

'Estebe knows who you are. His deputies know who he is. Their deputies, in turn, know who they are. For the authorities, it is simply a case of working their way up the chain. That is what they are busily doing right now.'

'Estebe would never betray me.'

'Isabella, the things they would do to him would make Estebe betray his own mother.'

'She is dead. Besides, he would not…'

'Aye, he would,' Finlay said firmly, and proceeded to explain, in graphic detail, exactly how they would set about it.

'You are making it up,' Isabella said faintly, when he was done. 'Or at the very least exaggerating. I may violently disagree with the government but we are Spanish, not barbarians. They would not treat one of their own citizens so inhumanely.'

'You give your government, all governments, come to that, too much credit. They will do what is expedient. The would not hesitate to use torture if necessary. I'm speaking from experience. Not of what I've inflicted, but of what I've witnessed,' he said implacably, refusing to allow himself to take pity on her. Taking pity on her could only harm her. 'What's more, your being a woman would not protect you. Quite the reverse. It would leave you open to other, even more degrading treatment, if you take my meaning.'

'No.' She jumped to her feet, her fists balled. 'No. What would be the point? If they had El Fantasma, if they really did manage to capture me, which I don't believe, why would they— What would be the point of torturing me?'

'For the love of God, woman! You said it your-self—people are listening to what El Fantasma has to say, and what he has to say is treason. It's not a case of simply shutting you up. They will want to make sure that there's no one left to fill your shoes. They will want names from you. As-sociates, contacts, sympathisers. Information. Such as the location of the printing press. Where the funding comes from. They know about your previous collaboration with the British. They'll want to know everything that went on back then. And when they've got all that—and believe me, you'll tell them everything they want to know, including my highly irregular and diplomati-cally explosive presence here—then they'll have done with you.'

'No! You are trying to frighten me. I won't listen.'

'Isabella...'

'No!' She turned on him, shaking his hand away from her arm, her face aglow with anger. 'You know, from the very start, I have been thinking, I have been asking myself, why are you really here?'

'What do you mean? I've told you—'

'Yes, that you are here to rescue El Fantasma from the Spanish government,' Isabella interrupted with a sneer. 'But why would you do that, Finlay? You are a soldier, an English—British soldier. You are here, by your own admission, under orders from the Duke of Wellington himself. But the Duke of Wellington does not care a fig about Spain. He stopped caring about Spain the moment he chased Napoleon across the border into France. No, Wellington does not give this,' she said, snapping her fingers, 'for what El Fantasma has to say now that we are no longer at war. He does, however, care very much about what El Fantasma could say about how that war was won here in Spain, yes? A campaign the duke himself had ultimate responsibility for.'

There was no point in pretending to misunderstand her. 'Yes,' Finlay said, 'you're quite correct. Whether as a result of his direct orders, or merely acts carried out in his name, there are many unsavoury aspects of the conduct of the war here that Wellington and his coterie would prefer left unsaid.'

'Especially now that he has hopes of becoming prime minister,' Isabella said, folding her arms across her chest and glaring at him. 'And he would go to some lengths to protect those hopes, I think. To the extent of sending one of his men here to Spain, even. To ensure the—what was your phrase—*diplomatically explosive* information does not fall into Spanish hands.'

'Aye, that he would.'

'Oh.'

His blunt admission took her aback. She had been a deal less certain in her accusations than she'd sounded, Finlay thought, but what the hell, the lass deserved the whole truth. 'You're right,' he said. 'Both our governments have the same aim, albeit for differing reasons. My orders were to get to you before they did and take you back with me. Whether you'd subsequently end up a prisoner in exile under house arrest, or whether you'd simply quietly disappear I don't know, but the net result would be the same. Silence.'

She put her hand to her breast, staggering away from him in horror. 'You knew that, and yet you—you tell me this, and you expect me to consent to—to allow you to—to abduct me? You have been lying to me all along. I don't understand. Why are you telling me all this?'

'To knock some sense into you!' He grabbed her, and when she shrank from him, gave her a tiny shake. 'Don't be so daft, lass. You can't possibly think I would harm a hair on your heid! I'm telling you what my orders were, but that doesn't necessarily mean I'm going to follow them.'

'You're not?'

'The Jock Upstart has a reputation for insubordination to uphold,' he said with a thin smile. 'I've told you the truth from the start. I'm not here to kill you. I'm here to save your life.'

'But how— What...'

'You have to get out of Spain, but there's no way I'm taking you to England. You're bound for America, lass, and safety,' Finlay said gently. 'You asked me why I was sorry for what happened there, between us. That is why. You have no choice but to make a new life for yourself a whole continent away, and I can play no part in that life, even if you wanted me to. The arrangements are already in place.'

He had said far more than he intended, implied far more than he would admit to feeling, made the matter personal when it should not be, but before he could regret it or retract it, Isabella pushed him away.

'America! I am not going to America. I am not going anywhere. Why would you think— No, wait. Something does not make sense. You had already made arrangements, planned to send El Fantasma to America, before you knew he was me—that it was me? That implies that you had always planned to disobey Wellington's orders.'

'I'm not here for Wellington. I'll admit, my orders originate from Wellington, but that's not why I'm here. I'm here because Jack asked me to come.'

'Jack.' Isabella stared at him blankly.

'My friend and comrade. Lieutenant Colonel Jack Trestain. Better known as Wellington's codebreaker. But then you know that because El Fantasma was one of his most trusted partisan contacts, although they never actually met. Jack says you've been responsible for saving literally thousands of lives, and now he feels he owes you yours. I've known him for the better part of a decade. We've been through some tough times together, so when he asked for my help I could not refuse him, despite the risks. Jack came up with the plan to send El Fantasma incognito to America. Wellington will be told El Fantasma perished in the course of the attempted abduction. Problem solved and everybody happy. A simple but elegant plan typical of Jack. But the key point is this. If Jack believes you are in mortal danger, believes it enough to ask me to risk my reputation and possibly my neck, then you surely need no further proof that the threat to your life is real.'

'I don't know. I need time to think about everything you have said.' She put her hand to her eyes, but he saw the sheen of tears lurking there.

He longed to comfort her, to allay her fear and distress, but he could not afford to risk diluting the message he'd hammered so brutally home.

'Isabella, that is a luxury we cannot afford. Time is of the essence.'

'No.' She threw her shoulders back and glared at him. 'This is my life we are talking about, Finlay, not yours. My life, and Estebe's and many others', too. I won't be rushed into a decision. I need time to think. At the end of the week…'

'No. Tomorrow,' Finlay said, hardening his heart. 'You have until tomorrow at the very latest.'

* * *

Isabella took another sip of cognac and stared into the fire. She had retired to her bedchamber immediately upon her return, both shaken and shocked by Finlay's words. For some time she sat, completely numb, almost unable to assimilate what he had told her, but as the hours passed and she replayed the conversation over and over, the truth began sink in. It was the manner in which he had spoken, almost as much as the words themselves that had finally convinced her. Finlay had laid out the detailed facts so clearly and concisely. He'd made no attempt to disguise the horrors, but nor had he overdramatised them. He had not been trying to frighten her, but to open her eyes to the stark reality of the situation.

As an upshot she was, nonetheless, extremely frightened. She had never thought of herself as a traitor. Listening to Finlay, she could only guess at the plethora of shocking, horrific experiences that lent credence to his words. Listening to Finlay, Isabella had been forced to concede to herself that she was not, as she had always imagined herself, a soldier fighting a noble fight. At least not a true soldier as he was.

She shuddered. She had thought, in the past few days, that she had come to know him, but it was difficult to reconcile the charming Finlay with the man who had sent her world crashing around her this afternoon. The horrors he must have witnessed. The savagery. The brutality. The bloodshed and suffering. He seemed quite untouched by it, yet she knew he was neither a brute nor a savage. He had come here, all this way, not because of an order but because of a promise he had made to his best friend and comrade. Finlay was an honourable man. Finlay was in many respects a gentleman. Finlay was also the most attractive man she had ever met. Her face flamed as she recalled her wanton behaviour this afternoon, but her unrepentant body began to thrum at the memory. He *had* wanted her—of that she had no doubt. But he had resisted the temptation, because he knew her fate was to lead a new life, in safety but in exile, on another continent. A life that he could have no part of, even if either of them wanted it.

Reality intervened once more, like being doused with a bucket of cold mountain water. Isabella threw back the remains of her cognac, coughing as the fiery liquor burned its way down her throat. Whatever her future was, wherever her future lay, it did not involve Finlay. Not only was it pointless to speculate, she had far more important things to think about now than her feelings for him. Whatever they were.

Jumping to her feet, she began to pace the floor, from the long doors that opened onto her balcony, to the door that opened onto the corridor, and back again. She no longer questioned the danger she was exposed to, but the consequences— No, she was not ready to accept those.

She threw open the windows and stepped out onto the balcony. A thin film of cloud covered the night sky, but a luminescent moon shone through it, bathing the vineyards below with a ghostly grey light. This was her home. She had never known another. Her family were here. And her life's work. She could not leave. There must be another solution.

A tap on the door made her jump. Isabella turned and saw her sister-in-law slip into the room. 'Consuela. What are you doing here so late—is something wrong? Is Ramon…?'

'My son is safe and well in his nursery. I intend to ensure that he remains so. Which is why I am here.' Consuela turned the key in the look and crossed the room, taking one of the chairs by the fireside. 'I would have come earlier, but I have had to spend the past hour with the wife of one of Xavier's tenants. It seems the man has disappeared off the face of the earth.'

'What man?'

Consuela waved her hand dismissively. 'I cannot remember the name. He works for Estebe. He will be off on a drunken spree, I don't doubt. Or run off with another man's wife. Of course, when I hinted at such, the woman became quite furious, claimed her husband never drank and never looked at another woman, but...'

They are working their way up the chain. That was what Finlay had said. No, she was being foolish. It was simply a coincidence. 'How long has he been missing?' Isabella asked.

'Almost a week. I don't know what the woman expects me to do. I told her to come back when Xavier has returned. But I did not come here to discuss missing farm workers. Sit down, Isabella, and pour me a glass of that cognac, if you please. It is time you and I had a little talk.'

'Can it not wait until morning? I am very tired.' The fact that the missing tenant worked for Estebe was a coincidence, nothing more. She was edgy, and no wonder. The last thing she wanted was to listen to another lecture on marriage. 'Really, Consuela, if you have come to further Gabriel's suit, I should tell you that you are wasting your time.'

'That is not why I am here, but that is indeed one of the things I suspected. Sit down, Isabella. I do not care how tired you are, this will not wait.'

There was something in her tone that made her heart sink. Consuela sounded quite implacable. She sounded horribly certain, just as Finlay had done earlier today. Isabella dropped abruptly onto the chair. 'What is it you wish to say?

Consuela took a measured sip of cognac. 'Why is Finlay Urquhart here?'

The question took Isabella utterly by surprise. 'To buy wine. But you already know that.'

'Do not play games with me. There is no time,' her sister-in-law said with an angry sigh. 'He knows even less about wine than I do. Xavier was suspicious from the first day—so much so, that he decided to check Mr Urquhart's credentials. What business did you imagine was keeping him so long in Pamplona?'

'I had no idea what my brother was doing since he rarely takes me into his confidence. Has Xavier proof that Finlay—Mr Urquhart—has he irrefutable proof that he is *not* a wine merchant?'

Consuela shrugged impatiently. 'What is he, Isabella? Who is he? And how is he connected with whatever it is you have secreted in my husband's wine cellars?'

A trickle of sweat running down her spine made Isabella shiver. Fear made knots in her stomach. 'What do you know of that?' she asked, the shock of this revelation on top of the tumultuous events earlier so severe that denial did not even occur to her.

Consuela curled her lip. 'You think you are the only one with eyes?'

'Clearly not.'

'I have watched you sneaking out of the house at night. At first I thought it was to meet a lover, but you had not the look of a woman who had experience of such matters until lately. You have allowed Mr Urquhart to take liberties, I think. That was foolish of you, but not, I think the most foolish thing you have done.'

Her throat was dry. She must not panic. She must—she must— Dear heavens, what was she to do? 'Consuela...'

'What is in the cellar, Isabella?'

Her life was crashing around her ears. She was beyond prevaricating. 'A printing press,' she whispered.

Consuela's hand went to her breast. Her eyes widened in horror. '*Madre de Dios*, are you insane?' She jumped to her feet, clutching at the mantel for support. 'It is illegal to merely own such a thing, far less print anything. If it is discovered, Xavier could be imprisoned. Worse. A printing press! And what is it that you are printing?' She swayed, the blood draining from her face. 'That madman. The spectre. No, that is not right. The Ghost.'

'El Fantasma.'

Consuela swayed. 'You are actually printing that man's material here, at Hermoso Romero? Has that man been here? Isabella, if you have— if they discover—it does not bear thinking about.

They would hang Xavier. They would hang us all. What have you been thinking?'

Not thinking. She had not been thinking. Finlay had tried to warn her, but she hadn't listened. Hadn't wanted to listen. Isabella felt sick. She felt faint. Dimly, she was aware that Consuela had not guessed the whole truth. Yet. 'I— It will— I will put an end to it,' she said. 'I am so sorry, I…'

'Sorry!' Consuela turned on her viciously. 'What good is sorry! Sorry will not save us.' She took a sip of cognac. The glass clattered against her teeth. A sob shook her, and the glass fell onto the hearthrug, splattering brandy over her feet. 'What have you done, Isabella? What are we to do?'

'Nothing.' Seeing Consuela so close to hysterics forced Isabella back from the brink of her own. She poured her sister-in-law another glass of cognac and held it out to her. 'You must do nothing. Say nothing. This is my problem. It is for me to resolve.'

'How?'

'The less you know the better, Consuela, but I promise you, you will all be safe.'

'What about that man? Mr Urquhart, what has he to do with all this?'

'It doesn't matter. He, too, will be—attended to, I promise. Now, if you please, go to your bed-chamber, and forget we had this conversation, and when Xavier returns, it would be much better if you did not mention any of it.'

'You think I am stupid!' Consuela drained the glass and got shakily to her feet. 'He will be back in two days, no more. Is that enough time for you to rectify things?'

'It will have to be,' Isabella said with grim determination. 'For all our sakes.'

Chapter Eight

As Finlay eased the chapel door closed behind him, the smoky scent of candle wax and the evocative, cloying aroma of incense caught him unawares, hurtling him back in time to the services he'd attended in his childhood with his mother and sisters. He closed his eyes, remembering the sense of defiance that had preceded each clandestine trip to the ramshackle longhouse that had served as their place of worship, for the Catholic religion was officially proscribed in Scotland. It shamed him now, thinking of all the years in the army when he had neglected his church, but it was crime enough to be the Jock Upstart. To proclaim himself a Catholic to boot—no, that would have been beyond the pale. His faith had never truly left him, but he'd kept it well hidden. It wasn't something he was proud of, looking back on it.

This morning, awaking from a fitful sleep, anxious as to how this pivotal day in his mission might play out, he had been drawn to the silence and sanctuary of the little chapel in the grounds of the estate. Leaning against the door, he drank in the stillness of the space, the hushed serenity he recalled from his youth, and which he had always found notably absent in the ceremonial services in huge churches and cathedrals he'd attended on regimental duty over the years.

This little church, though plain and modest on the outside, was rather ornate and beautiful inside. The nave was tiled with marble and flanked with a number of pillars, painted in bold, bright colours with scenes from the Bible. The vaulted ceiling was dark blue, speckled with stars and bordered with gold. The walls were a paler blue, hung with ornately framed paintings that looked, to his unpractised eye, to be of the Italian Renaissance period. The pews were padded with rich, crimson velvet. The candlesticks on the altar were wrought from solid gold. Above it, the stained glass would speckle the floor with vivid colours later in the day when the sun streamed in. So much wealth and opulence, left quite un-attended. Xavier Romero clearly considered his possessions inviolate. One must be very sure of one's position in society to be so complacent. Looking around him, Finlay was forced to re-consider the man's standing. If it was discovered that his sister was El Fantasma— No, the pos-sibility did not bear countenancing.

He did not notice Isabella at first. She was kneeling in the tiny chapel dedicated to St Vin-cent of Saragossa, the patron saint of winemak-ers, Finlay guessed, judging from the symbolism of the paintings. Her head was bowed low. Her hair was covered in a mantilla. There was some-thing so vulnerable about the fall of lace over her head, the slight curve of her shoulders as she prayed. Whether she was aware of him or not, Finlay decided not to disturb her, retreating into the nave to light a candle and to make his own request for divine guidance.

It was not that he lacked the resolution to act. The situation demanded it. His orders demanded it. His word of honour to Jack demanded it. He could all but hear his friend's voice in his ear.

Finlay, you must get El Fantasma out of Spain at any cost.

It was worth it. By doing so, he would save Isabella's life. In the light of this one salient fact, it was gie pathetic of him to wonder just how different his own life would be if circumstances had been different. Of all the women in the world to fall for, he'd chosen this one. Not that he had fallen heavily yet. No, a man did not fall in love in a matter of days. He had caught himself in time, but he'd be an eejit if he let himself fall any further in thrall to her.

He rubbed his eyes, gazing up at the beautiful stained-glass window in search of inspiration. He had wondered, in the middle of the night, if he dare enlist Romero's help. The estate owner could have the printing press broken up. He could certainly insist on an end to Estebe's participation, and force the winery manager to end all contact with his men. But Romero would most likely have his sister incarcerated in a nunnery as a consequence. Hidden away from the world she'd be safe, she'd be alive, but what kind of existence would that be for her? Finlay couldn't bear to contemplate it.

If Isabella was a man, he would not have to wrestle with his conscience like this, he thought, looking over at her still bowed figure. If she was a man, he'd not be taking any account of those beguiling eyes of hers, or that sensuous mouth, or that delectable body. Or that determined, clever mind of hers, either. He cursed, then raised his eyes to the altar and apologised.

He was going round in circles. A promise was a promise, and he'd given one to Jack weeks before he'd met Isabella. Jack was depending on him. Blast it, when it came down to it, he was under orders, albeit orders that he intended to bend to a more palatable shape. 'So stop dithering, laddie, and let's get on with it,' he muttered.

Isabella chose this point to get to her feet, and Finlay got up from the pew to join her at the font in the atrium. 'You are a Catholic?' she asked in surprise when he dipped his hand in the font to bless himself and genuflect.

'I was raised one,' he replied, stepping outside into the early-morning mist.

'Did you come to church this morning in search of divine inspiration?'

'Is that what you were praying for?'

'No, I was praying for the wisdom to find a successful resolution to this quandary. Consuela came to my room last night.'

Isabella's voice faltered several times as she recounted her sister-in-law's visit. There were shadows under her eyes, which were heavy-lidded. She'd likely had less sleep even than he, poor lass. Finlay's heart went out to her for the weight of the burden she was carrying, but he suspected that sympathy was the last thing she would want from him, and so he forced himself to listen in silence.

'I feel quite—quite appalled, to think of the danger in which I have placed my family. You are right. It is time to put an end to El Fantasma,' Isabella concluded. 'I do not yet know what that means for me, but...'

'It means you will have to quit Spain. You've no option.'

She flinched. 'Of a certainty, it means leaving Hermoso Romero. As to the future—that I will think about later. For the moment, I have other more important matters to attend to.'

He did not like the way she tilted her chin when she spoke this last sentence. He did not like the way the sadness in her big golden eyes turned to something like defiance. 'Such as?' Finlay asked.

'Such as Estebe,' she said, and this time there was no mistaking the stubborn note in her voice. 'It is my duty to warn him, to give him the chance to warn his men, too.'

'Are you mad, woman?'

'It is my duty to warn him,' she repeated. 'I would never forgive myself if I did not.'

Finlay rolled his eyes. It was exactly what he'd have said himself. 'I understand that you feel it's your duty, but it's too much of a risk,' he said. 'No matter what Señora Romero might have promised you in the middle of the night, do you really think she's going to keep something like this from your brother?'

'Xavier will not be home until tomorrow.'

'We can't rely on that. We need to be away from here now.'

She turned on him fiercely. 'I have been successfully running this operation for nearly two years without your advice. I do not require it now. If our situations were reversed, if Estebe was your second-in-command, you would not dream of leaving without alerting him to the danger he is in.'

She really was a feisty wee thing, and what was more she was in the right of it. But unlike Isabella, Estebe was a hardened soldier who knew the real risks. 'No,' Finlay said firmly. 'No, I'm sorry, but from now on you're following my orders. You need to go and pack. Take only what you can carry on horseback. And it might be an idea to bring anything valuable you have. Jack and I, we've made provision for you, but...'

'I do not need your blood money.'

Pick your battles, Finlay told himself firmly. 'Fine, then, have it your own way. I won't force it on you. Now will you go back to the house and pack?'

'What are you going to do?'

'Attend to that blasted printing press.'

'What is the point? Only Estebe and I know about it. Besides, it is far too big. You will never be able to destroy it on your own.'

'At the very least, I can put it beyond use, and get rid of that damned incriminating pamphlet.'

Isabella opened her mouth to protest, then changed her mind. Obviously she, too, was picking her battles. 'That is likely to take you some time,' she said.

'Aye, well, that's for me to worry about. I will meet you back here at noon, and then we'll take it from there.'

'Very well.' She turned on her heel and walked purposefully back towards the main house.

Finlay watched her go, allowing his gaze to linger only fleetingly on her retreating derrière, before turning away towards the winery. She had, he thought as he lit the lantern and made his way down the stone steps, accepted his orders with reasonably good grace, all considered. Poor lass. In fact she was bearing up remarkably well. She was not at all resigned to her fate, but she was at least finally reconciled to leaving.

He made his way towards the secret cellar with only one wrong turning. Señora Romero, now…she might pose a problem. It was a pity Isabella had let fall so much of the truth—though not the full truth, thank heavens for small mercies. The *señora* had no inkling that her sister-in-law was anything more than a conduit for El Fantasma. He'd have to find a way of keeping it that way. Would the cover story he'd dreamed up be sufficient?

He smiled grimly to himself. An elopement. Romero would be mortified at the idea of his sister and a wine merchant—a man who *claimed* to be a wine merchant. A word in Señora Romero's ear and Finlay was sure that she could be persuaded to drum up a witness or two, a maid perhaps, who might have seen one of their early-morning trysts in the cypress walk. It was a good story, and a far more likely explanation of Isabella's sudden disappearance than any link with El Fantasma. Xavier Romero and his family would be safe from questioning. Estebe...

Finlay paused in the act of moving the wine rack. If Estebe had been his deputy, he *would* have warned him, regardless of the risk. It was a matter of honour, as well as his duty as a commanding officer, just as Isabella had pointed out. And if it was his printing press hidden behind the wall here, he'd want to attend to it himself, too. The press, the pamphlets... Isabella poured her heart into them, yet she had not suggested...

'Ach, bugger it!' Finlay picked up the lantern and began to make his way as fast as he could back the way he had come. By God, he admired her. She was as stubborn as a mule, but her heart was in the right place. Even so, that lass had an awful lot to learn about insubordination. A smile crept over his face. *The Basque Upstart.* Aye, they were a well-matched pair, indeed!

Isabella brought her horse over to the mounting block in the courtyard and buttoned up the skirts of her riding habit before climbing agilely into the saddle. Today would be the last time, perhaps for years, perhaps forever, that she rode out to the village. Today she was leaving Hermoso Romero, leaving her family, leaving Estebe and El Fantasma behind. She couldn't take it in. She felt sick thinking about it. The unknown future loomed like a giant black mountain in front of her. She couldn't do it. She couldn't.

Her horse fidgeted. She gave herself a little shake and urged him into a canter. Best not to think too far ahead. Best to think only of this next step, and after that— No, she would not even think of that. She would instead concentrate on taking in all she could of her homeland, to impress it on her memory for a future when it might be of comfort. But she would not think of that future yet. 'Courage, Isabella. Courage.'

Her horse's ears twitched. They had reached the outskirts of the village now. It was very quiet. Smoke from some of the chimneys floated lazily aloft, for the air was quite still. Isabella dismounted, tethering her horse by one of the many streams that ran through the valley here. She paused to say good day to old Señora Abrantes, who was sitting on a stool in her garden, working on one of the beautiful pieces of lace she crocheted. Her latest grandchild was asleep in a wooden cradle by her side. Matai, Isabella recalled. He had been baptised in the estate chapel just a few weeks previously.

'He looks just like his papa,' she said encouragingly, though in truth all babies, boys and girls, looked to her like little old grumpy men.

'You've come to call on Estebe?' Señora Abrantes asked.

'*Sí.* My brother returns from Pamplona soon. He will be anxious to know how his manager fares.'

'He has been walking a little, with a stick. That doctor your brother sent, he has been here many times. I think that Señor Romero is worried for the health of his wine.'

'And the health of the man in charge of it,' Isabella said. Which was true, she thought as she made her way towards Estebe's house at the far end of the village. Estebe and Xavier were childhood friends. Xavier believed there was no one more loyal than Estebe. When she had tried to discuss this with him though, concerned at the possibility of Estebe being torn between loyalty to his employer and loyalty to El Fantasma, Estebe had merely shrugged. 'What Xavier does not know cannot harm him,' he had said. 'Xavier has everything, while we fight for those who have nothing. For me, there can be no question of which comes first.' In one sense it was flattering, but as his sister, she couldn't help feeling sorry for Xavier, who not only trusted Estebe completely, but whose affection for the man stemmed back to those childhood days, and—unusually for Xavier—existed regardless of the huge disparity in their stations in life.

The winery manager, standing in the doorway of his cottage, was, as Señora Abrantes had predicted, on his feet, supporting his splinted leg with a stick. In his early thirties, he had the swarthy skin and black hair typical of the Basque, and the laconic temperament also typical of the region. Estebe rarely smiled, but when he did, Isabella was reminded that underneath that slightly surly exterior there was a very handsome man. She had asked him once, in an unguarded moment, why he had never married. He had informed her curtly that he was a soldier, she remembered. Like Finlay, he believed that soldiers should not take wives.

'Is something wrong?' Estebe said guardedly. 'I thought we agreed it would be unwise for us to be seen together in public. It might arouse suspicions as to the nature of our relationship.'

'I am here on official estate business, at my brother's behest. He wants to know how your recovery is progressing, how soon you can return to work,' Isabella replied loudly, for the benefit of anyone who might be listening. 'I made a point of saying so to Señora Abrantes,' she added *sotto voce*.

'The doctor your brother sends says I must wear the splint a few more weeks, but I have told him the wine will not wait a few more weeks.

You can tell Xavier I will return to my duties next week. Tell him to do nothing with the vintage until then. Tell him that I said patience is a virtue.'

'Estebe,' Isabella said in an urgent undertone, 'I'm not really here for Xavier. I need to talk to you.'

'You should not have come. People will talk, and we cannot afford any talk. Have you heard that young Zabala has disappeared?'

The man Consuela had mentioned last night. 'He was one of ours?' Isabella asked, dismayed.

Estebe shrugged. 'It could be nothing, but—we will see. Since you are here, I want to talk to you about that man. The Englishman. I don't know why he is here, but is it a coincidence that one of our men disappears shortly after he shows up?'

'Estebe, Mr Urquhart is on our side. He's the reason I'm here, not to ask after your health. If I could just explain…'

Estebe's head jerked up. He pushed her out of the way, shading his eyes to scan the horizon. 'Señorita Romero, you need to get out of here at once.'

'What is it?' She screwed up her eyes in an effort to see through the dust being raised. It was some sort of carriage. 'I wonder...'

'Isabella!' Estebe grabbed her by the shoulder, dropping his stick. 'You have to leave immediately. Do not let them see you. Do not, whatever happens, show yourself to them. Do you understand?'

It was his use of her name rather than the tone that made her blood run cold. 'Are they— Do you think that they are...?'

'I don't know who they are, but I am certain it does not bode well,' Estebe replied, his voice clipped as he limped over to the wooden dresser, pushing it away from the wall and retrieving a pistol, which he proceeded to load with astonishing speed before aiming it at her. 'Get out. Believe me, if they capture you, you will wish I had put this bullet in your head.'

He meant it. Blood rushed from her head, making her stagger. She took a deep breath, clutching the door frame. The cart was at the other end of the street now. There were two men. Well dressed. She looked around frantically, wondering in terror if she had left it too late.

'The woodshed,' Estebe said, pushing her

down the steps. 'And remember, no matter what happens, you must keep silent. Promise me you won't do anything rash.'

Isabella dumbly nodded her reluctant assent and stumbled down into the dusty darkness of the woodshed as Estebe secured the door behind her.

Riding towards the village, Finlay spotted the dust cloud raised by the open, rather ornate carriage. It looked so incongruous in the midst of such modest surroundings of farms and cottages that Finlay's senses immediately went on high alert. Reining his horse back, he followed the carriage at a distance, taking care to keep out of sight, knowing that it could only be headed for the village, all the time hoping against hope that it was not. There were two male occupants. They could be here for any number of reasons, but he knew, with the sixth sense he relied upon when going into battle, that they were not. There was only one likely explanation, and it was an extremely alarming one.

When they turned into the village, Finlay tethered his horse by a ruined outbuilding and followed cautiously on foot. Isabella's horse was pawing the ground by the tethering post, confirmation that he had guessed her intentions correctly—as if he'd needed it confirmed. The carriage was drawing up at the top of the little street. As he made his way stealthily towards it, he could sense the eyes of the villagers peering from their cottages. An old woman holding a piece of lacework beckoned him, but he ignored her.

The two men who descended from the carriage were well dressed. They pounded on the door of the furthest cottage calling Estebe's name. 'Señor Mendi! Señor Mendi!'

The accent was not local. Finlay no longer had any doubts. Madrileños! As the door opened, he braced himself, drawing his *sgian-dubh* from his boot. In the rush to follow Isabella he had not had time to retrieve his pistol, but the vicious little knife, a coming-of-age gift from his father, had served him well enough in the past.

'Señor Mendi?'

Estebe, his leg in a splint, stood leaning on the door. 'Who wants to know?'

Finlay could see no sign of Isabella. Creeping

around the other side of the carriage, behind the backs of the strangers, he took a chance, allowing Estebe a brief glimpse of his presence. Either Isabella had briefed him, or Estebe, realising how dire the situation was, saw Finlay as the lesser of two evils. Whichever. The man gave him a tiny shake of his head, the smallest gesture to the side of the house where a lean-to stood.

Waiting for the coast to clear, he missed what the men said next, but it caused Estebe to open the door wider, ushering them into the cottage.

Isabella, her ear pressed to the adjoining wall of the cottage, had her back to the door, foolish lass. Finlay grabbed her from behind, covering her mouth before she could cry out. 'It's me,' he whispered, and her rigid body ceased struggling immediately.

'Government agents,' she whispered, her eyes wide with fear. 'Estebe said—he said that they may have taken one of his men a few days ago. Do you think that is why—how…?'

'Hush. Aye.'

She was shaking piteously. He took no pleasure in being proved correct. The Spanish government were working their way up El Fantasma's chain of command. The question was, would Estebe talk? Finlay pressed his ear up to the wall, but could hear only muffled words. Later, he would tear a strip or two off himself for not taking matters into his own hands much earlier. He could not find it in himself to be angry at Isabella, but he wished with all his heart that she'd been a wee bit less loyal to the man next door, and a bit more careful of her own safety. As he would have been? Aye, right enough.

He shook his head in frustration as the room next door went quiet. 'I can't hear a thing,' he whispered, just as a loud crash made Isabella jump, only his instinctive covering of her mouth once more preventing her from screaming.

It all happened so quickly after that. 'Careful, he has a gun. Put the weapon down, *señor,*' one of the Madrileños cried out, his voice ringing clearly through the connecting wall now. Then followed the sounds of a scuffle, another piece of furniture being upturned.

Isabella strained in Finlay's firm grasp, her eyes above his muffling hand pleading with him to go to the rescue, but he held firm, shaking his head. He could take them on, he might well overpower them, but his remit was to protect El Fantasma at all costs, which meant he could not take the chance in acting rashly, no matter what the collateral damage turned out to be.

The front door of the cottage flew open, and a shot whizzed out into the open air. For a moment, Finlay thought that it would be one of the Madrileños who would pay the price, but then he heard Estebe's voice. 'I am El Fantasma,' he shouted. 'I would rather die than fall into your hands.'

'We have good reason to believe that you are not. However, you can lead us to him. Put the gun down. Do not shoot. If you cooperate you will not be harmed. You have our word. Put the weapon down. There is no need for this.'

'I tell you, *I* am El Fantasma.'

This time, the sharp crack of the bullet came clearly from inside the cottage, followed by the dull thud of a body falling to the floor This time, it was not Estebe but the Madrileños who cried out, though frustratingly, Finlay could still make out nothing of what they said. Locked tight against him, Isabella was weeping silently. They waited for what seemed like hours, though it was only a few minutes. Finlay, holding his dagger in his right hand, motioned to Isabella to get behind the woodpile, positioning himself behind the door, ready to pounce, but more minutes passed, followed by the sound of the carriage being manoeuvred around in the narrow street.

He crept out, watching as the strangers drove back down through the village. Only when the carriage turned out onto the track heading west did the villagers start to emerge from their cottages. 'Wait here,' Finlay said.

The table in Estebe's cottage was overturned. Estebe lay on the floor, his splinted leg splayed at a very odd angle. A noise in the doorway alerted Finlay. 'Isabella, don't come any closer,' he said, grabbing the tablecloth, but it was too late. Isabella looked at the place where the wine manager's skull should be and screamed. It was a long, piercing, anguished scream that seemed to echo round the narrow village streets for an eternity.

Isabella sat slumped in her bedchamber, wrapped in a blanket, staring into the fire. She could not stop shaking. Again and again, she re-played the horrific scene in her mind, trying desperately to come up with a scenario in which she could have altered the outcome, trying equally desperately to assure herself there was nothing she could have done.

When the Madrileños had gone, her screams had given way to numb horror, leaving Finlay to deal with the situation. He had taken charge with an authority that was obeyed without question by the villagers. The version of events he presented them with had Estebe shot by the Madrileños as he'd attempted to escape captivity. Thanks to Finlay, Estebe's body now lay in the village church.

But Isabella knew the true story. Estebe was dead by his own hand. Estebe, a man she had come to think of as invincible, had chosen death and purgatory over captivity and torture. Her deputy had died trying to save her, turning his gun on himself rather than risk betraying her. A huge shudder ran through her. Finlay had been right when he'd said those men were ruthless. At least Estebe's suffering had been short-lived.

She could not bear to contemplate what he would have endured if the Madrileños had taken him.

They would be back. Without a doubt they would be back. They had not believed Estebe's claim to be El Fantasma. They would be back, and they would not give up until they found her. Fear clutched like icy fingers around her heart. Estebe had died trying to protect her. She could picture him all too vividly, lying there on the ground. The shockingly bright red of the freshly spilled blood. The unnatural angle of his splinted leg. And his poor head…

She shuddered so violently her teeth chattered. It was one thing to defy danger when it was merely an abstract concept, but to be confronted with the stark, terrible reality of it—that was very different matter.

She did not want to die. If they caught her, she was not sure she would be brave enough to take the option Estebe had done. The icy fingers closed tighter around her heart. Fear was a very, very cold creature, but anger, and action, they fired the blood. She could not allow his death to have been in vain. 'No, now is not the time for tears,' she told herself, getting up to pour a large measure of cognac with a shaky hand. 'Now is the time for courage, and resolve.' She swallowed the brandy in one cough-inducing gulp. Fire burned a path down her throat and into her belly. She poured herself another measure, and gulped it down, too.

'Courage, Isabella,' she muttered, pulling a portmanteau from a shelf in her cupboard and setting it on her bed. 'There is much to be done.'

Finlay prowled restlessly around his bedchamber dressed only in his breeches and shirt. Dealing as best he could with Estebe's tragic death had taken up too many precious hours already. Time was of the essence, with Romero due back imminently. Much more important, those Madrileños would be back. If only they had believed Estebe's last, valiant claim to be the man they sought, it would have solved a wheen of problems. But they clearly, very clearly had not. And Finlay had faffed around far too much. He felt sick to the stomach, thinking how close Isabella had come to being captured. A lesson sorely learned, putting his inclinations over his duties. He should have had her out of here and on her way to the boat the moment she'd confessed her identity.

Poor wee soul, she had been distraught at what she'd seen this afternoon, though it had certainly brought home all he'd been saying. She'd barely said a word on the ride home, staring sightlessly ahead, though she'd sat straight enough in the saddle. She'd had the stuffing knocked out of her. It made his heart ache to think that instead of comforting her, he was going to have to wrench her away from her home and her family without even the chance to say goodbye.

He paced restlessly around the room, from window to door, window to door, his mind whirring. The elopement story might just about hold if Señora Romero was prepared to cultivate it after they were gone. It would be better if he could find a way to speak to her, but short of breaking into her bedchamber...

Finlay laughed shortly. No, if he was to break into any bedchamber it would be Isabella's. Struck by this idea, he opened the window and stepped out onto the balcony. Isabella's room was two doors along. The curtains fluttered the window was open. He eyed the gap between the parapets. It was no more than five feet. And the fall was a good thirty, more than enough to break his legs if not to kill him. Anyone would think he'd not had enough high drama for the day. Returning to his bedchamber, Finlay decided he'd try the more conventional route.

'Finlay. I was on the point of coming to find you. Come in.'

Isabella ushered him in, closing the door softly behind her. She was fully dressed, though her hair was not up, but tied in a long plait down her back.

'How are you bearing up?' he asked her.

'I am sorry that I was of so little use to you earlier,' she replied, ignoring his question. 'I am very, very grateful for what you have done. If my brother knew— Xavier is—' she gulped '—was, extremely fond of Estebe. That you have spared him the truth… For that, and for the sake of all of Estebe's friends, I cannot thank you enough, Finlay.'

'It was nothing.'

'No. It was a great deal more than nothing. I

deeply regret that I was not of more assistance, but I assure you, I am ready now to do—to do...'

She broke off, screwing her eyes tight shut, but when he tried to take her in his arms, she shook her head. 'Please, do not—I do not deserve to be comforted. If I had listened to you, perhaps Estebe would still be alive. He is dead, and he died to save me. I owe it to him to try to save myself now. And I owe it to my family, too. My remaining here is dangerous for them. You were right. I did not truly understand the consequences of my—of El Fantasma's actions, but I do now. So, I am ready to go with you,' she concluded firmly. 'I am ready to follow whatever arrangements you have made for me.'

'America, I told you. It's the only place you can be safe.'

The very idea terrified her, but she nodded her head stoically. 'Then, I will go to America.'

Finlay bit his lip, eyeing her with some concern. 'Isabella, you could not have saved Estebe. His death is not your fault.'

She had picked up a hairbrush from the dressing table and was now putting it into the half-packed portmanteau lying open on the bed. 'If

I had listened to you earlier, I could have warned him.'

'They would still have come for him.' This time, when she tried to shake him off, Finlay resisted, putting an arm around her waist to anchor her to him. 'Even if you had warned him, what difference do you think it would have made. Would Estebe have fled?'

'Of course not, but—Finlay, do you think they will kill them all? If I could warn them—though I know only a few of the names—if I could warn them, give them a chance to escape…' she said, looking up at him pleadingly. 'Do you think…?'

'I think that Estebe's death is warning enough. I think your conscience is clear on that matter, and even if it were not—Isabella, my conscience will not allow you to devote any more time to such matters. I should have gotten you out of here days ago.'

'I would not have agreed to come.'

He smiled sadly. 'I should not have allowed that fact to make any difference.' She looked so vulnerable. His arms ached to embrace her. Catching himself in the act of bestowing a tender kiss on her forehead, Finlay let her go. 'Right, then,' he said brusquely, 'to work. I'm glad to see you've packed. I've been thinking about how best to leave things here. We need a story that will explain our sudden disappearance without linking it in any way to Estebe's death or, obviously, El Fantasma, so what I was thinking was, we could elope. Pretend to elope, that is. If you could write a letter...'

'I have every intention of writing a letter,' Isabella interrupted, 'but it will be the truth.'

He stared at her uncomprehendingly. 'The truth?'

'My confession. Those Madrileños did not believe Estebe when he said he was El Fantasma. They will be back, and they will be looking for a man close to Estebe, only more powerful. Who do you think they will settle on?'

'Xavier,' Finlay said with a sick feeling in the pit of his stomach.

'Xavier,' Isabella repeated. 'I will not allow my brother to pay the price for my actions.'

'Isabella, he's innocent.'

'Finlay,' she retorted with a sad smile, 'innocent or guilty, it makes no difference with those men. You told me so yourself. Once they have him, he will confess to anything. I will not permit that to happen.'

'No, I can see you wouldn't.' And he could see all his carefully laid plans toppling over like so many dominos. He could see the danger she was putting herself in. They'd have to flee north for their lives, for her confession would put those devils on their tails. She had no idea, and he had not the heart to tell her, that she was risking her own life for the sake of protecting her family. She was, however, once again doing exactly what he'd do himself.

Finlay sighed. 'I'd best see what I can do to cover up the evidence, then. I doubt there's much can be done with the press, but we must not leave that pamphlet.'

'I'll come with you. No,' Isabella said, smiling wanly, 'don't try to stop me. Two pairs of hands will be quicker than one, and it's time I started taking some responsibility for my actions. And I have you to thank for teaching that painful, but valuable, lesson.'

Chapter Nine

Four days later

They had ridden hard each day in their desperation to get as far away from Hermoso Romero as quickly as possible, stopping only for a few hours' fitful sleep and to rest and water the horses. The road ahead, the steady gallop of the steeds who carried them, were their only focus. The landscape thereabouts afforded little in the way of cover. The roads were no more than rough dirt tracks in places, meandering through the rolling hills, the lower slopes of which were covered in a patchwork of vines. This was her land, her home territory, but to Isabella it felt disconcertingly alien, almost as if she was the stranger here, not Finlay. Which she was, she supposed, since she had forgone the right to call it home. She forced herself to sit upright in the saddle, concentrating on looking forward, not back. Quite literally.

Pamplona and then north was the obvious and quickest route to the coast and the ship that would take her across the ocean, but Finlay insisted that was too risky, since any pursuers would know that and follow suit. No, better to take a more circuitous route. It might be slower but it would significantly improve their chances of avoiding capture. Isabella did not question him. In truth she did not care where they went. When he opted to follow one of the old pilgrim routes that lead to Santiago de Compostela, she did as he bid her. She had never been to the city. She wished fervently that it truly was their destination. She did not want to think about the country where she was to make a new life. Fear froze her imagination whenever she tried.

She barely spoke as they travelled. She had not cried, not since Estebe—no, she would not think of that. She did not deserve the release of tears. She did not deserve Finlay's sympathy, the comfort of his strong, reassuring embrace. Not that he offered it. The man who rode beside her was unquestionably a soldier. No trace in that steely expression of the sensual Highlander who had charmed her. This man had a duty to perform, and he was clearly set on executing it. Well, she, too, had a duty, to the memory of Estebe. He had died to protect her. She would not allow his sacrifice to have been in vain, so she could do nothing save put as much distance between herself and her family as possible, in order to protect them. There was nothing to be said, nothing to be done save do as Finlay bade her without question: eat what was put in front of her, lie down and close her eyes in whatever shack or shepherd's hut he found each night, feign sleep until he roused her at dawn, continue on in the saddle each morning without complaint. An obedient and uncomplaining trooper, that was what he required, and so that was what she would be.

They were following the River Aragon today, and reached the outskirts of the little town of Sanguesa in the late afternoon. One of the many overnight refuges for weary pilgrims that dotted the Camino Way, the jumble of white-washed houses was perched on the hillside looking, from a distance, like a set of steps leading up to the magnificent Romanesque church of Santa Maria la Real. Finlay reined his horse in, casting an anxious look at the sky, which looked as if it augured rain.

'I'm sorry, lass, but we can't risk staying in town,' he said regretfully, 'much as a proper meal and a comfy bed for the night would be a welcome treat.'

'No matter,' Isabella replied, casting an uninterested gaze at the town. 'If we follow the river, we can take shelter in the next valley.'

She had become so accustomed to spending long periods lying wide awake, alternated with fevered nightmares of trying to escape endless dark tunnels, that it was a surprise when Isabella struggled to open her eyes. She was lying on the wooden shelf that served for a bed in a ramshackle shepherd's hut. She could remember arriving here, remember Finlay lighting a fire, forcing herself to eat, forcing herself to lie down and close her eyes, waiting for the darkness and the guilt and remorse to envelop her. Instead, it had been as if all the bones had been removed from her body. She had slept dreamlessly. And now she felt—different.

She was warm, surprisingly comfortable. The blanket covering her smelled faintly of horse. She turned onto her side. The door of the shelter was ajar, giving her a glimpse of the grey, pre-dawn sky and Finlay a few yards distant, sitting by the horses, on guard as he had been every night. Did he ever sleep? For the first time, she wondered what it was he was watching out for, who it was he expected.

The dull stupor that had enveloped her since leaving Hermoso Romero had gone, and so, too, had the heavy pall of grief and regret, leaving her mind clear. Isabella counted the days since their flight, and was surprised to discover that this must be the fifth. Almost a week since Estebe died, since she left her home and her family, who were more dear to her than she had realised. But they would be better off without her. Consuela could have her sister come to live with her. Xavier would most likely mourn the loss of his winery manager more than his sister.

Isabella gave herself a shake. 'Be honest,' she told herself. 'Xavier will be so shocked at what he reads in that letter you left, he will be thankful you did not wait to say goodbye. "Finally," he will say to himself, "now I understand why my sister was such an unnatural woman. Gabriel has had a lucky escape.'" Which was very true, though she doubted very much that Xavier would go so far as to inform his friend of the exact nature of his good fortune.

Isabella sat up abruptly. She had been quite distraught when she had written the letter admitting to being El Fantasma, intent only on sparing her family by accepting sole responsibility. But what, exactly, had she imagined Xavier would do with such a confession? Show it to the government officials when they came calling, as they inevitably would? Why should they believe him? What credence would such a confession truly have, when Xavier was a much more likely candidate to be El Fantasma than his demure little sister?

The letter had made no mention of the printing press. The pamphlets she and Finlay had shredded, El Fantasma's last words, had been forced down the well, the pulpy mess anointed with ink and scattered with metal lettering. As she had pulled the wine rack over the concealed door for the last time, Isabella had wondered if any curious soul would ever discover it. Her nephew, perhaps? A few weeks ago, she would have smiled at the idea of passing on El Fantasma's legacy to an as-yet unborn niece. Now the notion filled her with horror.

The Madrileños would demand proof from Xavier, and when he had none to give them—what would they do to him? Remembering Estebe's determination not to fall into the men's clutches, Isabella shuddered. Consuela might tell them about the printing press, but would that not rather condemn rather than acquit him? Isabella clutched at her head. She had been so proud of the fact that no one would ever believe El Fantasma was a woman. Now—*Madre di Dios*, what a fool she was! No one would believe her confession. Pride truly did come before a fall.

'Finlay!'
The panic in Isabella's voice was unmistakable. He ran to the bothy just as she jumped out of the makeshift bed and grabbed him by the arm. 'What is it?'

'I have to go back. Xavier—they'll never believe him. I have to go back.'

She was dressed only in her underwear. Her hair was tumbling down her back, free from the long plait she usually wore. Her face, which had been so pale and set for days, was now flushed, her eyes bright. Thank the stars she was back to something like herself. He caught her hands between his. 'Wheesht, now, you know that's not possible.'

'I have to,' she said urgently. 'They will come for him, and even with the letter— Finlay, they won't believe him. They'll take him away. I can't let them take him away. I can't let them— We have to go back, Finlay.'

'We can't. There's no going back. I'm sorry.'

'But...'

'No, Isabella. Listen to me now,' he said, before she could speak again. 'You're in the right of it. That confession of yours won't protect your brother. It's an unlikely story, I'd be the first to admit, that the great El Fantasma is a mere woman. Indeed, I'd have had a great difficulty believing it myself, had I not become acquainted with you in that ditch beside an arms cache during the war.'

He had meant her to smile. Instead, she frowned deeply. 'No one will believe it. If only I had been Xavier's brother, and not his sister, things would have been so very different.'

'Aye, well, I'm not denying that would have made things a mite easier,' Finlay said, unable to suppress his smile, 'but a lot less interesting. I wouldn't have missed meeting you again for the world.'

'I have been a great deal of trouble to you. You told me not to go to Estebe, and…'

'Isabella, you did only what I'd have done myself, in your shoes.'

'You're not angry with me?'

'If I'm angry at anyone it's with myself for faffing about, for not getting you out of there sooner.'

'I made it very difficult for you. I was so stubborn, and I didn't listen, and I thought I knew best, and—Finlay, what will he do? Xavier, I mean. When they come for him, how will he save himself if they do not believe him?'

He had stupidly hoped she would not ask him

this question. No doubt about it, the shock had worn off, and her mind was as sharp as ever. He could lie to her, but she'd work it out for herself soon enough, and besides, he would not lie to her. 'Sit down,' Finlay said, steering her onto the bench and taking a seat beside her.

She did as he bid her, but without the docile obedience of the past few days. 'What is it? What do you know?'

'I don't know anything for sure.'

'You think they will discount my confession, don't you?'

'I do, I'm afraid.'

'So they will arrest Xavier? Finlay, I can't allow that.'

'Haud your wheesht a minute. The authorities have been meticulous and thorough in their pursuit of El Fantasma, Isabella, we know that. They might struggle to believe that a wee lassie could be El Fantasma, but they couldn't dismiss it out of hand. They'd be obliged to check it out—to eliminate the possibility. They are not the type to leave any stone unturned.'

'So they will be looking for me.' Isabella paled.

'And Xavier will— Do you think he will— What do you think he will do?'

'You know your brother better than I do, Isabella. What do you think?'

'I don't know!'

'Think about it,' Finlay said with a heavy heart. 'What is most important to him?'

'His son, his wife.'

'No, there is something even more important than that.'

Now she was nodding to herself, clearly beginning to follow his meaning. 'My brother has been raised to believe that he is the custodian of Hermoso Romero. It is his—I don't know what to call it—duty? His heritage? His destiny? If he was shamed, if they took him, accused him of being El Fantasma, he would lose everything.' Another little nod. 'So what you think is—what you think is that he would do anything to avoid that?'

Though she had paled, she looked him straight in the eye. 'Aye,' Finlay said. 'I do.'

'*Sí*. And the only way to avoid it, is to— You do not think he will try to stop them coming after me, do you?'

'I'm right sorry, but I don't see how he can. Even he has not that power, and frankly, it is not in his best interests.'

'I see.' Isabella clasped her hands together tightly. 'So that is why you have been so eager to put so many miles between us and Hermoso Romero. That is why you have been standing guard every night while I slept.'

'Aye,' he said, heart sore at watching it dawn on her just how alone she was.

'If they capture me, Xavier will be safe.'

'I've no intentions of letting anyone capture you, or me for that matter.'

Another faint smile greeted this remark. 'But if they do not, then suspicion will fall on my brother.'

Romero would be in the clear. The plan Jack had hatched would leave neither the British nor the Spanish in any doubt that El Fantasma had been silenced, but Finlay couldn't bring himself to explain this to Isabella just yet. She was only just recovering from one huge shock, only just starting to reassess her future. Time enough to explain just exactly what that future would entail another day. 'Your brother is a powerful man and not without influence. I wouldn't bet against him finding a way of convincing the authorities of his innocence.'

Her lips tightened. 'If that is true, then had there been a way to save me, he could have found it. The fact that you did not even consider giving him the opportunity to do so...'

Finlay managed a wry smile. 'Actually, I did, but I concluded the result would be your spending the rest of your life locked away in a nunnery.'

She stared at him in astonishment. 'You are probably right. I think you know my brother better than I. It would have been the perfect solution for you, too, I think. I could not betray the Duke of Wellington from a nunnery. You would not have been burdened with me. You could have gone back to England, having done your duty. Why did you not...?'

'Would you have *liked* to spend the rest of your life in a nunnery?'

'No, but—I do not *like* being a burden to you.'

'You're not.' He took her hand again, stroking the back of it with his thumb. 'You're not a burden.'

'But I am. My actions have put your life in danger as well as mine. I have been so blindly selfish. I am so very, very sorry.'

'Don't be daft. I was sent to protect you.' He carried on stroking her hand. Her fingers curled into his. 'And I won't be leaving your side until you're safely on that boat to America.'

'Because you promised your friend Jack?'

It was what he ought to say. It was the truth, but looking at her now, at those big golden eyes shadowed with lack of sleep, and the determined set of her shoulders, and thinking of the fearless way she had confronted the most unpalatable of facts, Finlay knew it was only a very small part of the truth. He could not tell her the whole of it, but he could not resist telling her a wee bit. 'Because you're a brave and honourable woman, the finest one I've ever met, and you deserve a future,' he said.

'I'm not feeling very brave right now.'

Her smile was shaky, but it was a smile. 'It's precisely because you're feart, and yet you are still ready to face the truth, that makes you brave,' Finlay said.

She touched his cheek, the pad of her thumb

soft against the roughness of his stubble. 'Almost, I believe you, but I think you are just trying to make me feel better.'

'And is my ploy working?'

'Yes.' She brushed his hair back from his brow. She leaned into him, and brushed her lips to his forehead. 'It is working, but I think I have an even more effective ploy,' she said, twining her arms around his neck and pressing her lips to his.

She'd caught him unawares. She tasted so sweet, he could not resist her. His arms slid around her back, pulling her tight up against him. Her tongue touched his, and his shaft sprang immediately to life. He ran his fingers through the long, silken weight of her hair, spanned the slim indent of her waist, slid them up to cup the swell of her breasts, covered only by her chemise. Her nipples were hard buds beneath the soft linen. She moaned, a soft, guttural sound that sent his blood racing.

Their kisses deepened, grew wilder. She lay back on the wooden bench. Tugging his shirt free from the waistband of his breeches, she stroked her fingers up his spine. He shuddered with delight. He kissed her throat. He kissed the mounds of her breasts above her chemise. He took one of her nipples between his lips and sucked. The fabric of her undergarments became damp from his mouth, making the dark pink nub beneath clearly visible. He turned his attention to her other nipple. She moaned again, digging her nails into his back, arching up under him, brushing her belly against the hard, throbbing rod in his breeches.

He had never wanted any woman so much. He ached to slide into her tantalisingly slowly, inch by inch by inch, relishing every single moment of it, until he was as high inside her as he could be, and then he'd tilt her delightful behind up and push deeper. His shaft pulsed in anticipation. As if she could read his mind, Isabella's hands roved down his body, cupping his buttocks, pulling him tighter against her.

'Finlay,' she said, in that hoarse, breathy voice that set his blood on fire. 'Finlay.'

He kissed her again, hard on the lips, and she met his passion with a fire of her own. If he could only have her this once… If they could make love just this once… He'd give almost anything for that.

Almost, but not quite. He tore himself away, too appalled at his lack of control to care how it must look, jumping down from the bench and tucking his shirt back into his breeches, swearing furiously in Gaelic.

Isabella sat up, pushing her hair back from her face. Her eyes were huge, desire giving way to confusion. Confusion! She should take a look inside his head! 'You are under my protection,' Finlay said raggedly. 'A fine way I have of discharging my duty, taking advantage of you like that.'

'I rather think that it was I who took advantage of you. I thought it might make us both feel a little better.'

'I've absolutely no doubt that it would, temporarily,' he said, running his hands through his hair. 'Isabella, I know that I have been— before— I know that I have been very much— Ach, for heaven's sake, you know perfectly well that I find it almost impossible to keep my hands off you. But the fact is we are fleeing for our very lives with half of Spain looking for us, so it's no surprise if neither of us is thinking quite straight. But that is precisely what we need to do. Keep our heads and focus on the task in hand.'

'So what do you propose we do?' Isabella asked.

'I don't know about you,' Finlay said, with as much gravitas as he could muster, 'but I'm going to sort the horses out.'

'Well, that certainly put me in my place,' Isabella muttered to herself as she stared at his retreating back in disbelief. 'Spurned for a horse!' Her body was still throbbing with unsated desire as she padded over to the doorway of the hut. Dawn was just breaking. In the growing light she could see that Finlay was not tending the horses, but standing on the banks of the stream that ran through the valley, less than ten yards away. *Which I suppose is some sort of consolation*, she thought, managing a self-deprecating smile.

She watched as he pulled his shirt over his head. He was close enough for her to see the ripple of his muscles as he stretched. Her breath caught in her throat. His skin was paler than she had imagined. His waist tapered down to the band of his leather breeches, which hung low on his hips. A silvery line of darker, puckered skin ran the full length from his left shoulder down close to the line of his spine. It must have been a horrific wound to leave such a scar. He rarely talked of the army, yet he had been a soldier his entire adult life. *It's not the same*, he'd told her, when she had compared her time as a soldier to his. She had been annoyed, she recalled. Looking at that scar, remembering how she had fallen apart when Estebe had shot himself, she was forced to acknowledge that she had been presumptuous. In fact, she knew very little about Finlay. Always, he turned their conversations away from himself. This man she was watching, this man who shared her biggest secret, whose body she ached for, was in many ways still a stranger. He joked about being called the Jock Upstart, but he was no mere soldier. A major, and promoted rather than commissioned. A hardened campaigner. A man accustomed to command. It was a wonder that he had tolerated her equivocation as long as he had. Not that he had any right to order her about, but...

Isabella sighed. Actually, under the circumstances, he had every right, and yet he had refrained from doing so. He was an honourable man. A very honourable man. An *extremely* honourable man. She had offered herself to him, and he had refused, not for lack of desire, but because she was under his protection. Even if she could persuade him that gratitude had played no role in her kissing him, he would still have torn himself free of her. She couldn't help wishing he was not quite so honourable. But then he would not be Finlay.

He had picked up the leather bag that contained his shaving things, and was heading a few yards upstream now, towards the small cascade that fed the stream. The water would be ice-cold. Isabella looked on, mesmerised, as Finlay undid the buttons of his leather breeches. She should not be watching. She should look away. This was an invasion of privacy. Her mouth went dry as he slid the last item of clothing to the ground. His legs were long and well muscled. There was a tan line that stopped just above the knee. His buttocks were unexpectedly shapely. She really should not be looking. He stepped out of his breeches, kicking them to one side, and she had a brief glimpse of him from the front. Colour rushed to her cheeks as she saw the jutting length of his arousal. Her knowledge of male anatomy came only from art. In the flesh—Isabella put a hand to her fluttering heart as Finlay splashed into the stream and stood under the waterfall—in the flesh, this man at least was quite blood-heatingly delicious.

Not a feast, but a banquet. She recalled Finlay's words in the printing-press room. He had his back to her now, stretching his arms high over his head, letting the freezing water fall in rivulets over his body. He seemed to be relishing the cold, embracing it. It occurred to her, with a shock, that the icy cascade was an antidote to his passion, and she looked with fresh eyes at the waterfall, thinking that she, too, could cool her throbbing body there. What would Finlay say if she joined him? She smiled, allowing herself to picture the scene, but she could not imagine having the nerve to carry it off, and even if she did, Finlay would most likely reject her.

He would be right to do so. Their perilous situation was clouding her judgement, making her foolish and rash, and she was neither. Her smile faded. As he began to lather himself, Isabella turned slowly and returned to the shack. The time had come to take back responsibility for her own life, for better or for worse. She had a lot to think about. Simple things, such as her entire future! Not to mention the small matter of getting out of Spain in one piece. No, Finlay was right. They needed to focus. She could not afford to be distracted by a pair of sea-blue eyes, a mane of auburn hair and a body that Michel-angelo himself could have sculpted.

Isabella, her skin glowing from the shower she had taken under the waterfall after he had returned from his own ablutions, her hair re-strained in a long wet braid, had a decidedly mulish look on her face. Trouble, Finlay thought, though he couldn't help but smile at this fur-ther evidence of the return of the feisty partisan he admired so much. Desired so much. No, he wouldn't think of that.

The sparkle had returned to her eyes. 'We need to talk,' she said.

'We do.' Finlay handed her a cup of coffee,

pleased to note the pleasure with which she took it, the admiring glance she gave the small portable trivet he always carried with him to heat the pot on. 'I always travel prepared for anything,' he said by way of explanation, 'although I can think of no item of field equipment that could have prepared me for you.' He was rewarded with a smile. 'Here, take this, you must be hungry.'

'Thank you. I am ravenous.' She took the toasted bread and cheese, sitting cross-legged on the hard-packed mud floor, looking quite at home.

'You'll have found bothies like these useful places during the war, no doubt,' Finlay said.

'Bothies?'

'A hut. A bothy is what we'd call it in the Highlands,' Finlay explained. 'A place for the cattle drovers to rest overnight on their way to market.'

'This land is too mountainous for cattle, but, yes, to answer your question, during the war, such places were often used for storing arms. And hiding partisans, just as this one is doing now.' Isabella finished her breakfast, and set her cup down, obviously bracing herself. 'You were right,' she said.

'In what way?'

'I was never a soldier as you were. I carried a gun, I witnessed some fighting, but I did not fight in the way you did. Estebe was not the first dead man I have seen, but it was the first time I had ever witnessed the barbarity of what a gun can do used in that way.'

'I regret that you did.'

'It is something I will never forget. Never.' She gazed into the fire, blinking rapidly. 'I know I was not wholly responsible for Estebe's death, but I must take some of the blame.'

'Isabella, Estebe was a grown man and he *was* a hardened soldier. He knew the risks and accepted them.'

'Yes, that is true, but I was his commanding officer, Finlay. He died for the cause, but it was under my watch.'

He could not argue with that, and it would be insulting to do so. At a loss, he poured her the last of the coffee.

She nodded her thanks and cupped her hands around the tin mug, staring into the fire. 'How do you reconcile that, Finlay? You must have sacrificed many of your men for the cause, the greater good. How do you do it?'

Her question caught him unawares. 'You do it by not thinking about it and simply obey the orders you are given. It is for others to weigh the moral balance,' Finlay said. It was the stock answer. The army answer. It was a steaming mound of horse manure, and Isabella knew it.

She drained her coffee again, and narrowed her eyes at him. 'You told me that if you had not been so insubordinate you would have been promoted beyond major by now. There are some orders you do not obey. You choose, on occasion, your own path. You follow your own instincts.'

He smiled wryly. 'I've always had a penchant for intelligent women, but until I met you, I never thought there could be such a thing as a lass who was too clever.'

'Don't mock me.'

'Isabella, I wouldn't dare, I was simply— You've a habit of asking difficult questions, do you know that?'

She raised her empty cup in salute. 'I am not the only one.'

'Aye, well, there you go.' Finlay picked up his knife and began to cut the piece of uneaten bread before him into smaller and smaller cubes. 'You're right. Of course I make choices. While there's always someone up the ranks to blame if things go awry, that's not my way, any more than it's my way to ask my men to do something I would not.'

'Such as cross enemy lines to reconnoitre a French arms dump?'

'Ach, that was more a case of my being bored and needing to see a wee bit of action. I'm wondering, though, if you were not in the habit of actually fighting, what you were doing there that night?'

'Ach,' Isabella replied in a fair attempt at his own accent, 'that was a case of my being bored and needing to see a wee bit of action, too. I did not fight,' she continued, reverting to her own voice, 'but I did try to ensure that El Fantasma's reputation for infallibility was preserved, since it was good for morale. It was my father, as usual, who heard the rumours of French activity. He thought that I had others investigate them, but towards the end of the war, more often than not

I did that myself.' Isabella gazed into the fire. 'I think—I thought that Papa would be proud of me, of El Fantasma, but Consuela, all the things she said…I don't know, Finlay. I am not so certain now. For Papa, his family came before everything, while I—I think, I think I have been putting myself first.' She sniffed. 'I am sorry. More self-pity. Excuse me.'

She got to her feet, but before she could move towards the door of the hut, Finlay caught her. 'How can you be so daft?' he said, pulling her into his arms, tilting her face up to force her to look at him. 'You've not been wielding a gun, but you've been fighting for your country all the same. You've put everyone *but* yourself first, Isabella. Selfish—that's the very last thing I'd call you.'

'Daft, that is what you called me. You mean stupid.'

'No. It can mean stupid right enough, but these auld Scots words, they've a wheen of other meanings.'

He was pleased to see that her tears had dried, her lips forming a shaky smile. 'Such as?'

'Such as *brave*, and *bold*. Such as *beautiful* and *bright*. Such as *surprising*.'

'Because I admit I was wrong?'

'Because you question yourself.' Reluctantly, he let her go. She was too distracting, and what was more she deserved an honest answer to her original question—or as honest as he could muster. He sat down on the mud-packed floor once more. 'You asked me how I choose between duty and human life, and I don't really know how to answer that. I've fought on battlefields where people make their homes. I've staged sieges in towns where women and children and old men and old women are living. I'd like to think that it's been worthwhile. Whenever my men have crossed the line in the aftermath of a battle— and there have been times—I've made sure they faced the consequences.' The memories of some of those times made him wince. Finlay rubbed his eyes. 'I've gone against some orders where my conscience has pricked me, but I've acted on others where I've been faced with the consequences only afterwards.' More images, worse ones, flickered through his mind. He shook his head in an effort to disperse them. 'I'm a soldier.

I am trained to obey orders. I'm not supposed to question them. I'm supposed to trust that my superiors will act honourably, in the name of our country, but war…it isn't like that, not all the time. Sometimes the lines are blurred and I—I have not always questioned as perhaps I ought.'

He had not noticed her sitting down beside him until she took his hand in hers. 'But you did question the orders you were given when you came here,' she said gently. 'When I told you who I was, you could have acted then, but instead of taking me by force you waited, tried to persuade me to leave voluntarily.'

'Not very successfully.' Her fingers were long and slender, so small compared to his.

'On the contrary,' Isabella said. 'You have saved my life.'

Gazing at her liquid amber eyes, holding her delicate hand between his, Finlay had the strangest feeling. Heartache? 'Not yet, I haven't. We're not out of the woods yet,' he said, as much to himself as Isabella.

'What is more, you are committing treason to protect me,' she said. 'Your orders from the great duke were to silence me.'

'Aye, well, that was one of those orders I'd never find it in my conscience to obey, but it's not treason, Isabella, not really. As far as the duke is concerned, El Fantasma will be silenced, just not in the way he's expecting.'

'But surely lying to the Duke of Wellington is as good as committing treason? Finlay Urquhart, I do believe you are a hero. Foolish, reckless, but a hero nonetheless.'

'Stop it, or you'll have me blushing like a wee lassie.'

Isabella's mouth curved into a smile. She closed the gap between them, reaching up to touch his cheek. 'You're no lassie. You're a man, a beautiful man.'

'Well, there, you see, you're wrong. Nobody could describe me as beautiful.'

'Oh, but you are.' She ran her fingers through his hair. 'The first time ever I met you, I thought, there is a man who will attract a second and a third glance.'

Her smile did terrible, wonderful things to him. It stirred his blood, that smile. It made him want to devour her. For she was a feast. A banquet.

Her mouth was only a few inches from his.

Her fingers were feathering the skin at the nape of his neck. 'You can't call a rough, burly Highlander beautiful,' Finlay said in a vain attempt to change the subject.

'I just did,' Isabella said with a mischievous smile. 'And I'm not referring to your appearance. You are a beautiful man, Finlay Urquhart, because you have saved my life. You have risked your life—are risking your life for me. I am completely in your debt, as are my family, though they do not know it. You will always have a special place in my heart because of that, regardless of what the future holds.'

'Then, that is all the reward I need,' Finlay said, surprising himself by the depth of emotion in his voice. Forcing himself to get to his feet, he stamped out the fire and began to pack up. 'As to the future, that can keep for later. We've a few more miles to put between us and Hermoso Romero first.'

Chapter Ten

They headed west once more, travelling at a fast pace for some hours, which precluded conversation, before slowing to a walk to give the horses a breather in the late afternoon. 'Tafalla is just ahead,' Isabella said. 'Were you ever there?'

Finlay shook his head. 'No. I think it was used as a garrison late in the campaign, but I was never quartered there.'

'It was one of the towns in the Navarre most heavily fortified by the French,' Isabella told him. 'Our partisan, Mina, he liberated it with the help of some of your British navy guns.'

'I've heard of Mina, though I have never met him.'

'Nor did I.' Isabella made a face. 'He would not have been interested in a mere woman, I don't think. Now, if he had known I was El Fantasma—but no, I will not talk of that. El Fantasma no longer exists. Now I am merely Isabella Romero—whomever she may turn out to be. A woman of means, you need not worry about that,' she said, with what she hoped was a reassuring smile. 'Not only do I have all my jewellery, which will fetch a pretty penny, but I have the bulk of this quarter's allowance. My papa left me well provided for, you know. I must find a way to make alternative arrangements with the bank to have the payments sent on to me.'

'Isabella.' Finlay drew his horse to a halt, leaning over to catch her reins at the same time. His expression was stern. 'You can't touch that money.'

All morning, as they rode, she had been trying to imagine herself in America, but the more she tried, the more terrified she became. She had promised Finlay she would go, she desperately wanted to fulfil that promise, but as the prospect became more real with every mile they travelled—the sheer terror of being on her own, of a future without shape ate away at her resolve. Her courage deserted her. 'Finlay,' she beseeched him now, unable to stop herself, 'is there no alternative to my going to America? May I not remain in Spain and make a new life for myself where no one knows me? It is a big country.'

His expression became grim. 'Not big enough. I thought I'd made it clear—those men will not give up. I know this is hard for you, and I'm right sorry to have to be the one to open your eyes, but you can't carry on living as Isabella Romero.'

'You mean I must take a new name, a new identity?'

'Aye.'

'That is why I cannot claim my allowance?'

'Not the only reason.'

There was a horrible sinking feeling in the pit of her stomach. Finlay looked like a man trying to swallow poison. 'What are you trying to tell me?' she asked.

He ran his fingers through his hair, then straightened his shoulders, giving her a direct look. 'Isabella Romero has to die. There's no other way to put an end to this.'

'Die.' She clutched at her breast. For a horrible moment she thought he had tricked her and meant it literally. But this was Finlay; he would not harm her, she knew that instinctively. She furrowed her brow. She remembered, vaguely, that conversation on the hillside the day before Estebe died. It seemed so long ago. 'You mean that the world—Xavier, Consuela, my nephew, even the bank—must believe that I am dead?'

'It is the only way to guarantee your safety. I thought you understood that. I thought I'd made it clear.'

'Did you? I don't know. I can't remember. No, that is not fair of me, I know you did, only...' Her voice was rising in panic. She tried breathing deeply, tried to remember. 'I can't go to America, Finlay,' she said. 'Please, there must be another way. I know that's what you said, I know it's what I promised, but I didn't think— I mean, I have not thought— Surely there must be a safe haven somewhere that does not require me to go halfway across the world.'

Her horse was twitching nervously. Finlay dismounted and pulled her unresisting from the saddle, tethering both sets of reins to the stump of a fallen tree before taking her hands in his. 'You can't stay in Spain. You can't come to England with me. I know a wee bit of the ways of these government men, Isabella, from my friend

Jack. Their reach is frightening, and those in power across the Continent, they're all in each other's pockets. I doubt very much that there would be anywhere in Europe safe for you.'

'But America!'

'The New World, they call it. Think about it,' he said, with a reassuring smile. 'A place where you can start again, completely afresh. A place where none of the old rules apply, where the restrictions you've been fighting don't exist. They say a man—or a woman—can do anything, achieve anything there, just by dint of hard work. It's a land of equal opportunity, a blank canvas. Isn't that precisely what you've been fighting for?'

'I've been fighting to have such a society in my own country.'

'A country that regards you as a traitor. You could help shape society in America, Isabella, not waste your time trying to dismantle the existing one in Spain.'

'You make it sound like utopia.'

Finlay's smile faltered. His grip on her tightened. 'I'm sure it's not, but there exists the opportunity to make it so. If anyone can contribute to that it's you.'

'You're just saying that to reassure me.'

His eyes darkened. His smile disappeared all together. For a moment, she thought he looked quite desolate, but then he shook his head. 'I'm saying it because I believe it to be true. You're apprehensive, and no wonder. It will be a—a challenge. You'll be lonely. Things will be strange and unfamiliar. But you'll be alive, Isabella. I look at you, and I know you can do anything you set your mind to. Take this chance, lass, I'm begging you to take this chance, because it's the only one you have.'

He meant it. He was telling her the plain, unvarnished truth, just as he had told her the plain, unvarnished truth about the horrors she'd be subjected to if she was captured. If she did not leave Spain, she would die. If she went to England, she would die. If she travelled to France or to Italy, or to Prussia, or even Russia, they would find her eventually, and she would die. She did not want to die. Faced with the very real prospect, she was filled with defiance and determination, and a very strong will to live, indeed. 'I don't want to die,' she said.

He pulled her into his arms and held her so tight she could hardly breathe. 'You won't. I won't let them get to you. I'll keep you safe, I promise you.'

Her face was muffled against his coat. She could feel his heart beating against her cheek. She knew he would lay down his life for her if he had to. She had already witnessed one life sacrificed for her. She could not risk another. And especially not this one. 'I'm sorry,' she said wretchedly. 'I'm so sorry, Finlay. I will do as you say.'

'Don't cry. Oh, God, Isabella, don't cry.'

'I'm not crying.'

'You've every right to.' Finlay mopped her tears with his handkerchief. 'You're being so brave.'

'I'm not. I'm being—what is it? Feart. I am feart.'

'If you were not, I'd worry about your sanity. If it was me, I'd be feart. If I could find a way to escort you myself...'

'Don't be daft,' she said softly. 'You have to

arrange El Fantasma's tragic death, and then you have to go back to England and tell the great duke what has happened, and then you have to go back to the army and once again become Major Finlay Urquhart, the Jock Upstart, and forget all about me.'

'I'll never forget you, Isabella. I will never, ever be able to forget you.'

'I can see how it might be difficult to forget a woman who put your life in mortal danger,' she said lightly, in an effort to lighten the mood.

'It's not that I will remember. I have much more pleasant memories of our time together than that to keep me warm at night.'

Isabella felt herself blush slightly. His visage was no longer grim. His sea-blue eyes were no longer pained. She would have to be very careful not to make him fret for her. She did not want to be a source of worry. She had caused him enough worry. She would do her very best to be the bold, bright, brave partisan he thought her. She would not only comply with the future he had arranged for her, she would embrace it. 'So I'm to sail for America,' Isabella said. 'Should we not then be heading north, for the coast?'

'In good time. They will be searching for us there. It's the obvious place to look.'

'Which is why we're heading west. For how much longer?'

'It's been nigh on a week and there's been no sign of any pursuers. Another day and I think we will be safe enough.' Finlay looked up at the sky, which had turned from blue to grey, with clouds like lumps of charcoal. 'In fact, I see no reason why we should not sleep in a decent bed tonight, partake of a decent dinner.'

'You think that's wise?'

'I reckon you deserve it.' Finlay touched her cheek. 'Not a word of complaint have I heard from you about living and sleeping rough for the past week. You've been a trooper.'

Isabella beamed. 'That is the best compliment you could pay me, but I do not need a feather bed and a proper dinner if you think it is too risky.'

'You shall have both. And a bath, too, in water that's a wee bit warmer than melted ice. It's the least I can do.' He leaned into her. She thought he was going to kiss her, but his lips brushed her forehead, and then he let her go, turning toward the horses. 'To Tafalla it is, then.'

* * *

The town was set on a wide cultivated plain, reached by traversing another ancient trail over the Valdorba Mountains. The warren of narrow medieval streets clustered with houses built from mellow honey-coloured stone rose steeply up towards a citadel. The more modern part of the town was built on the flatter land around the Cidacos River, and it was here that they had found lodgings at a small inn, hiring a private salon and two bedchambers. Finlay had made all the arrangements, under the name of Mr and Mrs Upstart, in his halting Spanish. 'Just my little joke,' he had told her with a grin.

Now clean, shaved and dressed in fresh linen, he waited for her in the small salon, gazing morosely into a glass of sherry that he had barely touched. With every passing day she was becoming more precious to him. And yet, with every passing day, the inevitability of losing her forever loomed larger. Their worlds had collided all too briefly, but soon, very soon, they would part forever. Isabella was destined for a brand-new world, and he to return to his old, familiar one, where his career and his family awaited.

It made him heartsore to think of it, and pointlessly so. He would not think of it.

Instead, he would make the most of what little time he had in her company. He would make the most of tonight for this bonny, clever, brave lass, who deserved so much more than the hand that fate had dealt her, and who was facing the dangers and the fears of the great unknown with such fortitude it made him want to weep like a bairn.

Fresh from her bath, Isabella wore a pretty olive-green gown trimmed with bronze that made her skin seem golden. A woollen scarf in the same shades was draped around her shoulders. She had braided her hair around her head in a way that reminded Finlay of images of Greek goddesses, though there was nothing at all ethereal in her smile, nor in his reaction to it. 'You look ravishing,' he said.

She blushed endearingly. Such a bonny thing, and yet she had not a trace of vanity in her. Finlay took her hand, pressing a kiss to her fingertips. 'Thank you,' she said. 'You look very…'

'Do not dare try to tell me I'm beautiful,' he teased.

She laughed. 'It's an insult, I remember. May

I be permitted to say that you look very dashing instead?'

He grinned, holding out his arm. 'I'll settle for that. Shall we go for a stroll before dinner?'

'I would like that very much,' Isabella said.

Braziers and lanterns were already being lit in the Plaza Mayor. It was time for the traditional evening *paseo* or promenade. They did not join in, Finlay being all too aware that his distinctive auburn hair might draw unwanted attention, so they watched from the shadows. Couples and families strolled, exchanging greetings, passing comment on the unseasonably mild weather, speculating on the possibility of rain. Women compared *toilettes*, children ran laughing round and round the square in excited clusters, while the smaller ones gurgled from their carriages or their mother's arms. Young and old, well-heeled and down-at-heel alike, everyone congregated in the square in the early evening.

'It's a right social mix, isn't it?' Finlay marvelled. 'In London, Hyde Park is where they promenade, but it's more of a fashion parade for the toffs than anything, and you certainly wouldnae get the— I don't know what it is here. There's no sense of people sticking to their own kind.'

Isabella chuckled. 'You have met my brother. There is plenty of that behaviour to be found in Spain, but not for the *paseo*. Do they have such a custom in Scotland?'

'No, we have not the weather for it,' Finlay replied. 'I think I told you we have more than our fair share of rain. Mind you, when there's a wedding, then you'll get everyone out parading in their finery. That's a sight to behold.'

'Tell me about it.'

'Well, now, I'm talking about a kirk wedding mind. The last one I attended was for my youngest sister Sheena—I missed all the others, but I was home on leave for that one. My mother was baking for days before it. My mother makes the best scones in Scotland. They are a sort of cake, though not sweet, like a soft biscuit, and you eat them hot from the griddle with butter or crowdie, which is cheese.'

'What other foods do they eat at wedding feasts? What does the bride wear? And the groom, does he wear the plaid? Me, I like the plaid very much,' Isabella said, her eyes dancing, 'though not, I think, on a man with thin legs. Or fat legs.'

'A lady should not comment on a gentleman's legs,' Finlay said with mock outrage.

'Ah but since you have told me that I am dead, then I am no longer a lady and therefore free to state that I think that you have a fine pair of legs and look most becoming in your kilt,' Isabella retorted with a mischievous twinkle in her eye.

He smiled down at her. 'Then, since I'm not and never have been a gentleman, I'll take the liberty of reminding you that you have a very delightful derrière.'

Colour tinged her cheeks. Her eyes sparkled. Her mouth was curved into the most tantalising, teasing smile. He spoke without thinking. 'If we were not in the midst of half the population of Tafalla, I would kiss you.'

'I don't know if you've noticed, but half the population of Tafalla have just spent the past hour kissing each other.'

'I didn't mean that sort of kiss.'

Isabella held his gaze. 'I know you didn't,' she whispered.

His breath caught in his chest. He had the oddest sensation, as if he were falling head first from a cliff. She was teasing him. Flirting. But as he gazed down at her, his chest tightened, and he knew, clear as day, what it was he felt for her, and it bore no relation at all to what he'd felt for his other flirts.

He would not name it. If he did not give it a name, there was a chance, a tiny wee chance, that it would pass, because what point was there in him feeling…that, when he was about to pack the object of his—that thing, off to America?

'I don't know about you, but I'm ravenous. We should eat. What do you think of that place over there?' Finlay said, steering a slightly bewildered Isabella towards a brightly lit tavern on the corner of the square.

By the time they had gone through the ceremony of being formally seated at a table in the *commodore*, the back room reserved for diners in the tavern, and consumed a complimentary glass of the local aperitif, the awkward moment had passed. The dining room was basic, the food simple but excellent. They ate hungrily, enjoying a range of dishes. *Morcilla*, a variety of spicy blood sausage that reminded Finlay very much of the black pudding to be found back home in Scotland, *menestra de verduras*, a mixture of local vegetables and salty ham, a braised quail with tiny pale-green beans cooked in tomato, simply grilled lamb chops served with potatoes and cabbage, and the famous *pimientos de piquillo*—red peppers preserved in oil and stuffed with salted cod. The wine, Isabella informed him, was not as good as her brother's. Finlay, who had always been a moderate drinker, partook sparingly, but Isabella, like many Spanish women he had met, seemed to be able to consume quite a few glasses without it having any noticeable effect.

They chatted about the food, relishing the first proper meal in over a week. They speculated about their fellow diners. Then, when they had been served an extremely good *roncal* cheese, Isabella raised the subject of his sister's wedding again. Accustomed as he was to having his origins mocked, Finlay automatically embarked on one of his usual, heavily embroidered tales.

'I think you are making this up,' Isabella interrupted halfway through the yarn.

'Not at all. Well, maybe a bit, but not all of it.'

She frowned. 'Why would you do that? I am not a child, to be told stories. I do not want to hear family secrets or—or confidences. I was not prying. I simply wanted to understand you more. You have seen my home, you know so much about me, yet you tell me almost nothing about yourself.'

He had offended her. 'I'm sorry. I'm not used to talking about myself.'

Isabella propped her hand on her chin and studied him across the table. 'The Jock Upstart,' she said. 'Was that one of the stories you tell in your officers' mess?'

'They would not be interested in the truth,' Finlay said awkwardly, though he wasn't sure, now he came to think about it, that he ever told anyone the truth, save Jack.

'I am interested,' Isabella said. 'What is it like, to have three sisters? Consuela is very fond of hers. She is always writing letters to them. Do your sisters write to you?'

'Aye, once every few months, with news of all my nephews and nieces. I've twelve of them,' Finlay said with a grin.

Isabella's eyes widened. 'Twelve!'

'And counting. Mhairi was expecting another the last I heard.'

'I wonder sometimes what it would have been like, to have a sister.'

'Someone to confide in?' Finlay laid his hands over hers. 'Your mother died when you were a bairn, didn't she? It must have been hard, growing up without any female company.'

'You said that to me that first night we met. I did not think—but now, I don't know. Do you miss them, your family?'

He opened his mouth to assure her that he did, of course he did, then closed it again, frowning. 'Honestly?' He quirked his brow, and Isabella nodded. 'I've been away for so long, that in a way they are strangers to me. They are my blood, I love them, but I'm no more part of their lives than they are mine. Aside from kinship, we have little in common.'

'Though it must be a comfort to know that there are people who care for you, who would be there if you needed them.'

'Aye,' Finlay agreed with surprise, 'that is true. The letters they write, they don't make me want to go home, but it is a comfort indeed, seeing a picture drawn by my nephew, or reading one of my niece's stories. Or reading about the fishing, and the peats and the tattie howking, whatever is the latest gossip my mother thinks fit for my ears,' he said, smiling nostalgically. 'It is good to hear that life can go on in that way, that people can be happy, when you are sitting in a foreign field in the aftermath of battle.'

'What will you do now, Finlay? Now that Europe is at peace, and there are no more battles to fight?'

A damned good question. One of the many lessons this mission had taught him was that he was no peacetime soldier. 'There are always other wars,' he said, thinking, with little enthusiasm, of the rumours he'd heard about India. 'When Wellington hears of my success in silencing El Fantasma, perhaps there will be other such missions, too.'

'You think he will believe you? You have not told me what it is, exactly, that you will tell him.'

'That's Jack's territory.' The light had faded a wee bit from her big golden eyes. She was tired. And he'd been prattling on about his family, and his damned career, when all the while the poor lass had no family now, and much less of a clue than he about her future. 'Let's get you back to the inn,' Finlay said, pressing her hand. 'I'll just go through and pay the shot.'

They were standing at the bar when he opened the connecting door. Two men, dressed in the uniform of the Spanish army, drinking a glass of wine. Not officers, but guards, Finlay reckoned. Their boots were dusty. He heard only one word. 'English.' But it was enough.

Retreating quietly back into the *commodore*, Finlay returned to the table. 'We have to leave. Quietly. Don't panic,' he whispered into Isabella's ear, putting her shawl around her shoulders and throwing some coins onto the table. Fortunately the room had emptied, the few diners left talking intimately over their wine and cheese. Even more fortunately, Isabella asked no questions, doing exactly as he asked, getting to her feet, following the pressure of his hand on her back, to the door that led to the kitchens.

'Soldiers,' he said, as the door closed behind them. 'Spanish army. Two, looking for us. I don't know if there are any more. I'm sorry, but it looks as though you won't be able to enjoy the luxury of a feather bed tonight after all.'

She had not quite believed they were after her. Despite what Finlay had said, despite the urgency with which they travelled, despite the unequivocal evidence of their existence that fateful day at Estebe's house, Isabella had been unable to wholly credit the tenacity of the Spanish government in tracking down El Fantasma, unable to believe that the pamphlets she had written, printed in the cellars of Hermoso Romero, could result in this merciless vendetta. As she scurried along at Finlay's side through the back streets of Tafalla, her heart in her mouth, she no longer doubted. Finlay's concerns were very real. America seemed, of a sudden, a very attractive prospect, if only because it was so very far away. She did not want to be caught. She desperately, desperately did not want them to catch Finlay.

'Should we separate?' she panted. 'Finlay, I don't want them to…'

'Isabella, I'm not going anywhere without you.'

'But they are looking for two of us.'

'An Englishman and a Spanish woman, that's

what they said. If anything, it's me who's putting you in danger.'

Isabella's hands tightened on his arm. 'You won't leave me,' she said, before she could stop herself.

He smiled down at her. Even as they fled for their lives, that smile did things to her insides. 'I won't leave you.' His smile faded. 'Not until you're safe on that boat. And the sooner we get you there the better. We'll start to head for the north coast tonight.'

'You said that is where they would concentrate the search for us. But now here they are in Tafalla in the west.'

'They've clearly enough men spare to cover all the options. Ours is not the only army kicking its heels in peacetime. King Ferdinand's men haven't enough to do, either, by the looks of it.'

She was going to be sick. Fear, such as she had never felt during the war, made her break out in a cold sweat. She stumbled, and would have fallen if Finlay had not had her anchored firmly to his side. 'Courage, lass,' he said.

Isabella managed a weak smile, swallowed the

nausea and picked up the pace again. 'I won't let you down.'

'You couldn't.'

His faith, whether misplaced or not, kept her going through the next fraught hours as they hurriedly reclaimed baggage and horses from the inn. They were heading home, east, Finlay told the landlady, a family crisis. He did not pretend that the false trail was likely to do anything other than give their pursuers a choice of three alternative directions. 'And if there's only the two soldiers, we might just get lucky, though we can't count on it,' he'd said.

They rode through the darkness, across the flat land that spread out to Logrono, for the route directly north was too mountainous. Towards dawn, as the horses were flagging and the terrain was becoming more difficult, they quit the main road and stopped to rest in the shelter of a valley where the mountains rose steeply around them. Shaking, exhausted and oddly exhilarated, Isabella sat huddled in a blanket coaxing a tiny fire into life while Finlay tended to the sweating horses.

'We are likely safe enough here for a few hours,' he said, sitting down beside her. 'You should try to sleep.'

'I don't think I could.'

He put his arm around her. 'Try.'

She did because he wanted her to, without any expectation of success.

When she opened her eyes it was daylight, and the smell of coffee brewing on the trivet greeted her. Finlay, astonishingly clean-shaven, his hair damp, handed her a tin mug. 'I have some good news,' he said.

'Let me guess, there has been an uprising in Pamplona and all the soldiers in the area have been recalled to suppress it.'

'Now, that would be remarkably good news,' he said, sitting down beside her and stretching his long legs out in front of him. 'Mine isn't quite in that category. How are you feeling?'

'You let me sleep for the whole night.'

'What little was left of it.'

Noticing that there was only one cup of coffee, Isabella handed Finlay the mug. 'We can share,' she said, when he looked as if he would refuse.

'Thank you.'

He took a sip and handed it back. She took a sip, putting her mouth where his had been. He was watching her. She took another sip. His hand lingered on hers when she handed the mug back. His eyes lingered on her mouth. Her breath caught. Finlay sipped, placing his lips exactly where hers had been. Her heart bumped. She leaned towards him. He leaned towards her. He handed her the mug. His lips brushed hers. He tasted of coffee. She felt the sharp intake of his breath. He kissed her, slowly, his tongue licking along the inside of her lower lip. Then he handed her the mug. 'You finish it.'

At least he did not walk away, or head off to tend to the horses. Isabella finished the coffee. 'You haven't told me the good news.'

'I recognise this place. I've been here before, during the campaign. There's a mountain pass we can follow, well away from the main routes, that will take us towards Vitoria, and from there we can head to San Sebastian.'

'Vitoria. It was a very bloody battle for the English—British, I think.'

Finlay grimaced. 'I confess, it's not a place I've any yearning to see again.'

'You have seen such terrible things. That day, when you opened my eyes to reality, when you told me what they would do to me if they caught me…'

'I'm sorry I had to do that.'

'I know you are,' Isabella said, setting down the mug and touching his hand. 'I know what it cost you to speak as you did, and I am very grateful. If you had been less blunt, I would have been less convinced. How do you do it, Finlay? How is it that you seem so—so divorced from what you have seen, what you have had to do? You are not a savage. You have a conscience, stronger than most, I think.'

'If you're talking about guilt, I have plenty of it.' He frowned down at the dying fire. 'You don't think of it, not when you're on active service. You think only of the next manoeuvre, the next battle. You can't afford to look back. That way can lie madness—and I mean that.' He glanced up at her, his eyes dark. 'You must have heard something of what our men did after Burgos. Some of the atrocities. I was there in the aftermath, Isabella. There was no stopping them. The lust for blood, it wasn't just revenge, it went deeper than that. It was as if some of them—it was as if they were possessed by an evil spirit. I sound like your Inquisition, but it's the only way of describing it.'

'Though, you never took part in such things,' Isabella said. It was not a question. She was absolutely certain of it.

Finlay shook his head. 'No, but my men did. I carry some of the blame.'

'No!'

'I was their commanding officer. I seem to remember you saying some such thing with regard to Estebe.'

'I will always have that guilt as part of me. Is that what you mean?'

'I won't lie to you, that's what I mean.'

'Finlay, one of the things I like so much about you is that you don't lie to me. Not even when you want to.' She touched his hand again, and this time he turned it around to clasp her fingers. 'You treat me as if I have a mind of my own.'

'A very decided one,' he said.

She smiled softly. 'Like the Jock Upstart, I do

not take kindly to being given orders. We are very alike in that way.'

'Who'd have thought it?' He raised her hand to his lips, pressing a kiss onto her palm, allowing his mouth to linger for a moment, warm on her skin. 'We must go. We've a few days yet before we reach the coast, and the path is treacherous so we need to make the most of the daylight.'

They travelled all day, leading the horses over the roughest terrain, making slow but steady progress north. It was hard going, but Isabella made not a word of complaint, and though her steps flagged as dusk approached, she insisted on continuing for another mile, until darkness prevented them travelling further. Cheese and stale bread were all they had to eat, but she made no protest about this meagre fare, either.

There was sparse shelter provided by an over-hanging rocky outcrop. 'You take the blankets,' Finlay said. 'I'll keep watch.'

'There is no need. No one is following us up here. You will feel better for a sleep, and we will be warmer if we share.' She smiled up at him, her face shadowed by the flickers of the tiny fire they had lit. 'We did it once before, do you remember?'

'I do.' His heart gave a painful twist as he sat down beside her. More than two years ago, it had been. Against all odds they had met in the strangest of circumstances, and here they were again about to huddle under a blanket together for warmth. He hadn't thought himself a man who believed in destiny. He wished fervently that fate had drawn him a kinder hand. Twice, he had crossed paths with the woman who owned his heart, and soon they would be parted forever. He could not resist putting his arm around her and drawing her closer. He loved her. Pointless to deny it any longer. Time to stop pretending it was anything else. He loved her, and he always would.

'It is a strange coincidence, being here like this for the second time, is it not?' Isabella asked.

'I was thinking the very same thing myself.' Finlay shifted on the hard ground, tucking the blanket around them. Her cheek rested on his shoulder. Her hair tickled his chin. He breathed in the sweet, familiar scent of her, and closed his eyes, trying to etch the feel of her body against his, the softness of her, the shape of her, deep in his mind, achingly conscious that he would have so few chances left just to hold her like this.

'We talked of America that night,' Isabella said. 'I never thought I would travel there. I never imagined it would be my home.'

'Isabella, if there was any...'

'Wheesht,' she said, putting her fingers to his mouth, her accent making the word sound like a caress. 'I have been thinking of what you said. America is a new world. A country where ideals are not simply dreams. You are right, Finlay. It is a country where I can start again. I don't know what I will do, but there are so many possibilities. You were right. It is a good place for me to go. Thank you.'

He knew she was trying to make him feel better, but there was a note of real enthusiasm in her voice that was surely not manufactured. She was not simply making the best of things, she was trying her wee heart out to embrace her fate. He loved her so much. *Gràdh, mo chrìdh*, he said to himself, touching his lips to the silky mass of her hair. 'You should sleep now,' he added aloud. 'We've a way to go in the morning.'

'*Buenas noches*, Finlay.'

'*Oidhche mhath*, Isabella.'

'*Oika va?*'

He chuckled softly. 'Not bad. You've an ear for the Gaelic. Goodnight, lass.'

She nestled her head into his shoulder. He kissed her hair again, tightening his arm around the slim curve of her waist. Her breathing slowed. She was asleep almost immediately. '*Gràdh, mo chrìdh,*' Finlay whispered, wanting to say the words to her just once, though she could not hear. 'Love of my heart you are, Isabella. Love of my heart.'

Chapter Eleven

Isabella awoke from a deep slumber to find that her head was cushioned on Finlay's chest. She was lying on her side, with one of her legs wedged between his. His arm anchored her to him; his other hand was splayed across her bottom. She could feel his heart beating, slow and steady, through his shirt. She listened, keeping quite still, to his breathing. Also slow and steady. He was asleep. She did not want to move and risk waking him.

The cloud had cleared while she slept, and the stars were out, huge disks of silver in the inky blue sky, the half-moon glowing milky white. Finlay said the stars in Scotland seemed much farther away. She couldn't imagine how that could be. He stirred, tightening his hold on her. She felt safe here with him. She wished the night would go on forever. She did not want to think of the morning, which would bring her another day closer to the coast, and to the ship that would take her to her new life. If she was not so completely alone, she might be looking forward to it almost as much as she had tried to persuade Finlay she was. A new world. Perhaps there would be an opportunity for a new El Fantasma. Not a partisan, but perhaps— Her mind skittered to a halt. Something. She would think of something tomorrow, and she would tell Finlay, and she would enthuse and speculate, and the guilt he was so patently feeling about sending her off alone to her fate would hopefully abate a little.

She owed him so much. She owed him her life. She couldn't bear to think that he'd be fretting about her once she had sailed. He had his own life to be getting on with. He would be off to fight another war soon enough. Or off on another mission for the Duke of Wellington. She hoped for Finlay's sake that he would be given something constructive to do. Though she hated the idea of him being in danger, she knew he would be miserable kicking his heels in the officers' mess. The Jock Upstart was a man who thrived on action. Her heart lurched at the real-isation that she would never know what he was doing, who he was with, what country he was in, even.

Perhaps he would, after all, return to the High-lands and raise a family. She could imagine him, very easily imagine him, with a brood of chil-dren—bairns, as he would call them. She could imagine them surprisingly easily. Their bairns. Hers and Finlay's. She had never really thought about children, never imagined herself as a mother. Now, for a fleeting moment, the notion filled her with some soft and warm emotion that she'd never experienced before. 'Stupid,' Isabella muttered to herself. 'Stupid, stupid, stupid!'

She was torturing herself. Better to focus on the real future, whatever that would be. It would be empty of Finlay—that was the only thing she knew for sure. Perhaps she should suggest they correspond, once she had settled in America. But she dismissed the idea immediately. A con-solation to her, those letters might be, but they would be a burden to Finlay. The break, when it came, must be clean. In a few more days, only a few more days, they would part, and she must make very sure that the parting was as painless for Finlay as it could be. As to herself—no, truly, there was no point in thinking about her feelings.

She flattened her palm on his chest. He was so solid. She had never lain like this with a man. Slept with a man. It was such a very intimate thing to be doing, despite the fact that they were both more or less fully clothed. Asleep, even Finlay was vulnerable. In a sense, sleeping together was more intimate than making love. Not that anyone would believe that all she had done was slept in his arms. If it were discovered, her reputation would be ruined. If she had any left to ruin, that was. Though her reputation would not matter at all in the New World she was headed towards. No one would know anything about her past history. They would not know that she had spent the night alone, in a Highlander's embrace. It was a terrible pity she had not anything more scandalous to conceal. Almost a waste.

Somehow her hand had slipped inside the opening of Finlay's shirt. The rough hair of his chest prickled her palm. His nipple was unexpectedly hard. Was it as sensitive as hers? When she touched it, did it tingle the way hers did?

Was there that shivering connection between his nipple and his—his arousal? There was certainly a connection between his nipple and her arousal. If she turned her head just the tiniest fraction, she could put her lips to the skin of his throat. It was a very, very appealing idea, but she dared not move lest she wake him. Though it was so very tempting. But it would be wrong. He had made it clear, very clear, that he would not make love to her. She was under his protection. She was an innocent. He was not a seducer of virgins.

In a few days' time, she would be alone on a boat, and she would never see him again. No one save Finlay cared about her virginity. She would certainly be more than happy not to have to take it with her. Without her dowry and her pedigree, her virginity was not even a marketable asset. She turned her head a tiny fraction. Just a kiss. But she did not want to wake him. Just one tiny kiss. What was the harm in that?

Her lips touched his throat. His skin was warm. She licked him. He tasted slightly salty. A trickle of perspiration ran down her back. She kissed his throat again. She could feel his pulse beating against her lips. His hand tightened on her rump, and she knew he was awake.

She froze, horrified. She lifted her head to apologise, but Finlay smiled softly. 'Isabella,' he said, 'lovely Isabella. You've no idea how lovely.'

'Finlay.' In the moonlight, his skin was pale, his eyes dark. She reached up to touch his hair. 'The colour of autumn leaves,' she said. 'All that time ago, when first we sat under the stars like this, that's what I thought. That your eyes were colour of the summer sea. And your hair the colour of autumn leaves.'

He laughed softly. 'I wanted to kiss you, that night. Under that blanket. Under those stars. I wanted very much to kiss you.' His hand was caressing her bottom, the flat of his palm smoothing delightful circles. 'I regretted the fact that I didn't,' he said.

'And I, too.' She smoothed her hand over his chest. She felt his heart leap, beat faster than before. Longing, so deep that it was almost painful, overwhelmed her. 'I have so many regrets, Finlay. I don't want this to be another. Make love to me.'

'Isabella...'

'Please,' she interrupted, desperate to quell his conscience before it could put an end to things. 'This has nothing to do with gratitude or guilt, Finlay. I know what I am doing. You will not be stealing my innocence. I am giving it to you. I *know* you want me. I know, too, that it can mean nothing.'

'You're wrong. Isabella, you are so wrong. It means everything. But I can't resist you. I don't want to resist you. I want you more than I've ever wanted anything.'

He loved her so much. *I love you*, he thought as he kissed her. *I love you, Isabella, I love you.* He poured his heart into his kisses. It would be his only chance to love her, to worship her, to show her how he felt. He kissed her hungrily, passionately, then softly, tenderly. 'You are so beautiful,' he said. 'I want you so much.' *I love you so much.*

He rolled her onto her back. He kissed her mouth, her throat, her neck, her shoulders, the mounds of her breasts above the neckline of her riding habit. She tugged at his shirt, slipping her hands beneath the fabric to stroke his skin, making his muscles clench in response, sending the blood shooting to his groin.

He eased her up, sitting her between his legs, and kissed the nape of her neck. Slowly, he began to unbraid her hair, teasing it loose with his fingers. Long, silken strands spread over her shoulders. He pulled her up against him, her back against his chest, cupping her breasts, kissing her neck, then began to unlace her riding habit, taking his time, planting kisses on every inch of skin revealed, slipping the top over her arms, kissing her shoulders, the crook of her elbows, before unlacing her stays and sliding her chemise down. He kissed the knot of her spine. He could feel her breathing, fast and shallow. He cupped her breasts, exposed now, rolling her nipples between his fingers, relishing the small moans of pleasure his touch elicited.

Hot skin, cold air. He pulled his shirt over his head and drew her back against him. The silken touch of her hair caressed his chest. He whispered her name, feathering kisses across her narrow shoulders. She arched back against him, her breathing more ragged. He wanted to see her face. Gently, he rolled her onto her back again.

Another long, deep kiss, her tongue on his, making his shaft pulse and throb. He ached to be inside her, but he would not rush this, his one unique opportunity to make love to the woman he loved.

'You are a banquet,' he said, smiling down at her. 'A feast.'

Her response was a sensuous smile that sent his pulses racing. She ran her hands over the breadth of his chest, pressing her mouth to his throat. 'You are not the only one with an appetite.'

'I have never been so ravenous in my life,' Finlay replied, taking her nipple into his mouth.

She gasped with pleasure. He tasted her lingeringly, licking and teasing her, first one nipple and then the other. Her fingers dug into his back. She arched under him. He kissed the delicate line of her ribcage, licking into the hollow of her navel, murmuring her name over and over. Her hands fluttered frantically over him, her untutored touch rousing him, the guttural little moans she made heating his blood, making his pulses race.

He pulled her habit and her petticoats off together. Her skin was creamy white in the moonlight. Her slim beauty, her delicate curves, were almost too much. 'You are so lovely. I have never seen anything to match your loveliness,' he said. He kissed the back of her knee, her calf, her ankle, as he removed her stocking. Then the same for the other leg. Isabella was watching him, wide-eyed, intent. He adored the way she watched him. Not a trace of modesty, as if she, too, was savouring every precious moment, as if she, too, was trying to memorise every inch of him. He could not resist claiming her lips again. She wrapped her arms around him, pressing her naked breasts to his naked chest. Her nipples grazed his skin. He had never felt anything so arousing.

More kisses, far headier than any of the region's wine. He could drink of her and drink of her and never have his fill. Easing her back down, he kissed his way down her body, the valley between her breasts, the dip of her belly, to the apex of her thighs. She was panting now, her fingers clutching at the edge of the blanket on which they lay. The flesh here was sweet, soft, faintly scented with her arousal. He eased her legs farther apart, and slid his tongue inside her. She bucked under him. The taste of her, the heat and wet of her, was heady.

He thought he might come. It took him every bit of self-control he possessed to wait, to get himself under control, but he did it. She was a feast he had waited a long time to consume. He wanted to enjoy every morsel. He slipped his hands under her bottom, tilting her towards him, and licked. She was already tight. Already on the brink. He was careful not to send her over, slowly licking and stroking just enough, then moving away, sliding his fingers inside her, thrusting slowly, carefully. Her moans had become pleas. Her hands were in his hair, on his shoulders, his arms. He licked again. He thrust again with his fingers. She cried out his name, a desperate sound. He licked again, slowly but relentlessly, and she came with a loud cry, pulsing against him, the taste of her so unbearably sweet, so uniquely his lovely Isabella, that he closed his eyes to relish it, telling her again and again, to the rhythm of her climax, whispering so softly that she could not hear him, that he loved her, loved her, loved her.

When the pulses faded to ripples, Finlay looked up to find her watching him again. He smiled. Isabella smiled back, a slow, sensuous, sated smile. He could call a halt now. He thought about it. But then she reached for him, pulling him towards her, her hands on the waistband of his breeches, shaking her head as if she had read his mind. 'I am hungry, too,' she said. 'Take them off. I want to see you naked,' she said urgently.

He wanted her to look. It was strange, he'd never felt like that before, but he wanted her to see him. He kissed her again before dragging his mouth from hers and hurriedly divesting himself of the last of his clothes. Even in the moonlight, he could see the flush of colour tingeing her cheeks. It was delightful. She was delightful.

'May I touch you?'

'You need to ask? I can think of nothing I want more.' He knelt before her, once more between her legs. She sat up. Her blush was quite distinct now, but she was still looking at him in that intent, sultry way that made him ache with the need to be inside her. She touched his belly. With her finger, she traced the line of hair that arrowed down to his groin. She stroked his flanks. She traced the line of his buttocks. His muscles tightened in response. She reached for his shaft. He inhaled sharply, praying for self-control. Her touch was the faintest feathering, tracing the length of him with her fingertip. 'Dear God,' he said.

She yanked her hand away. 'I'm sorry.'

'No.' He couldn't catch his breath. 'No. I'm just— It is just…'

'You like it?' Her smile became feline. Predatory. She touched him again, feathering up and down the length of him. 'I think you like it a lot?'

'Aye,' he said, snatching a kiss from her, 'a lot.'

'And this?'

She circled her fingers around his girth. He nodded, gritting his teeth.

'And this?'

A slow stroke of her hand. Finlay nodded again. Pain and pleasure; he'd no idea they were such bedmates.

'And this.'

Another stroke, more sure, but still slow. And

another. He was going to come. He would not come. Not yet. 'Isabella.'

She stopped at the warning note in his voice. Then she smiled at him again.

'And this, Finlay?'

Her lips touched the tip of his shaft. He felt her tongue, hot on the most sensitive part of him. With a long, low groan of ecstasy and regret, he pulled himself free of her and laid her down, covering her body with his. 'You are a sorceress,' he said. 'You are the most delightful, delicious, desirable sorceress, and you have me under your spell and I can't wait any longer. Do you still want this, Isabella? Because if you don't, now is the time to say so.'

For answer, she put her arms around his neck and kissed him. 'I want this. I want you. More than anything.'

Her words were no lie. She ached in a way she had never ached before, her body yearning for him in a new way. She wanted him inside her. She wanted that sleek, silken part of him inside her. She tilted herself towards him in open invitation, worlds beyond modesty or embarrassment, caring nothing for her utter lack of experience, surrendering completely to her body's instincts. His kiss was hard and deep. His tongue thrust into her mouth. She was hot, fevered, tense, urgent, but he entered her slowly. She opened her eyes to watch him. His gaze locked on hers as his body became part of her until he filled her. There was no pain. There was only delight. And more tension. Her muscles clenched around him. He pushed higher inside her, and she felt an odd fluttering sensation. Then he waited, watching her. She pulled him towards her for another kiss. 'Yes,' she said. 'Yes.' Permission for anything. Everything. She wanted all of him.

'Yes,' he whispered. 'Oh, yes.'

His first thrust was careful. The effort of control was etched on his face. Another thrust, harder this time. She was learning how to hold him and release him. Another thrust, and she felt the tension inside her building. They were finding a common rhythm now. Thrust, cling, release, thrust. Still he watched her. Still she held his gaze, seeing her pleasure reflected on his face, the power of giving that pleasure making her bolder, making her match his thrust with a tilt of her hips, holding him higher, clinging to him tighter, until her climax took her, sending her spiralling higher than she had ever flown, and Finlay cried out, pulling himself free of her to spend himself with an equally hoarse cry that was her name, and something in his native tongue she did not understand.

Afterwards, she could not sleep. She was afraid to speak. They lay entwined, skin on skin, watching the stars, listening to the whickering of the horses, the gentle burble of a distant stream. Finlay held her as if she was made of glass and he was afraid she might break. She clung to him as if she was afraid she would drown in a sea of emotion. As the waves of pleasure ebbed and the euphoria of their coupling faded, she was left feeling oddly desolate.

She felt the brush of his lips on her hair. His hand tightened possessively around her flank. She moved, burrowing closer. If she could climb inside his skin, she would. If she could live inside his skin, she would. That was when it struck her.

'*Madre de Dios.*'

'What is it?'

'Nothing.' Her heart skipped a beat, then began to beat harder, as if she had been running. *Madre de Dios.* She was in love. Isabella closed her eyes in pain. How could she have been so stupid? How could she have been so blind? Of course she was in love with this man. Had she not just made love to him with her body and her mind, too? She was in love. Of all the foolish things she had done, surely this was the worst.

Finlay's lips brushed her hair again. She found his hand, twining her fingers in his. Tears stung behind her lids. She could not let them fall. He would think she regretted what they had just done. Her heart began to slow. She did not regret it. She lifted his hand to hers and kissed his knuckles. She would never regret it, but he must never find out. She had already given him enough to feel guilty about. This— No, he must not know this. He cared deeply for her, she did not doubt that, but there was no question, none at all, of any possible future for them.

Despite this, she allowed herself to dream for a few precious moments. To imagine that they could lie like this every night, wrapped in each other's loving embrace. That he could make love to her every night, spending himself inside her, in the hope of creating a new human life forged by them both. She allowed herself to dream of a little farm—no, croft—in the Highlands. They would attend the church in the longhouse he had described to her. Their children would play with the children of his three sisters. Everyone from the village would dance at their wedding. She would learn to cook, and to weave, and Finlay would...

Enough of this schoolgirl fantasy! The cold reality was that it was impossible for her to set foot on British soil. Furthermore, if it were known that he was harbouring El Fantasma, Major Finlay Urquhart would be court-martialled and most likely hanged. No, she had to vanish off the face of the earth and resurface in America under an assumed identity, and Finlay had to return to Britain in order to complete his mission and convince Wellington that El Fantasma had been eliminated. Failure to do that would also likely lead to him being hanged, this time for desertion.

Isabella sighed. If only things were different, he could sail with her to the New World. In America, there would be opportunity for any number of adventures. *Stupid!* If things were different, she would not have to go to America. If things were different, she would not have met Finlay again, and she would not be lying here under the stars, her body still tingling from his lovemaking. Time to stop dreaming and face facts. She was leaving everything behind, including her country and her family, everything she knew and loved. She had kept the pain of this at bay by simply avoiding thinking of it, but she knew, when she was alone, that it would come. She loved Finlay with all her heart. Which did not mean asking him to give up everything, as she had, and come away with her. No, what it meant was to ensure the exact opposite was the case. For his sake. And she'd better make damned sure she remembered that over the next few days.

The stars were beginning to fade. Isabella turned her face into Finlay's chest. An errant tear escaped. She rubbed her cheek against the hard wall of muscle, hoping he would not notice.

He pulled her closer. 'Try to sleep for a bit,'

he said softly. 'We've a long day ahead of us tomorrow.'

And a long, empty future ahead of her after that, Isabella thought. But she was not given to self-pity, and would not indulge in it now. 'In less than a week, I will be at sea,' she said with forced cheer. 'If the boat is still waiting.'

'It will be there. Jack gave his word,' Finlay said heavily, unwittingly killing the tiny spark of hope.

'Good,' said Isabella bracingly. 'That is at least one less thing to worry about.'

They were on their way before dawn had fully broken. The mountains to the east obscured the sunrise, and the dull, tarnished silver clouds above absorbed much of the sun's light when it finally did make an appearance. Finlay fought the desolation that threatened to envelop him. He was not by nature morose, nor given to railing against fate, but as he looked at the woman riding by his side and tried to imagine life without her, his rage verged on the biblical.

Why the devil had the fates thrown them together like this, if they were so intent on pulling the pair of them asunder? Bloody fates. And bloody Wellington. The man was power mad. And he was a mite too bloody cautious. What did it matter that El Fantasma could tell a few tales that would embarrass him? True, a few of those tales would stir up quite a storm, but the duke was riding so high on the wave of triumph fuelled by the victory at Waterloo that Finlay reckoned even the revelation that Wellington was in the habit of eating bairns for breakfast wouldn't cost him the political career he was hankering after. Bloody Wellington.

And while he was at it, bloody Jack, too. Jack could have told Wellington to stick his orders where the sun didn't shine. Jack wasn't even in the army anymore. But no, Jack and his principles had to take up El Fantasma's cause, and Jack knew Finlay a bit too damned well, catching him when he was kicking his heels, desperate for orders. Any orders. Some bloody friend.

Finlay's hands tightened on his reins, and his horse started. Quick as a flash, Isabella's hand reached for his rein. 'It's fine. I was dwamming,' he said, getting the horse back under control. 'It means daydreaming.'

She smiled at him. It was a forced smile. Her big golden eyes were shadowed with something that looked distinctly like unhappiness. 'You looked angry. I am sorry if...'

He was immediately contrite. 'Don't apologise. I'm like a bear with a sore heid, but it's not your fault, Isabella.'

'You do not regret last night?'

'No. Dear heavens, no.' He pulled up beside her, and she brought her horse to a halt. 'Isabella, last night was— It was...' *Everything.* The urge to tell her was powerful. 'It was perfect,' Finlay said. 'I only hope that you do not...'

'No, I don't regret it. For me it was also—perfect. Only today, I think that I am a little sad, knowing that soon I will be saying goodbye to you.' Her voice wobbled, but she smiled again valiantly. 'Of course I am very much looking forward to my new life, but I will—I will miss you, Finlay.'

Dear God. There was a sheen of tears in her eyes. She was so brave. He loved her so much. He should thank Jack and Wellington and the fates for throwing them together instead of cursing them for it. If he had not come here to Spain, he would never have known what love was. And if he had not come here to Spain, Isabella would have…

Finlay shuddered. She was safe. They would not get their hands on her, even if he had to die saving her. She was safe and she was getting the chance of a new life. Without him, but a life. He must remember that. He leaned over in the saddle to kiss her softly. 'I will miss you, too, Isabella. You are a woman like no other. I am glad, and I am honoured, that I have had the chance to know you.'

So much less than he felt, but it was enough, it seemed. She blushed. 'And I, too, Finlay. Glad and deeply honoured.'

Chapter Twelve

They descended from the heights of La Puebla down a steep zigzag path and into the valley below through which the Zadorra River flowed, the site of the bloody Battle of Vitoria. It was a peaceful place, nature having reclaimed the battlefield, leaving little trace of the countless lives lost and the oceans of blood spilled more than two years before. Peaceful now that was, but Isabella sensed a certain melancholy linger in the air. Perhaps she was being fanciful, but she gave an involuntary shudder as she took in the scene.

'It is hard to believe that this particular engagement could have been so decisive,' she said, making a sweeping gesture.

'There were more than ten thousand casualties in total,' Finlay said grimly. 'Our army lost three and a half thousand men. Five hundred Spanish died. Can anything be worth so many lives, so much sacrifice?'

The British and their allies had been positioned on the western banks of the river, he had told her. Isabella stared at the rural scene, trying to imagine the serried ranks of soldiers numbering in the thousands, the field-gun placements firing salvo after merciless salvo, the sound of muskets, the acrid smell of gunpowder as it drifted across the battlefield in a thick pall of smoke. She could not, but Finlay, his eyes blank, staring off into the distance, clearly could. 'They say it was a pivotal moment, the turning point in the war,' Isabella offered.

'Aye. That's what they always say when the body count climbs that high.'

'But in this case, surely it is true. Not long after the Battle of Vitoria was won, Napoleon's army was in retreat. The occupation of Spain was over.'

'And you were free to build a new world, eh? Remind me how is that working out again.'

The bitterness in Finlay's voice took Isabella aback. The viciousness of his barb stung. 'You think it would have been better if the French had won?'

'I think it would have been better if we had not had to fight at all,' he said. 'The French left wagons full of the spoils of war behind as they fled, did you know that? Not just gold, but all sorts. Our men plundered it. They went mad. Discipline broke down entirely. There was no stopping them. Bloodlust, that's what it was. I hope you never witnessed it, Isabella. War can make a man less than human. I saw it with my own eyes but it is only now, with the benefit of some perspective that I begin to see how distasteful the whole bloody enterprise is. An enterprise that I was proud to be part of.'

'But you did not behave…'

'No,' he said tersely, 'I did not. Wellington called them the scum of the earth in a dispatch. The common soldier, who had won his precious victory, who had followed orders that took him hundreds of miles from home, tramped hundreds of miles across this country of yours, starving at times, suffering illness at others, frozen to the marrow often enough. Their wives trailing in their wake, too, some with bairns, having to suffer the same privations. And Wellington rewards them by calling them the scum of the earth.'

'Because they committed atrocities, Finlay.'

He looked at her bleakly. 'What is war itself, Isabella, if not an atrocity, an affront to humanity?'

'No. Don't say that. Don't talk like that.'

'Why not?'

'Because you are a soldier, and fighting wars is what you do. You have spent your life saving the lives of others, forging peace, making the world a safer place, a better place. The wars you have fought have been just wars, Finlay. You are an honourable man, a brave man. You are Major Urquhart, the Jock Upstart. All your life, you have served your country, done your duty. You should be proud of that legacy.'

She finished in a rush, eyeing him anxiously. Every word she had spoken was true, but this rousing little speech had not the effect she intended. If anything, Finlay looked even more bleak. 'In England, all anyone wants to talk about is the great victory of Waterloo. Children re-enact the battle with their little toy soldiers. If you tell a woman you were there, you're guaranteed a grateful embrace. Wellington is toasted at every dinner party in London. Yet the men who won that battle for him, many of them are starving now. So many died or were wounded in all these wars we fought against the French, the country can't afford to pay the pensions they're entitled to. They'll do anything to wriggle out of paying a widow, you know. They'll tell a man it's his own fault that he lost his legs, not the army's. Jack was railing against the injustice of it when we discussed my mission here. I begin to see that he was absolutely right. You are not the only one, Isabella, whose hopes of a better future have been dashed.'

'If Napoleon had not been defeated, the world would most likely be a worse place.'

He smiled at her wryly. 'You don't really believe that, do you? Spain was on the winning side, was it not? And by your own admission, your country has gone backwards and not forward.'

She took his hand in hers, though she doubted the small gesture afforded him a tithe of the comfort she longed to give him. 'You cannot mean that you wish Wellington had been defeated.'

'No, of course not. But I wonder, I am truly beginning to wonder, if I have it in me to fight any more wars on his behalf. Or anyone else's. I am getting tired of taking orders. I'm thinking it might be time I took my life into my own hands.'

'Come with me to America, then,' she said, before she could catch the words.

He touched her cheek. 'They'd execute me for desertion if they caught me, not to mention the shame it would bring to my family and the stain on my character. No, whatever I do, I have to go back.'

'You are not a man to run away from anything, are you, Finlay?'

'You know me very well. Indeed, I am not.'

'I wasn't being serious about you coming with me,' Isabella said, who had actually never been more serious in her whole life. 'The Duke of Wellington might very well be persuaded that El Fantasma has been killed, since it is what he fervently hopes to hear, but his Jock Upstart leads a charmed life. He would know it was a ruse if you did not return.'

'Aye, like as not.' Finlay tucked a strand of her hair behind her ear, and kissed her forehead. 'I'm sorry. This morning I was a bear with a sore heid, and now I'm having a fit of the blue devils. You'll be glad to see the back of me.'

'Aye,' she said, 'like as not.'

He was forced to laugh. 'I'm thinking, once we leave Vitoria, it will be a hard and dangerous push to the coast. The boat will be waiting on standby at San Sebastian. She's a fishing boat. The captain is one of Jack's connections. A fine sailor, he assures me. He'll take you on to Lisbon, where you'll pick up a cargo ship bound for the New World. I'm afraid I don't know the detail—that has been left in the hands of the fisherman. You can trust him with your life, Jack says...'

'Finlay, you need not worry about me. I am perfectly capable of looking after myself. Trust me.'

'I do. I have every faith in you. But I wish...'

'No.' Isabella put her finger to his lips. 'Wheesht, now,' she said. 'You have saved my life. You have given me the chance of another life. That is a priceless gift, Finlay. I promise you, I will make the most of it in return.'

'I know you will.'

'So let us have no more of it.' She looked up at the lowering sky. 'It's going to rain. We should think about finding somewhere to camp for the night.'

'We'll not be camping rough. Tonight you'll have the bath and the feather bed I promised you.' He shook his head when she made to protest. 'It's the last chance you'll get for quite some time. Like I said, the authorities are likely to be hot on our tail all the way to the coast.'

'Then they are likely to be here, in Vitoria, Finlay.'

He smiled at her. 'One advantage I have, of having been in this place before, is that I made a few trustworthy acquaintances, and one of them just happens to be an innkeeper. You shall have a hot bath and a comfortable bed, and you shall be quite safe.'

'Will you share it with me?'

He raised a quizzical brow. 'The bath?'

'I meant the bed, but you are welcome to share

both. More than welcome. Very much more. It will be our last chance. I would like…'

'Yes.' He caught her in a tight embrace. 'Yes. I would like that. More than like that. Very much more.'

Alesander Gebara, proprietor of the Hosteria Vasca, greeted Finlay like a long-lost brother, and seemed not at all surprised when informed of the need for discretion. 'They are looking for an Englishman, the soldiers. You,' he said, poking Finlay playfully in the chest, 'are Scottish. So when they come again tonight, I can say no, no, I have seen no English. But it will be best, I think, if I serve you dinner in the privacy of your chamber.'

The inn was ancient, a veritable warren of narrow corridors and rickety staircases, but it had a charm all of its own. The bedchamber Señor Gebara ushered them into was low ceilinged, the heavy, dark oak exposed beams ran at odd angles and a massive stone fireplace dominated one wall, while an imposing tester bed took up most of the floor space, leaving room only for a small table and two chairs set in the window embrasure, and a chest of drawers tucked into a corner.

The innkeeper set about a flurry of activity, summoning a chambermaid to air the bed and set the fire. Another maid was put in charge of the bathing arrangements while Señor Gebara himself brought refreshments from the taproom. 'The finest Rioja in the region,' he said, pouring a glass for each of them.

Isabella took a sip and smilingly informed her host that it was indeed the best she had ever tasted, but she could not help thinking of her brother as she did so. Xavier would be safe as long as the Spanish soldiers were searching for her, but when they were forced to admit defeat, what then? Would the influence her brother wielded really be sufficient to keep him safe from harm?

She would never know. The knowledge gave her a sickening jolt. She would never know. A mixture of panic and fear made her feel faint. She couldn't do this. She had thought herself so strong; she had prided herself on her courage and her daring. What a fool she had been. She was absolutely terrified. She couldn't do this. She simply couldn't.

A warm hand slid around her waist, pulling her up against a strong, solid body. Finlay's smile was warm, too, his sea-blue eyes reassuring. He believed in her. When she had told him how worried she was about letting him down, he'd said she could not. The mist of her panic began to recede. She wouldn't let him down. She would never let him down. Isabella smiled back. Finlay settled her more firmly against him, and returned to his conversation with Señor Gebara.

Isabella listened, sipping at her wine, enjoying the comfort of Finlay's physical proximity, gradually beginning to relax again. It took two maids to carry the enormous copper bath into the room, which they then placed behind screens in front of the now blazing fire. The room was becoming delightfully warm. Steam rose from behind the screens as bucket after bucket of hot water was poured into the bath. The two men were talking of Spain, the changes since the British army and the French had left. The innkeeper sounded very like Estebe. It was not only his accent but the repressed passion that underscored his words. She wondered if he had ever read any of El Fantasma's pamphlets. But Señor Gebara was clearly a prosperous man, his business thriving. He had a wife and a child now, he'd told Finlay. Such a man would not risk all he'd built, would he?

He caught her staring, and smiled warmly at her. He had a very nice smile. He was not much older than Finlay. 'Forgive me, *señora*, I have allowed my tongue to run away with itself, talking of the old days. So many times, I have wondered what became of the Jock Upstart. Not that I doubted he would survive, because—what is it you always said, Finlay?'

'A man who is born to be hanged can never be drowned.'

Señor Gebara laughed. 'That is it, that is it. I am very pleased indeed to see that you are still evading your fate. Those soldiers… If they knew they were chasing the Jock Upstart, they would give up and go back to Madrid. You need have no fear, *señora*. While you have this man to protect you, you are perfectly safe.'

'Ach, you don't know the *señora* here,' Finlay said. 'She's more than capable of protecting herself.'

'A fellow soldier.' The innkeeper nodded. 'I see now why she has your heart, my friend. I am very glad that you, too, have found a woman to share your life.' He turned to Isabella. 'I lost my betrothed in the war,' he said sadly. 'I thought I would never love again, but my Maria, she has shown me that the human spirit is a strong thing, the human heart even stronger. I hope you are as happy with this Jock Upstart, *señora*, as I am with my Maria.'

Isabella did not need Finlay to caution her. She was pleased to be able to maintain the innkeeper's misapprehension, to speak the truth for once. 'I can think of no other man capable of making me this happy,' she said. 'None.'

Alesander left with promises to serve them the best dinner the region could provide in an hour. It was good to see his old friend and ally so happy, but Finlay couldn't help envying the man, too. Alesander had made a new life for himself. Who'd have thought that the wild, bold and fearless guerrilla fighter he'd known would be so content running an inn? Though the way he'd spoken, Finlay would not be surprised to hear that Alesander was still, in his own quiet way, fighting for a better life for his wife and child. Not so very different after all from the man he'd known? Perhaps.

'I like your friend very much,' Isabella said. She was standing at the window, her cheek on the pane. 'Finlay, do you not think that he is in the right of it? The human spirit is a very strong thing. Your friend has made a new life for himself. I would like it so much—so very, very much, if I could believe you could, too.'

He joined her at the window. She clutched his hand tightly. There were tears sparkling on her long lashes. She looked up at him beseechingly. *I can think of no other man capable of making me this happy*, she had said to Alesander. She had said it to maintain their cover, he knew that, but her words had, to his pathetically desperate heart, seemed to carry an undertone of truth. She did care, though. Best not to think about how much; he was heartsore enough.

'Finlay?'

She wanted an answer. She needed the reassurance of an answer. He tried, he tried bloody hard, but he could not imagine what kind of new life he'd forge for himself, and he would not lie to her. 'Isabella,' he said, kissing the tears from her lids, 'we've only got tonight before we spend a lifetime apart. Let's not think about anything else. Not tonight.'

Her lips were soft, sweet, shaped perfectly for his. He ached for her in a new way. The desire was just as fierce, but his need to cherish her, to meld himself to her, to be as one with her, was so much stronger. They would make love, but not yet. He wanted to spin out every single moment of time with her, to be everything to her as she was to him, just for tonight, because tonight was all they would have. He had to make it enough for the memory to last forever.

He had never shared anything so intimate as a bath before. They undressed each other slowly in the fading light, lit only by the glow of the fire, and Finlay discovered that he was wrong about the urgency, the need, the desire, as they touched and stroked, and kissed and licked. The pace was not only his to set. Isabella, his beautiful, feisty Isabella, had a passion to match his.

When she pulled him down onto the rug by the fire, he was hers to command. Her mouth, her hands, her hips, captured him as no other had. When she lowered herself onto him, taking him inside her inch by gut-wrenching, achingly delightful inch, he moaned her name, could not resist telling her, in his own language, how much he loved her. They found their rhythm quickly. She seemed to know him instinctively, when to rock on top of him slowly and when to buck and thrust urgently. She came with wild abandon, her climax making him lose control, his own so powerful that he managed, only just, to lift her safely from him at the last second.

She would shed her skin for this man. There was nothing she would not do for him. Lying in his arms, her heart thudding wildly, her body singing with pleasure, Isabella closed her eyes, pressed her cheek to his heartbeat and whispered her love. She had behaved without any inhibitions because, quite simply, she had none with Finlay. He knew her as no one else ever had. Or would.

Pushing this last mournful thought to one side,

Isabella sat up. They would have tonight. She was going to make the most of it. 'The bath,' she said, smiling at him. 'You promised you would join me.'

'It will be a tight fit,' he said, smiling back.

It was his wicked smile. It seemed she was not, after all, completely sated. 'I think you have already proved that to both our satisfaction,' Isabella said with a wicked smile of her own.

He laughed then, getting to his feet, his muscles rippling, picking her up and holding her high against him, flesh to flesh, skin to skin, and stepped with her into the bath. He set her down carefully. They stood facing each other and kissed again. The water was still warm. After the icy streams they had washed in of late, it felt hot.

Finlay picked up a tin pitcher and poured water over her. Her skin, alight with his lovemaking, felt every trickle. Another pitcher full. Then the soap. The lather made his hands slippery. His fingers slid over her shoulders, down her arms, back up to her breasts. Her body thrummed with anticipation.

Isabella picked up the jug. There was a delicious ache in postponing pleasure. Water trickled down Finlay's chest, clinging to the rough hair there. Another pitcher full of water. She took the soap from him and began to lather. Her fingers slipped and slid over his skin, finding the ridges of old scars. They were long healed. Some were just the faintest of shadows; others ran deeper.

'Where did you get this one?' she asked, and he told her. 'And this one?' she asked. 'And this one?' There were scars on his shoulders. On his belly. On his thighs. The long, vicious scar on his back was from Corunna, he said. She kissed each one. When her lips reached the base of that worst marking, he turned her round, taking her into his arms. Their bodies slid together, against each other, adhering to each other with the soap-suds, and she forgot about the scars and concentrated on kissing him. By the time they finally stepped from the tub, the water was cold.

Dinner was, as Alesander had promised, excellent. Hearty Basque cuisine, venison in a rich wine stew flavoured with the blood sausages that reminded Finlay of home. They ate at the little table by the window, watching the bustle on the street below, for it was the hour of the *paseo*. Isabella wore one of his shirts. Another first. They'd also managed a couple of other firsts in the bath there, he thought with a grin.

'What are you thinking about?' Isabella asked.

'What do you think?'

She chuckled. 'I think that we are not going to be doing much sleeping in that big comfortable bed.'

'You're not tired, then?'

She shook her head. 'I have the rest of my life to catch up on my sleep.' Her smile wobbled, and his heart lurched in response, but before he could say anything, she had recovered, and took a reviving sip of wine. 'I was thinking,' she said, 'that your scars, they are like a chart of all the places you have been, all the battles you have fought.'

'My body is like a campaign map, right enough,' Finlay said, twirling his half-empty glass around on the table. 'I'm thinking that I've scarcely room for any more entries, nor desire for them.'

Isabella reached for his hand and gently moved

the glass away. 'Today, at the site of that terrible battle, and seeing Señor Gebara, too, has brought back horrible memories, things you do not want to think about. I am so sorry.'

Finlay shook his head firmly. 'I'm not.' He stretched his legs out, and pushed his plate aside. 'It's how we keep going, when we're at war— not thinking about it. It's a habit they teach you in the army, not thinking about it, for if you do, you'd not survive. Or you'd run. Or worse.' He glanced over at Isabella. 'Some men can't live with the memories, you know.'

She paled. 'I did not know. Finlay, I...'

'Don't worry. I've no intentions of doing anything daft. Quite the opposite.'

'What do you mean?'

'I told you, it was a good thing, seeing that place again. And seeing Alesander. It's given me pause for thought.' He twined his fingers in hers. 'You've made me question things. Right from the first moment we met, to be honest, you've forced me to confront a lot of unpalatable truths.'

'Me?'

He smiled at her incredulous tone. 'Aye, you. You've a habit of asking the kind of awkward questions that I prefer to avoid. Such as what I'll do now that Wellington has brought us a peace that seems like to last.'

'There will always be other wars to fight, Finlay.'

'There will,' he said sadly. 'Indeed, there will, but I'm done with fighting other people's battles. If this battered body of mine has to be inflicted with any more scars, I'd like them to be of my own devising.'

'What does that mean?'

He frowned, shaking his head. 'I've absolutely no idea, lass. Despite my nickname, I've never really been an upstart, never been anything but unswervingly loyal to my country and my so-called superior officers, but where has it got me? And then there's you. Look at you. Look what a love of your country has made of you. An exile. A traitor.'

'Our cases are not the same.'

'They are more similar than I'd have thought

when first I came here. Like you, I'm done with soldiering.'

Across from him, Isabella looked shocked, though when she made to speak, Finlay shook his head. 'I mean it,' he said, and found with surprise that he did. 'I've never in my life thought to be anything but a soldier, but now I'm done with it, and what's more, I'm looking forward to telling Wellington so.'

'What will he say?'

The question gave him pause, for despite his opinion of the man, as a soldier, Finlay had never had anything other than respect for the duke, and—if he was being really honest, which he might as well be now—no little awe. Not that he'd have to actually face the duke if he resigned. But would he feel he'd truly resigned unless he did? Wasn't it his duty, and didn't he always do his duty? He'd not be letting himself down at the last, that was for sure. Finlay shook his head again. 'I don't know what he'll say, though I'll find out soon enough.'

'So you will confront him, then,' Isabella said, with that uncanny ability to read his mind. 'Even though you do not need to?'

'As you said, I'm not a man to run away.' Finlay got to his feet and began to stack the dishes onto a tray.

'No. You are a man who does his duty. Even when he does not wish to.'

Thinking of tomorrow, he thought she'd never said a truer word. He did not want to think about tomorrow. Finlay set the tray outside the door. 'Talking of wishes,' he said, turning the key in the lock, 'I've a few you could help me with, if you're so inclined.'

He was relieved to see the shadow of melancholy leave her eyes, the sensuous tilt return to her lips. 'Your wish is my command,' she said, giving him a mocking little salute.

Finlay picked her up, setting her gently down on the bed. She stretched her arms over her head, stretching the hem of his shirt she wore up to the top of her thighs. He could see the shadow of her nipples, dark through the white cotton. Her hair was spread out like silk on the pillows.

'I await your orders,' she said.

Finlay pulled his shirt over his head and hurriedly stepped out of his breeches. 'Then, lie back,' he said, kneeling between her legs, 'close your eyes and surrender.'

The following morning Señor Gebara brought their breakfast personally, tapping softly on the door just before daybreak. Finlay set the tray down on the table by the window and returned to the bed, pulling Isabella back into his arms. 'The horses will be ready in half an hour. Alesander has provided us with some supplies, enough to get us to the coast, he says. We'll be two, maybe three days, on the road.'

'Then, we should make haste,' Isabella said, making no move.

'Aye.'

Finlay pulled her tighter. They had lain like this all night, in the sleepy intervals between their passionate lovemaking. Time had seemed suspended; the hours had stretched, seemingly endlessly ahead, until now. Now, as he ran his palm over her flank, as he nestled his chin into her hair, as she pressed herself closer, close enough for their hearts to beat against each other, time began to gallop out of control.

A few more minutes, Isabella thought. She just

needed a few more minutes, and then she would be ready. She wrapped her arms tighter around Finlay's waist. She pressed her lips to the hollow of his throat. She felt the stirrings of his arousal and pressed tighter. His erection hardened. She wriggled. She felt his sharp intake of breath. And then his resolute shifting.

'Isabella…'

She leaped from the bed, tearing herself away from him, because the alternative was to cry and to cling, and she would not do that to him. She had promised she would not let him, or herself, down. 'Is that fresh coffee? Would you like some?'

She began to dress. The very thoughtful Señor Gebara had had her undergarments laundered, her habit and boots brushed clean of the dust of the road. She was aware of Finlay watching her as she snatched at clothes and pulled them on, pouring coffee, wittering on about the fresh bread, the salty cheese, the smoky ham, as if she cared about anything other than the fact that every minute, every second, took them inexorably towards their separate fates.

She sat at the table and managed to force down

her breakfast without choking. Her smile was manic, she knew that even without the look Finlay gave her, but he said nothing, eating his own breakfast steadily, taking a second cup of coffee, a faint frown furrowing his brow. She had no idea what he was thinking. He had that locked-away look, already putting a distance between them as he shaved. She knew he cared for her—how could she not, after the intensity and raw emotion of their coupling? She suspected he cared more than he would ever allow her to know. But she knew, too, with absolute certainty, that he would not allow himself to care enough, and she knew with equal certainty that she would never wish him to. She was not worth the sacrifice, and he would be sacrificing everything. His family. His career—even if he no longer wanted it. More important, his honour, and Finlay was a man who must always be honourable. A man who would always do his duty. As he was doing now.

As she must do hers. Last night was their goodbye. She had vowed she would make it as easy, as painless, as guilt-free as possible for him. He was not detached; he was not indifferent.

He was trying to make it easy for her. Isabella pushed her coffee cup aside and got to her feet. 'Time to go,' she said, straightening her shoulders, head back, like the trooper he expected. 'Time to face the future.'

Finlay stuck to the bargain he'd made with himself for the three days and two nights it took them to reach San Sebastian. He played the soldier, as he had always played the soldier, thinking only of executing his orders as best he could, of protecting and defending Isabella's liberty, wary at every second of potential ambush, dragging his mind back again and again to the task in hand whenever it strayed into dangerous territory. He would not think of their impending parting. He would not allow his heart to ache. He would not wish for anything other than Isabella's safe delivery to the waiting fishing boat, and then his own execution of the final elements of Jack's plan, which would ensure her future safety.

They stood on the final crest above the fortress town of San Sebastian, the scene of the last battle he'd fought in Spain before heading for the

Pyrenees in pursuit of the retreating French army. Below, the bay was fringed by a perfect, beautiful crescent of golden sand. A small islet was set like a jewel in the middle of the bay, breaking up the softly rolling waves. It reminded him of Oban bay, in some respects. The distinctively shaped Basque fishing boats, their hulls, to his Highland eyes, so vertiginous and bulky that he found it difficult to believe, looking at them bobbing in the protective embrace of the harbour wall, that they wouldn't simply topple over in the lightest of swells. Isabella was bound for one of those boats. Isabella was bound for that sea, in the directly opposite direction he would take.

Isabella, his lovely Isabella, who had been so brave and so stoic, these past few days. Not a tear had she shed, nor a word of complaint had she uttered. Not a mention of that perfect night they'd shared had she made. No regrets. No looking back. Only onward, forward, to the new life she would forge. A new life in a new world. A world he would not inhabit.

His gut clenched. He thought he might be sick. The breeze ruffled her hair. She dipped her head to make some adjustment to her reins, and he thought he caught a glimpse of tears. Though it might be the wind. His heart contracted. His stomach roiled. It took him a moment to recognise it for what it was. Fear. He was desperately afraid of losing her. He knew at that moment, knew despite all, that he could not let her go.

'Isabella.'

She turned to face him. Tears. They were tears, but she forced a smile. 'I'm fine. I will be fine. It is just—I will be fine,' she said.

She was trying to reassure him. Hope did not spring, it burst forth like the first snowdrop of the year. A fragile shoot, but determinedly pushing itself towards the sun. He hadn't allowed himself to consider how deeply her feelings for him ran; he had been too concerned with damping down his own, but if she cared even a fraction as much as he did...

'Isabella...'

'Finlay, don't worry. I won't let you down. I am—I am ready.'

She straightened in the saddle, determined to play the soldier she thought he expected, and it was his undoing. 'Isabella, I love you so much. My own heart, I love you. I can't let you go without me.'

* * *

She thought she had misheard him. She must have misheard him. She opened her mouth, but no words came. She could only stare stupidly.

'Isabella.'

Finlay jumped down from his horse and pulled her from the saddle. These past few days, in their wild race across the mountains, his face had been set, his expression steadfastly distant. He had played the commanding officer, she had played the foot soldier, just as they had agreed. Now the light was back in his eyes. They were the colour of the sea below. Her heart, her poor about-to-be-broken heart, began to beat faster. She couldn't possibly hope. There was no hope. None.

'Isabella.' He took her hands in his. The horses were untethered, she noticed, and then immediately lost interest. 'Isabella.' He shook his head, grinned, shook his head, frowned. 'I've never said the word before.'

Say it again, she prayed, but said nothing, in case her prayers were misguided.

'Never. I don't know if I should... It's—it's likely all wrong, only— Ach, what a blithering eejit I am. I love you. I love you with all my heart, and no amount of telling myself all these other things matter more makes a whit of difference. I love you, lass, and I don't want to have to live without you. I don't know what that means. I can't make any promises, I can't even...'

'I don't care!' Isabella threw her arms around him. 'I don't care what or how or if. All I care about is that I love you, and if you love me, too— Do you? Do you truly love me?'

Finlay laughed. 'Could you ever have doubted it?'

'Yes! You never once...'

'I could not. And you...'

'I could not. Oh, Finlay, how could I tell you that I loved you, how could I ask you to come with me, when it would mean you giving up everything that is important to you?'

'You are everything. You are the only thing that is, or ever will be, important to me.'

'But your family. The army. You will be court-martialled.' Cold reality hit her. She dragged herself free of his embrace. 'Finlay, I love you so much. Too much. I could not do this to you, put your life in danger, ask you to...'

'You haven't asked me,' Finlay said gently, pulling her back into his arms. 'I'm offering. I don't have much, or I won't, not if—when—I leave with you, but without you, I have nothing. I don't know what kind of life we'll make, lass, but I'm asking you for the chance to build it together. Will you give me that chance?'

She wanted to. Her heart cried out yes, but her head…her head needed some convincing yet, it seemed. 'You said it yourself, Finlay, you're not a man to run away. You have a duty to go back, even if it is only to resign. You cannot blight your honour with the shame of desertion, and you cannot take the risk of them catching you, for you will be hanged.'

'I will not lie to you, I would wish it otherwise. I would wish that we could both go to England together, that I could put a clean and honourable end to my career, but I can't. There are some sacrifices worth making. I love you. My duty is to my heart now, and not my country.'

She swallowed the lump in her throat that his words, his beautiful, heartfelt words caused. 'But your family?'

Now he did flinch. She sensed true pain there,

but still he shook his head. 'I will be sacrificing no more than you, my love. We will make a new family together. If you'll have me. It won't be easy. It won't be painless. We'll miss what we've lost, but we won't have lost the most important thing of all.'

'Each other?'

'Each other.'

She could resist no longer. The future, which had seemed like a huge, black abyss, now spread golden before her, not perfect, not rosy or easy, but one redolent with promise. 'I love you, Finlay Urquhart, with all my heart.'

'And I love you, Isabella Romero, with every fragment of mine.'

Epilogue

Oban, Argyll—six months later

The fishing village of Oban reminded Jack Trestain a little of San Sebastian. Funny how things sometimes came full circle. The same horseshoe bay, the island a short distance off-shore, the sheltering haven of the harbour, the cluster of white houses lining the front. Admittedly the gently bobbing fishing boats were shallower, longer, the sky was a paler blue and it was significantly colder, but all the same…

Had the similarity struck Finlay when he had sailed for Lisbon with his Isabella all those months ago? He had not mentioned it in his letter, but then he'd had rather more important matters to occupy him. Such as how to arrange his death, along with the death of El Fantasma.

Jack smiled wryly to himself. Who would have thought that the partisan Finlay had encountered all those years ago would turn out to be a blue-blooded Spanish lady? And who would have imagined that the blue-blooded Spanish lady would turn out to be one of Spain's most wanted rebel partisans? 'No one, and it's just as well,' he said to himself as he stepped out of the fishing boat that had carried him here, after agreeing a time for his return journey with the captain, for his visit was a fleeting one with a sole but crucial purpose.

Jack sat on the edge of the harbour wall to garner his thoughts. It had been Celeste's idea that he come here in person. 'For you cannot write such things in a letter, *mon amour*,' she had said. It was true. What he had to say was far too politically sensitive to commit to paper, but that wasn't what his lovely wife-to-be had meant. Finlay's family had already received one tragic letter out of the blue, posing more questions than answers, something Celeste was only too familiar with. On this occasion, he would be there in person to answer all their questions, ease their concerns. This time, they would get the truth. Or as much of it as was prudent to furnish them with.

Finlay's missive had come to him via heaven knew what circuitous route, but by some miracle it had not, to Jack's very experienced eyes, been tampered with. Short and pithy, it had been shocking, but it had also made Jack smile. Clearly, Finlay was head over ears in love with his partisan, though he had naturally said no such thing. Love, as Jack had recently learned, was capable of making a man do all sorts of rash and mad things. Such as ask his best friend to fake his death. *You're a master strategist*, Finlay had written. *I rely on you to give me a suitably fitting end.*

Well, he'd managed that, all right. The fate that had met the brave Major Urquhart in the remote, rocky mountains of Spain, was deemed heroic when reported in the British press. There had been no overt mention of El Fantasma, of course, but there had been sufficient hints to entice the Spanish chaps to ask the English chaps for more background, and the top-secret information they'd received had convinced them. El Fantasma was dead, and Major Urquhart had died, presumably at the hands of the cut-throat partisan's accomplices, but not before successfully completing his mission. The Romero family were safe from prosecution, just as Finlay had insisted. More important, Wellington had fallen for the story, relieved that a potentially awkward political scandal had been avoided, and had even been persuaded to grant Finlay a posthumous honour.

Jack looked at the medal now, sitting in its leather case. Finlay wouldn't be interested in it, but his father would, and Jack was pretty sure that Mr and Mrs Urquhart would be able to put their son's military pension to good use. It had taken a good deal of strong-arming to secure that pension. Jack had to make an effort to unfurl his fist, thinking about that. It shouldn't have proved so difficult.

He patted his coat pocket, though there was no need. The paper with Finlay's new name and whereabouts in America was safely tucked away there, along with the letter from the bank with the arrangement for payment of the monies due each quarter. It was a risk, telling these strangers that their son was alive, but one Jack was certain to be worth taking. Secrets and lies, he had learned from his lovely Celeste, could tear a family asunder. Finlay's family might never see him again, but their love for him would reach across the oceans that separated them in the letters they could write, and one day, perhaps, Finlay and Isabella's children would be able to visit their father's Highland homeland. That was a thought to warm the heart.

Jack smiled. Mawkish idiot! Love had made him a sentimental fool. His smile widened. No, love had brought him happiness. He hoped Finlay and his Isabella were as happy as he and his Celeste. Reading between the lines of that letter, he'd wager that they were.

* * * * *

Historical Note

The inspiration for Finlay Urquhart, the Jock Upstart, arose when I was reading Richard Holmes's excellent book *Redcoat* while researching my previous book in this series, *The Soldier's Dark Secret*. It was, I discovered, extremely unusual for a man of humble origins to work his way up through the ranks in Wellington's army. He'd have to have been exceptional in every way—brave, bold and bright—but he'd always have remained an outsider to the establishment elite. I do love an underdog, and so Finlay was born.

The main part of my research for the partisan war in Spain came from Ronald Fraser's book *Napoleon's Cursed War*. There were indeed female partisans fighting what was referred to, for the first time, as a guerrilla war—including Catalina Martin, who was promoted to second lieutenant, and Dominica Ruiz, said to have killed three imperial soldiers with her own hands.

Isabella's alter ego, El Fantasma, was a spy rather than a *guerrillero*, her values influenced by what I was hearing in the news—which at the time I was writing, focused on the conflict between matters of state security and freedom of speech and information: the so-called 'enemy within'.

I already knew that Finlay would be disillusioned by the lack of any meaningful change for the better wrought by peace, just as his comrade Jack was. I began to wonder about Isabella, too. My reading implied that in many ways Spain regressed, in terms of social justice, after the end of what they called the War of Independence. I wondered how my heroine would feel, forced to take a back seat in the country she'd fought so hard to liberate.

As always, I've strived to set this story in as accurate a historical background as possible. In July 1813, when the story opens, the French had been driven into the north-eastern corner of Spain after the bloody Battle of Vitoria. Wellington was forced to withdraw from his attempt to storm the fortress town of San Sebastian, and it was not until September that the town finally surrendered, and was immediately sacked by the British—forcing the French to retreat across the Pyrenees. Any mistakes or inaccuracies are entirely my own fault.

Finally, a note on Finlay's accent. He is a Highlander. His family come from Oban, in Argyll, not far from my own home, and he would, of course, have been a native Gaelic speaker. His English would have become fluent in the army, giving him, more than likely, an English rather than a Scots accent. But I wanted my hero to be unmistakably Scots—gritty and a bit rough round the edges—so I'll put my hands up right now and confess that the slang he uses has large elements of straight, modern-day Glaswegian.

Anachronistic, completely historically incorrect, I know, but I hope it works. I leave it up to you to decide.

MILLS & BOON®

Why shop at millsandboon.co.uk?

Each year, thousands of romance readers find their perfect read at millsandboon.co.uk. That's because we're passionate about bringing you the very best romantic fiction. Here are some of the advantages of shopping at www.millsandboon.co.uk:

* **Get new books first**—you'll be able to buy your favourite books one month before they hit the shops

* **Get exclusive discounts**—you'll also be able to buy our specially created monthly collections, with up to 50% off the RRP

* **Find your favourite authors**—latest news, interviews and new releases for all your favourite authors and series on our website, plus ideas for what to try next

* **Join in**—once you've bought your favourite books, don't forget to register with us to rate, review and join in the discussions

Visit **www.millsandboon.co.uk**
for all this and more today!